CHRISTOPHER BUSH
THE CASE OF THE CARELESS THIEF

CHRISTOPHER BUSH was born Charlie Christmas Bush in Norfolk in 1885. His father was a farm labourer and his mother a milliner. In the early years of his childhood he lived with his aunt and uncle in London before returning to Norfolk aged seven, later winning a scholarship to Thetford Grammar School.

As an adult, Bush worked as a schoolmaster for 27 years, pausing only to fight in World War One, until retiring aged 46 in 1931 to be a full-time novelist. His first novel featuring the eccentric Ludovic Travers was published in 1926, and was followed by 62 additional Travers mysteries. These are all to be republished by Dean Street Press.

Christopher Bush fought again in World War Two, and was elected a member of the prestigious Detection Club.

He died in 1973.

CHRISTOPHER BUSH

THE CASE OF THE CARELESS THIEF

With an introduction
by Curtis Evans

DEAN STREET PRESS

INTRODUCTION

Rosalind. If it be true that good wine needs no bush [i.e., advertising], 'tis true that a good play needs no epilogue. Yet to good wine, they do use good bushes, and good plays prove the better by the help of good epilogues.

—SHAKESPEARE, Epilogue, *As You Like It*

THE decade of the 1960s saw the sun finally begin to set on that storied generation which between the First and Second World Wars gave us detective fiction's Golden Age. Taking account of both deaths and retirements, by the late Sixties only a bare half-dozen pre-World War Two members of the Detection Club were still plying their deliciously deceptive craft: Agatha Christie, Anthony Gilbert (Lucy Beatrice Malleson), Gladys Mitchell, John Dickson Carr, Nicholas Blake and Christopher Bush, the subject of this introduction. Bush himself would pass away, at the age of eighty-seven, in 1973, having published, at the age of eighty-two, his sixty-third Ludovic Travers detective novel, *The Case of the Prodigal Daughter*, in the United Kingdom in the spring of 1968.

In the United States Bush's final detective novel did not appear until late November 1969, about four months after the horrific Manson murders in the tarnished Golden State of California. Implicating the triple terrors of sex, drugs and rock and roll (not to mention almost inconceivably bestial violence), the Manson slayings could not have strayed farther from the whimsically escapist "death as a game" aesthetic of Golden Age of detective fiction. Increasingly in the decade capable of producing psyche-delic psychopaths like Charles Manson and his "family," the few remaining survivors of the Golden Age of detective fiction increasingly deemed themselves men and women far out of time. In his detective fiction John Dickson Carr, an incurable roman-tic, prudently beat a retreat from the present into the pleasanter pages of the past, setting his tales in bygone historical eras where he felt vastly more at home. With varying success Agatha Christie made a brave effort to stay abreast of the times (*Third Girl*, *Endless Night*), but ultimately her strivings to understand what was going on around her collapsed into the utter incoherence of *Passenger to Frankfurt* and *Postern of Fate*, by general consensus the worst mystery novels that Dame Agatha ever put down on paper.

In his detective fiction Christopher Bush, who was not quite two years older than Christie, managed rather better than the Queen of Crime to keep up with all the unsettling goings-on around him, while never forswearing the Golden Age article of faith that the primary purpose of a crime writer is pleasingly to puzzle his/her readers. And, in contrast with Christie and Carr, Bush knew when it was time to lay down his pen (or turn off his dictation machine, as the case may be), thereby allowing him to make his exit from the stage on a comparatively high note. Indeed, Christopher Bush's concluding baker's dozen of detective novels, which he published between 1957 and 1968 (and which have now been reprinted, after more than a half-century, by Dean Street Press), makes a generally fine epilogue, or coda, to the author's impressive corpus of crime fiction, which first began to see the light of day way back in the jubilant Jazz Age. These are, readers will find, "good bushes" (to punningly borrow from Shakespeare), providing them with ample intelligent detective entertainment as Bush's longtime series sleuth Ludovic Travers, in the luminous twilight of his career, makes his final forays into ingenious criminal investigation.

*

In the last thirteen Ludovic Travers mystery novels, Travers' *entrée* to his cases continues to come through his ownership of the Broad Street Detective Agency. Besides Travers we also regularly encounter his elegant wife, Bernice (although sometimes his independent-minded spouse is away on excursions of her own), his proverbially loyal secretary, Bertha Munney, his top Broad Street op, Hallows (another one named French, presumably inspired by Bush's late Detection Club colleague Freeman Wills

Crofts, pops up occasionally), John Hill of the United Assurance Agency, who brings Travers many of his cases, and Scotland Yard's Inspector Jewle and Sergeant Matthews, who after the first of these final novels, *The Case of the Treble Twist* (in the U.S. *Triple Twist*), are promoted, respectively, to Superintendent and Inspector. (The Yard's ex-Superintendent George Wharton, now firmly retired from any form of investigative work whatsoever, is mentioned just once by Ludo, when, in *The Case of the Dead Man Gone,* he passingly imparts that he and Wharton recently had lunch together.)

For all practical purposes Travers, who during the Golden Age was a classic gentleman amateur snooper like Philo Vance and Lord Peter Wimsey, now functions fully as a professional private eye—although one, to be sure, who is rather posher than the rest. While some reviewers referred to Travers as England's Philip Marlowe, in fact he little resembles the general run of love and leave 'em/hate and beat 'em brand of brutish American P.I.'s, favoring a nice cup of coffee (a post-war change from tea), a good pipe and the occasional spot of sherry to the frequent snatches of liquor and cigarettes favored by most of his American brethren and remaining faithful to his spouse despite encountering a succession of sexy women, not all of them, shall we say, virtuously inclined.

This was a formula which throughout the period maintained a devoted audience on both sides of the Atlantic consisting, one surmises, of readers (including crime writers Anthony Berkeley, Nicholas Blake and the late Alan Hunter, creator of Inspector George Gently) who preferred their detectives something less than hard-boiled. Travers himself sneers at the hugely popular (and psychotically violent) postwar American private eye Mike Hammer, commenting of an American couple in *The Case of the Treble Twist*: "She was a woman of considerable culture; his ran about as far as Mickey Spillane" [a withering reference to Mike Hammer's creator]. Yet despite his manifest disdain for Mike Hammer, an ugly American if ever there were one, Christopher

Bush and his wife Florence in the spring of 1957 had traveled to New York aboard the RMS *Queen Elizabeth*, and references by him to both the United States and Canada became more frequent in the books which followed this trip.

Certainly *The Case of the Treble Twist* (1957) features tough customers and an exceptionally cruel murder, yet it is also one of Bush's most ingeniously contrived cases from the Fifties, full of charm, treacherous deception and, yes, plenty of twists, including one that is a real sockaroo (to borrow, as Bush occasionally did, from American idiom). Similarly clever is *The Case of the Running Man* (1958), which draws, as several earlier Bush books had, on the author's profound love and knowledge of antiques. By this time Bush and his wife, their coffers having burgeoned from the proceeds of his successful mysteries, resided in the quaint medieval market town of Lavenham, Suffolk at the Great House, a splendidly decorated fourteenth-century structure with an elegant Georgian-era façade which he and Florence purchased in 1953 and resided in until their deaths. The dashing author, whom in 1967 *Chicago Tribune* mystery reviewer Alice Crombie swooningly dubbed "one of the handsomest mystery writers on either side of the Channel or Atlantic," also drove a Jaguar, beloved by James Bond films of late, well into his eighties.

The Case of the Running Man includes that Golden Age detective fiction staple, a family tree, but more originally the novel features as a major character a black American man, Sam, the devoted chauffeur of the wealthy murder victim. Sam, who reminds Ludovic Travers of Rochester, "Jack Benny's factotum of television and radio," is an interesting and sincerely treated individual, although as Anthony Boucher amusingly pronounced at the time in the *New York Times Book Review*, he speaks "a dialect never heard by mortal ear"—an odd compounding of "American Negro" and London cockney.

The Case of the Careless Thief (1959) takes Ludo to Sandbeach, "the Blackpool of the South Coast," as the American jacket blurb puts it, with "a dozen hotels, a race track, a dog track, a music hall and two enormous dance halls." Anthony Boucher deemed this hard-hitting, tricky tale, which draws to strong effect on contemporary events in England, "one of Ludovic Travers' best cases." Likewise hard-hitting are *The Case of the Sapphire Brooch* (1960) and *The Case of the Extra Grave* (1961), complex tales of murderous mésalliances with memorably grim conclusions. The plot of *The Case of the Dead Man Gone* (1961) topically involves refugee relief groups, while *The Case of the Heavenly Twin* (1963) opens with a case of a creative criminal couple forging American Express Travelers Checks, concerning which Americans of a certain age will recall actor Karl Malden sternly enjoining, in a long-running television advertising campaign: "Don't leave home without them." In contrast with many of his crime writing contemporaries (judging from the tone of their work), Bush actually learned to watch and enjoy television, although in *The Case of The Three-Ring Puzzle*, a tale of violently escalating intrigue, Travers dryly references Scottish philosopher Thomas Carlyle's famous observation that England's population consisted of "mostly fools" when he comments: "I guess he wasn't too far out at that. But rather remarkable an estimate perhaps, considering that in his day there were no television commercials."

Of Bush's final five Ludovic Travers detective novels, published between 1964 and 1968, when the Western World, in the eyes of many, was going from whimsically mod to utterly mad, the best are, in my estimation, the cases of *The Jumbo Sandwich* (1965), *The Good Employer* (1966) and *The Prodigal Daughter* (1968). In *Sandwich* a crisp case of a defrauded (and jilted) gentry lady friend of Ludo's metamorphoses into a smorgasbord of, as the American book jacket puts it, "blackmail, black magic, a black sheep, and murder." It all culminates in a confrontation on a lonely Riviera beach in France, setting of some of Ludovic Travers' earliest cases, between Ludo and a desperate killer, in which Bernice plays an unexpectedly active part. Ludo again travels to France in the highly classic *Employer*, which draws most engagingly on the sleuth's (and the author's) dabbling in the world of art and is dedicated to his distinguished Lavenham artist friends, the couple Reginald and Rosalie Brill, who resided next door to Bush and his wife at the fourteenth-century Little Hall, then an art student hostel for which the Brills served as guardians. In *The Guardian* Francis Iles (aka Golden Age crime writer Anthony Berkeley) pronounced that *Employer* represented Bush "at his most ingenious."

Finally, in *Daughter* Travers finds himself tasked with recovering the absconded teenage offspring of domineering Dora Marport, sober-sided head of the organization Home and Family, which is righteously devoted to "the fostering, so to speak, of family life as the stoutest bulwark against the encroachment of ever-more numerous hostile forces: sex and violence in literature, films and on television; pornography generally, and the erosion of responsibility and the capability for sacrifice by the welfare state." Can Travers, a Great War veteran who made his debut in detective fiction in 1926, bridge the generation gap in late-Sixties London? Ludo may prefer Bach to the Beatles, but in this, the last of his recorded cases, he proves more "with it" than one might have expected. All in all, *Daughter* makes a rewarding finish to one of the longest-running and most noteworthy sleuth series in British detective fiction.

Curtis Evans

1
MERELY BURGLARY

I suppose one could stretch a point and call it a coincidence, but even then I doubt it. The Broad Street Detective Agency is concerned with practically nothing but crime of one sort and another, and even when I'm away from the office my mind is very often working, as it were, on the same wave-length. In other words I might at any time have been thinking about crime—in general or particular—and have had my thoughts interrupted by a telephone call that itself was to deal with crime. Still, that's how it was.

It was the 21st of March, raw and foggy, and ironically described on the calendars as the first day of Spring. My wife was away on yet another of the periodic calls to an elderly, ailing aunt, and I had the flat to myself. I'd intended to have an easy day. so I'd got up rather late. I'd made myself toast and coffee—breakfast is not one of my meals—and I was looking through one of the morning papers when I saw quoted again that trenchant summary, appraisal or dismissal if you like, that had been made some months before by Lord Chief Justice Goddard.

"The causes of crime today are the same as they were in the days of the Old Testament—greed, love of easy money, jealousy, lust and cruelty."

I think I smiled somewhat ironically as it suddenly struck me that the shrewd impact of that statement lay as much in what it omitted as in what it said. After all, in Old Testament days there were no psychiatrists, penal reformers or even well-intentioned cranks to unearth the causes of crime or to howl in protest against the convenient simplicity, as a deterrent, of an eye for an eye and a tooth for a tooth. Then, more personally, it struck me that in the course of my life I must have dealt over and over again with crimes that had had one or other of those starkly simple motivations. I was even wondering if there could be a crime that was permeated with all five of them, and it was just then that the telephone rang. I know now that I'd have been the most startled man in all creation if, as my hand went out to the receiver, some unquestionably authoritative voice had whispered that I was within a second of being brought into contact with just that kind of crime.

"Hill here, Travers. I thought I might catch you at home."

That was John Hill of United Assurance. It's the contract work that puts the jam on the bread and butter, with United Assurance the most valuable contract of all. And John Hill happens also to be a friend of mine.

"Started early this morning, haven't you?" I said. "Something in the wind?"

"Maybe only routine. A jewel robbery. About eighteen thousand pounds. At Sandbeach."

"Like to give me the picture? Or would you rather see me?"

He said he'd like me to come along, so I picked up the car at the garage and made for Lombart Street. The old Bentley was running superbly. And it ought to have done. It had just come back from a complete face-lifting at the works, and we could have bought one of the cheaper cars with what that overhaul cost us. But it's a fine car for our kind of job—fast, quiet and absolutely unobtrusive.

I went straight up to Hill's office. We had a sort of general chat while coffee was coming in, and then we lighted our cigarettes and got down to business. The few documents he had on his desk had come from his Sandbeach inspector, a man named Plygate. In any case the amount involved automatically took the whole thing out of Plygate's hands. Hill had also had a telephone conversation with him that morning.

I had a look first at the list of missing jewellery as set down in the policy inventory. There didn't seem a lot for eighteen thousand pounds, but since the company's own appraiser had been satisfied, that was not my concern. I put the copy in my wallet: two rings, one diamond and one diamond and emerald; two matching sets of ear-rings; a diamond rivière and brooch, and a diamond and emerald bracelet.

"You know Sandbeach?"

"In a way," I said. "I haven't been there for some time, but I do seem to remember that I'd hate to be found dead in it."

"Yes," he said. "Brighton and Hove has a few redeeming features, but Sandbeach is sheer blatancy. A ghastly place. But about this burglary. The insured was a Mrs. Mona Dovell. Her husband is a Charles Dovell and they live at Laneford Hall. That's about ten miles out of Sandbeach back among the Downs. The husband's much older than she is, according to Plygate. Also he's an important figure: county magistrate and so on, but he's over seventy and crippled with arthritis. That's why he didn't accompany her on Saturday night to a gala ball, held in aid of local charities. An annual affair, so I gather. At the Regency Hotel, by the way, which is also where the burglary took place.

"At any rate, Mrs. Dovell drove her husband to Sandbeach on Saturday morning and the jewellery was collected from their bank—Barclays in Duke Street. It was handed over to the manager of the Regency where Mrs. Dovell booked a room for the night. She drove herself in at about half-past seven and the jewellery was taken up to her room. I don't think I made it clear that it was a fancy-dress ball and she was going as a ranee or oriental princess or something of the sort: at any rate she'd only to do some final titivating and then walk down to the ballroom. There's a private entrance to that, by the way, and the general business of the hotel wasn't in any way disorganised. I just mention that to give you a picture.

"The ball was over punctually at midnight and Mrs. Dovell handed the jewellery back personally to the manager—a man named Sellman—who put it in the safe in his office, and half an hour later the hotel was asleep. Then at about half-past three the night porter woke up with the hell of a crack on his skull. He says he doesn't even remember being hit, but at any rate he roused the manager and the burglary was discovered. The police were called in and it was found an entry had been made through the service door to the kitchens."

"Just a minute," I said. "I know it's a question of adjustment between companies, but doesn't liability fall on the hotel?"

Hill smiled dryly.

"In this case, unfortunately not. The hotel was insured with us, too. They changed over from General Liabilities to us about a couple of years ago. That's one of the things Plygate ventured to call my attention to."

"Yes," I said. "Couldn't have been handier from the hotel's point of view. Anything else missing, by the way?"

"Takings since the bank closed. The two bars and drinks at the ball brought in quite a lot. The total hasn't been accurately worked out yet but it'll be between four and five hundred pounds. The burglar left the cheques."

"Sensible man," I said. "Anything else did Plygate mention as being at all unusual?"

"Yes," he said. "This was the third year of that ball, and always at the Regency. Mrs. Dovell was there all three times, but this was the first time she'd slept at the hotel and left her jewellery there. And it was a brightish night, cold but fine. She could have been home in twenty minutes."

I grunted.

"Well, there may be something in it and there may not. Any previous burglaries there?"

"Nothing of this sort. I haven't got the full details but I gather there've only been the usual thefts from rooms, and none of them very recently."

I couldn't help smiling. Time and time again John Hill and I had sat in that room and looked through preliminary reports and found all sorts of things which, at a distance, looked as if they needed a pretty careful investigation. And nineteen times out of twenty the suspicious had turned out to be just nothing at all.

He must have guessed my thoughts.

"I know," he said. "A couple of hilarious days for you, if you can't spin it out to three, and then a bill as long as my arm. Any idea where you're going to stay?"

I hadn't a notion, but he recommended the Clarendon, at what he called the quieter end of Duke Street. He'd ring them up and engage a room. I told him to make it two rooms. I wasn't so young as I was and I might like an operative to do the leg work.

"What about the police? Got any names with whom I ought to get into touch?"

He said he'd find out and have someone waiting for me by the time I got there. I thought that would be by mid-day.

"Any other information?"

There was nothing he could think of, so I checked my notes to see that I had everything relevant and in five minutes I was on my way. I drove round to Broad Street and saw Norris, the manager. Things were a bit slack, so he wasn't sorry to hear about the job. We've done pretty well in our time out of United Assurance, especially when we've been lucky enough to collect a ten-per-cent recovery bonus. And an excellent thing about John Hill is that he doesn't hire a dog and then start barking himself. Once he puts you on a job it's entirely up to you.

I collected a few of those cards which describe me as a Chief Inspector for United Assurance and then I asked him about Hallows. He's our best man and the specialist in insurance jobs. My guess is also that he's the best paid operative in town. Norris said he could take him off the job he was on and have him at the Clarendon by late afternoon. It might be as well, I said, if he drove down in his own car.

I went on to the flat, packed a bag, and well before eleven I was heading for Sandbeach. I heard a clock strike twelve as I entered the town.

There was an immense new roundabout as I came to the town proper, to control the traffic that converged at the end of Duke Street and the Esplanade. In the centre of Duke Street I passed the showy front of the Regency Hotel, and about two hundred yards further on, on the south side, was the Clarendon. It occupied a corner with Henry Street, leading back to the front and the sea.

The Clarendon seemed a quiet, family sort of hotel. I parked the car in the hotel garage, and when I went to the desk to see about the room there was a message for me. It was from a Detective-Sergeant Blayde, and written on official paper, and it said that unless he heard from me to the contrary, he would see me at the hotel at two o'clock. Police headquarters, according to the heading, were in Henry Street and that meant that Blayde would have only a few yards to walk. I don't know why, but I didn't feel happy somehow about having the police almost breathing down my neck. There was something vaguely hampering about it, a kind of loss of freedom of movement, though why I should have thought so I still haven't the least idea.

I had a good room on the second floor, and there was a lift that stopped virtually opposite the door. Hallows's room was just on the left. When I'd unpacked my bag and had a quick clean up, I took a look out of the window that overlooked Duke Street. I hadn't dreamt of such a panorama. Across the lower building that faced me I could see almost the whole sweep of the town as it rose up the slope to almost two miles away towards Laneford. It never pays to make an assignment look too easy, and maybe that had been at the back of my mind when I'd let John Hill assume that I wasn't too well acquainted with Sandbeach. In fact, a case there some two years previously had forced me to know it pretty well.

Your motoring handbook will tell you that Sandbeach has a hundred thousand people; that it is about an hour from London by train and its early closing day is on Wednesday. It will give a list of a dozen hotels, from the four star of the Regency to the two star of the Hampton, and it will add a formidable list of garages. But that doesn't even scratch the informatory surface. Sandbeach has far more than that. Plenty of people will claim that it has everything.

For instance, it has a race-track, a dirt track and a dog track, and a professional football team. It has two enormous dance halls, a dozen cinemas, a music-hall, a couple of theatres, an ice-skating rink, four or five amusement arcades and a huge fun-fair at the end of Carter Street. It has two piers like spatulate fingers pointing out to sea, two municipal car parks and what is probably the ugliest railway station in Europe. I almost forgot the two golf courses: Havington, near the race-course, and another as you come in by the London Road.

Sandbeach calls itself the Blackpool of the South. In the season its population may be more than trebled, and its long mile of beach so chock-a-block that from a distance it seems impossible to make room for yet one more deck chair. But Sandbeach is never empty; it is far too near London for that, and trains too frequent. And there is something cosmopolitan about it, not that it envies Brighton its title of New Jerusalem, but when you see the names above the shops in the back streets, you think straight away of Soho. That's about the one part of the town that I like, with its little restaurants and its junk shops. It's noisy and colourful but orderly enough. There was a time when the track gangs made plenty of trouble but now it's scarcely sporadic.

From my window I naturally couldn't see the sea-front: that wide, mile stretch of road that's called the Esplanade, where the larger hotels are interspersed with the showier shops and boarding houses, and at night the gaudy signs and the coloured lights make a kind of homespun Broadway. But when I raised the window and looked out I could see the whole length of Duke Street. It runs due east and west; north of the Esplanade and parallel. Its centre is the fashionable shopping area, but at each end it tapers off into smaller shops, cheap restaurants and cafes and catchpenny arcades. It was a cold, clear day, and behind Duke Street I could see the terraced streets, boarding houses for the most part and less pretentious shops. Then, fanning out towards the far height of ground were the new housing estates like huge splashes of vermilion, and between them a greyish green which was probably a new park. And still farther back, like pink tendrils, I could trace the lines of bungalows, streaks at first and then mere isolated dots. Compressed, as it were, in the middle of it all, was the small grey mass of the factory section, with its warehouses and market area. And everywhere in that conglomeration beyond Duke Street there would be small garages, pubs and, at midday and evening, mingled, if the wind was right, with the faint smell of the sea, would be the overpowering smell of fried fish.

I thought I could even smell it at that moment, and it reminded me that I was ready for a meal, so I went down to the dining-room. I've eaten better food but it was good enough and there was quite a reasonable choice. There was, at least, an excellent Stilton, and after I'd sampled it I glanced at my watch and was surprised to see that it was almost two o'clock. The waiter told me I could have coffee in any of the lounges, so I went to the large foyer which also served as a lounge and found a table towards the back from which I could watch the door. It was two o'clock to the dot when Blayde came in. Hill must have described me, for he came straight towards me.

"Mr. Travers?" he said, as I got to my feet.

"Yes," I said. "And you're Detective-Sergeant Blayde?"

"That's right, sir." He smiled as he held out his hand.

I'm speaking after the event, as it were, but John Blayde was thirty-two, and if anything he looked younger. He was about five foot eleven, judging by my six foot three, but whereas I'm lean as a lamp-post and on the wiry side for all that, he was slimly built with almost a frailness as in the slight stoop of the shoulders. His brown hair had a natural wave. The warm brown eyes were the best part of him, for there was something too pretty and almost effeminate about the shape of his mouth and the dimpled chin. His manner was assured enough, and when I said I was just about to have some coffee and would he join me, he said at once that he would, and began taking off his heavy tweed coat.

I gave the order to a waiter. Under the coat Blayde had on a brown tweed jacket and a reddish tie, a rust-coloured pullover and light brown dacron slacks. His shoes had the polish of a mirror and, as a colour scheme, the whole get-up was highly effective.

"You know Sandbeach, sir?" he wanted to know as he sat down.

"Not too well," I said. "Are you a native?"

"Born and brought up here."

I smiled.

"Lucky I didn't say anything against it. Seems a much bigger place, though, than when I saw it last."

"It keeps on growing," he said, and gave a kind of approving sideways nod.

The coffee came. He had his white, with sugar: I had black. It was uncommonly hot for hotel coffee and he grimaced as he took too careless a sip. I passed my cigarette case and held the lighter.

"Thanks," he said. He let out a puff and leaned back.

"Now about business, sir."

I told him what reports I'd seen and I gave him one of the cards. He studied it as if it were far more important than it was. It turned out that he was rehearsing his speech.

"This is just sort of a preliminary," he said, "if you know what I mean. But about the Regency job, you can take it from me that everything's in order. I was the first one on the spot and everything was plain sailing from the very first. Entry was made by jemmy-ing the service door, and then the night porter was slugged and after that it was easy. The safe was old fashioned and wouldn't have given any trouble to the sort of one who planned that job. The really amusing thing is that after pulling off the job he went and bitched the whole thing up. Know what he did?"

I shook my head.

"Left a torch behind with a nice set of prints. They went up to the Yard yesterday morning in case he has a record."

That was news. It looked, in fact, as if Hallows and I could be back in town by next morning. Or did it?

"Well, that seems to settle everything," I said. "But let me make something perfectly clear, Sergeant. We're only too delighted to have you people help us, but our own investigation has to go through, though it'll be only perfunctory in view of what you've told me. Call it red tape or what you will, but every claim over a certain amount has to be investigated and every person at all concerned has to be seen. That's just for the records. Every important company follows the same procedure." I tried another smile, this one a bit wistful. "Strictly between ourselves, I'd rather counted on spending a nice quiet three or four days down here; now it doesn't look as if I shall. Have some more coffee?"

"Thank you, sir, no." He was very pleased somehow with what I'd just said, and he gave me quite a grin. "Reckon you could spin the job out, couldn't you? Seems a pity now you're here."

"We'll see," I said. "So long as you people don't give me away. Sure you won't have some more coffee?"

"Sorry, but I can't." He reached for his overcoat. "This is actually my afternoon off. Which reminds me. My inspector would like to have a word with you in the morning. Chief Inspector Overson. He's actually in charge."

"Very good of him. At what time?"

"Well, sir, if you could come along to his office at about half-past nine. It's only a few yards round the corner. He'll probably have some news then about those prints."

"That'll be fine. A tough character, is he?"

He laughed.

"What, Dave?" He chuckled again. "He can be, of course, but you needn't worry."

"You work with him?"

"That's right," he said. "We're a sort of pair. Been working together the last four years. Practically brought up together."

"Good," I said. "Nothing like a good team, even in my job." Then, as I helped him on with his overcoat, "You're a married man?"

An almost startled look came over his face.

"Yes," he said, after a moment, and when I was beginning to think I must have dropped some kind of brick. And then, without saying anything else, he held out his hand.

"Nice to have seen you," I said. "Tell your inspector, if you see him, that I'll be along at half-past nine."

He gave a farewell wave of the hand and made for the swing doors. Just short of them he put on the brown felt hat with the snap brim. He went through without looking back.

I poured myself out another cup of coffee, tasted it and found it lukewarm. I got out my pipe, stoked it and lighted it. A snappy dresser, Blayde. Good clothes that had cost good money, not that that was any business of mine. But I thought of one or two sergeants I'd known at the Yard who'd come up the hard way, and Blayde didn't show up too well by comparison. Somehow he struck me as miscast.

Take that business of a left torch and fingerprints. Why hadn't Blayde seen that he was contradicting his own statement? First the man was someone to whom the safe would have presented no difficulties: in fact, a first-rate professional. And yet that professional had not only worked without gloves, but, with all the time in the world to do the job, had been so grossly careless as to leave behind his torch! To me that didn't make sense.

There was one other thing and whether or not it was an asset I didn't know, but I rather thought it was. That case that had brought me to Sandbeach two years previously had not necessitated any contacts with the local police: in fact, I'd been careful to keep out of their way. All the same, in my time I'd done quite a lot of more or less official work at the Yard, and, if I'd ever been at all top-heavy about it, then Blayde would have deflated me, for he'd taken me at the face value of the card. And that had described me simply as L. Travers, Chief Inspector, Investigation Department, United Assurance. And if Blayde took me as merely that, then it was almost a certainty that his inspector was also unaware of any connection of mine with the police.

Then suddenly I couldn't help smiling. The only way to conduct an investigation is to come to it with an open mind, and there was I, coming over all secretive and thinking only in terms of fraud. That's the worst of that flibbertigibbet brain of mine. It picks up an idea, twiddles it round, finds a fit with something that's no more substantial and it's tally-ho for cloud-cuckoo land.

So I knocked out my pipe and went up to my room. From there I telephoned to the Regency. Sellman, the manager, said he was quite free to see me. Inside five minutes I was on my way.

2

LOOKING FOR FACTS

I CAN'T say that I felt too happy. If the prints on that torch were really those of a man with a record, then the rest of what I had to do would have about it something of the perfunctory, however conscientious I tried to be. But as I left the Clarendon the sun came out and thoughts switched in sympathy to the brighter side. After all, in the course of the job I should have to see new scenes and new faces. Even the Regency which I was approaching would be new to me. I'd passed it more than once when I was in Sandbeach before, but I'd never been in. All I knew about it was that it had two hundred and fifty bedrooms and its charges were as high as the best hotels in town.

Plenty of people were about in spite of the shrewd east wind, and the pavement was quite crowded. I think that was why I turned off at Hanley Road along which the Regency ran back from Duke Street. Some thirty yards down was the other entrance which gave access to the ballroom, but the swing doors were locked. Still further along was a private entry to a spacious paved yard at the back of which was a long range of garages. In that extensive wing of the hotel there seemed to be three or four service doors and I wondered which was the one where the entry had been made, but there were people about and I was under observation from the kitchens, so I turned back.

I went through the main doors to the enormous late-Victorian foyer, all gilt and scrolls and mirrors. Quite a few people were sitting about in the leather chairs, and I had to stop and look about me till I could see the reception desk. When I said I had an appointment with the manager, the woman on duty had hardly time to speak before a man came through from a room in the rear and introduced himself as Sellman.

He was in the early fifties; tallish and well-built. I'd call him distinguished-looking; well-spoken and beautifully mannered. I gave him a card and he smiled in the most charming way and asked if he might keep it. Then we went through to the room from which he had emerged, which was his office.

"Do sit down, Mr. Travers. A cigarette?"

The silver box held a special brand. No sooner had I taken one than he was flicking on his lighter. Then he took the seat at the desk and swivelled it round to face me.

"You like your job?" he said, and as if he were really interested.

I smiled. I said it was always a change. Always new places and new people. "But not a very pleasant business for you, this burglary."

He shrugged his shoulders. "Just one of those things. It might have been more unpleasant still."

He caught my questioning tilt of the head.

"I mean there seems quite a likelihood that the jewellery may be recovered. From what the police tell me they've every hope of laying their hands on the man concerned. But you'd like to see everything. The safe there, for instance."

There it stood, alongside the desk; a big, solid, old-fashioned safe that was new when the hotel was built. He produced a key, put it in the lock, turned it and there it was—open. It was so simple as to be laughable. I had a look at the lock and put my glass on the scratch marks.

"The police say it was opened with a bent wire." He smiled as he caught my eye. "A hopeless sort of affair, really, but then one never expects burglaries—at least, not here."

"Because of the night porter?"

"Well, yes. The man on night duty comes on at half-past ten, but of course we don't close down so early as that, except the bars."

"Look," I said, "I'm sorry to be a nuisance but would you mind telling me the exact procedure after half-past ten?"

"My dear fellow, you're not a nuisance at all," he told me. "I'm only too glad to help. As for the procedure, that's very simple. The reception closes officially at eleven, but I'm always about till twelve. The last thing I do is to look round and see that everything's in order. If there should be any late and unexpected arrivals, the night porter lets them in and deals with them. Arrangements are always made for that. There's a light on in reception and that's where he spends the night." He smiled dryly. "He's not supposed to sleep but naturally he does. Then at six-thirty he reports anything there is to report and then he goes off duty."

"I could have a word with the one who was on duty on Saturday night?"

"Of course," he said. "If it's at all urgent, by the way, you'll have to see him at his home. In view of that blow on the head I thought he'd better take a day or two off. An excellent man, by the way; an ex-sergeant-major with a first-class record."

He gave me the name and address—William Hiddon, 33 Denmark Road, Beacon Housing Estate. He said it was easy to find: due north from the roundabout.

"About the missing cash," he said. "I think we have the figures now if you'd care to go into them."

I told him I was expecting my assistant at any moment and, if it was all the same to him, he'd come round later and do any checking. Not that there'd be any argument.

"But one other thing I would like to see, and that's the door where the entry was made."

He got up at once. There was another door just to the left of where I was sitting and we went through it and along a corridor. We turned left again and passed a long range of kitchens. Chefs were already at work and there was the heavy smell of cooking. A yard or two on was the door. A new lock had already been fitted and the jemmy marks touched up with paint.

"Not much harder than cracking a nut," I said. "But the bolts at top and bottom? Why weren't they drawn?"

"Don't think I haven't made my own enquiries," he said. "It's the duty of the second chef to see that everything's in order here." He shrugged his shoulders. "This seems to have been one of those cases when someone assumes that something is being done by someone else. Nearly always I check up myself, but Saturday night was an exceptional night on account of the ball. I was far too busy."

"Of course. I just asked the question. Not that the bolts would have made all that difference." I added a little more placation. "If a professional burglar had made up his mind to make an entry, you bet your life he'd have made it. But one thing does puzzle me. How on earth did the burglar know that the safe would hold what it did?"

"In my view, just a chance guess," he said. "After all, he could reasonably assume that some of the guests at the ball would be staying the night. It was a very well-publicised affair and the actual charges made it unusually select." He was looking at that door and gave a wry shake of the head. "Strictly without prejudice, I think that the question of the bolts amounts to gross negligence."

"I don't think I'd worry," I told him placatingly. "This your first experience of the kind, by the way?"

"Not by any means," he said, and gave a reminiscent smile. "Many years ago when I was second chef at the Carlton there was a very big robbery. There was another when I was assistant manager at the Royal, and, now I come to think of it, entry there was made through the kitchens."

I told him he sounded as if he'd had a varied experience, and he smiled. He said his father had been manager of the Splendide at Cannes and his maternal grandfather—his mother was French—had owned a hotel at Grasse. Once a hotel career had been planned for him, he had had to get experience of every side of the trade.

"What we call coming up the hard way," I told him. "And you like it here?"

He did. The Regency, now it had been thoroughly modernised, was as fine a hotel as any in the provinces. He hoped to make it still better.

"Who actually owns it?"

"A private syndicate," he said. "The chairman is a Mr. Garlen. I don't know if you know him?"

I said I didn't, and as he'd glanced at his watch I thought I'd take up no more of his time. As we walked back I said I doubted if I'd have to worry him very much again unless anything most unusual arose. And the odds against that were pretty big. I shook hands, thanked him and said a temporary goodbye in the office, and then, as we turned to go out, the door opened and a man stepped in.

He was tall and his shoulders were broad. Under the black homburg hat his hair was greying, and there was something arresting about the look of him—the beak of a nose, the cold, grey eyes and the grooves that ran deeply by the hard mouth.

"Sorry, Sellman. I didn't know you were engaged."

"That's all right, Mr. Garlen." Sellman seemed quite pleased. "You're just in time to see Mr. Travers. He's a chief inspector on the investigations department of United Assurance."

"Glad to meet you. Mr. Travers." Garlen held out a hand. "I hope Mr. Sellman has been able to help."

Sellman had been most co-operative, I said, and switched at once to that spiel about red-tape. Garlen listened and, where most people would have smiled, he moved never a muscle. It was like playing to a dead audience. Only when I added that plaintive quip about losing an anticipated three-day holiday did he relax—if one could call it that. The lips bent slightly in what was meant for a smile.

"All work and no play doesn't go well in Sandbeach." There was a hard, dry quality about the voice. "Take my advice and treat yourself to a day or two. You're staying here?"

I said the company had arranged for accommodation at the Clarendon.

"A nice little hotel."

The comment seemed impersonal rather than disparaging. Then he turned to Sellman who'd been hovering on the fringes of things.

"Mr. Travers must try dinner here. As a guest."

"That's very handsome of you," I told him. "Tonight I'm engaged, but tomorrow night, perhaps?"

"We'll be glad to have you." He waved a hand at nothing in particular and turned to Sellman again. "I think I'll come back later. You were actually going, Mr. Travers? If so I'll go with you."

I shook hands with Sellman, and Garlen and I went out to the foyer.

"A first-class man, Sellman," he told me. "We're very lucky to have him here."

"Most competent, I should think."

It wasn't a remark I was proud of but it was difficult making conversation with a man like Garlen, and all the time he was talking his eyes were going round that foyer as if looking for someone. Or perhaps he was just checking up.

"I'd like your opinion on the food here. I'm told there's none better, even in town."

He drew back to let me pass through the swing doors. Drawn up at the kerb was a black Mercedes-Benz. At the sight of us the man at the wheel slid across, got out and stood by the door: a shortish, thickset man of about forty.

"Can I take you anywhere?" Garlen asked me.

"Good of you, but I have to get back."

"Well, anything I can do for you, let me know." He made a move towards the car and then turned back. "You think everything will go through smoothly? No difficulties?"

"Probably none whatever."

"Glad to hear it." The corners of the lips drooped again in what was meant for a smile and he held out his hand. "Have a good time here. That's what we're here for."

I said I'd do my best. He nodded and turned back again to the car. He took the front seat, the driver closed the door and went round. The car glided away and Garlen didn't look back.

I walked on to the Clarendon and somehow I couldn't get the look of Garlen out of my mind. Hard as nails, I thought, and I didn't mean physically. As for that meeting with him, everything had been far too pat. Sellman must have had instructions to let him know at once when a representative of the company turned up. And my guess was that he had been waiting in the reception area till we returned, and pretty close to the door of Sellman's office. What was behind that offer of a free dinner I didn't know. It might have been genuine and a kind of courtesy, but somehow I couldn't see it that way. And yet one couldn't call it bribery. It had all been too suave for that.

In the Clarendon I thought I'd find out what I could about Garlen. The elderly clerk at the desk seemed unoccupied and I went across. He looked up and gave me the official smile. "Hallo, sir. Enjoying yourself here?"

"Haven't had time yet," I said. "And, by the way, I just met a man named Garlen. Met him at the Regency. Do you know him?"

He gave me a shrewd look. "A friend of yours, sir?"

"Not in the least. I was introduced to him, that's all. What's he do exactly?"

"Sammy Garlen?" His lips drooped. "A commission agent, sir."

"You mean a bookmaker?"

"A cut above that," he told me. "No, sir. He has a big office in Warren Street. Haven't you ever seen his advertisements? He trades under Holmes & Co."

"In a big way?"

"I'd say in a very big way. This is a rare betting town, sir. Wait a minute."

He fiddled about under the desk and came up with that day's early edition of the Sandbeach *Evening Gazette*. He had a quick glance through and found what he was looking for.

"There you are, sir. One of his advertisements." He waved the paper away. "Keep it, sir. There'll be another edition later on."

I went through to the lounge and ordered tea. While I was waiting for it I had a look at the paper. Its eight pages were almost all racing news: lists of runners at the three jumping meetings and the opening of the flat season at Lincoln. General news was used for a series of fill-ins, and a third of the whole space was taken up with advertisements. Garlen's was as large as any. Holmes & Co., "THE FIRM YOU CAN TRUST", invited bets on the Wednesday's Lincoln Handicap and gave a list of runners and prices. There was a similar list for the Saturday's Grand National. It gave preliminary prices for the Two Thousand Guineas and announced a Grand Competition for all regular clients—a hundred pounds for predicting the first three in the Derby. No entrance fee. Particulars in next Monday's issue. "WATCH THIS COLUMN!!" I'm no authority on the economics of a turf commission agency but it looked to me as if Garlen owned a money-spinner. I wondered who did the prodding of welshers and bad payers. If Garlen himself took a hand in it, then I guessed there wouldn't be many. That man who'd been driving his car looked pretty hard-bitten, too.

I had a couple of cups of tea and a cake and went up to my room to do some telephoning. I got Norris first and asked him to do a quick check-up on a Bernard Sellman who'd been assistant manager at the Royal. What I wanted was an authoritative opinion as to his integrity. Then I looked up the Dovell number at Laneford.

A man's voice was on the line, a butler's by the sound of it. He asked me to hang on and in a couple of minutes I was hearing another voice: elderly, scholarly and faintly blurred. It was Charles Dovell. I explained who I was and asked when it would be convenient for me to see his wife. He was most courteous. Mrs. Dovell would not be in till late that evening and he thought she was engaged again in the morning. But he was sure she would be in during the afternoon since some people were coming to tea.

Would two-thirty be convenient for me? I said it would, thanked him and that was that.

I looked at my watch and it was still short of half-past four. There was no sign of Hallows so I suddenly made up my mind to see that night porter, Hiddon. I don't like night interviews. The night obscures all sorts of little things that may give a clue to this and that. And now the evenings were drawing out and I'd all the time in the world before dusk.

Sellman had said that Denmark Road was easy to find. It might have been for him, but I came to a fork and went right instead of left. In a couple of minutes I knew I'd gone wrong. It wasn't the smart maisonettes that I came to first that made me uneasy: they were comparatively new and might well have been the beginning of the Beacon Estate. What did put me wise was the Avenue into which I turned next. Wellbrook Avenue gave me my bearings and I knew from the last time I'd been there that I was making for the London Road. All that area was the high-class oasis of big houses and bigger gardens, homes of the Sandbeach elite. From then on I was looking for a private roadway into which I could turn and back. I found one, and was just drawing into it when I saw a car that I thought I recognised. It was, in fact, that Mercedes-Benz.

The house before which it was drawn up was a sprawling affair in Edwardian Tudor. Fifty yards along the well-kept drive was a double garage, separate from the house itself. At the far end of the house the sun was reflected from the glass of a large lean-to conservatory. The gate bore the name Wellbrook Lodge, but I didn't stay to investigate further, for coming out of the front door was the man who'd driven that car from the Regency. I shot the Bentley back and then went on.

I came to a left turn and took it. It was Rutland Avenue and I knew where I was. All I had to do was go straight on and I'd be back at the fork. Just short of it I saw a telephone kiosk and I drew the car in. The directory told me that Garlen hadn't been visiting. Wellbrook Lodge was the private address of Garlen, S., and the telephone number, Sandbeach 244.

Three minutes later I was in Denmark Road: all semi-detached houses whose longish back gardens met those of a similar road further up the rise. Hiddon's front garden was well kept. He'd already pruned his roses, and in the bed round the table-cloth patch of lawn, daffodils were just coming into bloom. I pushed the door-bell; pushed it again and decided no one was in. Then I saw no harm in trying the back, and there, at the end of the garden, was a man digging. He was a big, broad-shouldered man wearing an old pair of trousers and a short-sleeved sweater, and it wasn't the first time he'd dug a garden. His movements were too rhythmical for that.

I gave a cough as I neared him down the path. I'd waited till he'd come to the end of a row, and now he turned leisurely round. He looked in the late fifties and as he straightened himself and used the spade as a scraper for his boots, he was full-face to me. Everything about him from the set of the head to the moustache proclaimed the old soldier.

"Nice to see someone working," I said. "I thought no one ever worked in Sandbeach."

"Wish it was true," he told me. "Give me five hundred a year and I wouldn't be getting this here bit o' ground ready for potatoes."

"You're Mr. Hiddon? Or is it Sergeant-Major Hiddon?"

"Just plain Mister."

He took the card and read it.

"Oh, yes," he said. "That Mr. Plygate said someone would be seeing me. And you're the one, sir?"

I said I was. And I held out my hand. He looked at his own hands, gave them a quick rub on the old flannel trousers and gave me the devil of a grip.

"I shan't keep you long," I said. "Just want to hear your account of what happened on Saturday night."

"No hurry, sir," he said. "My missus has gone to the pictures so we've got the whole place to ourselves. I can clean the spade later."

We went down the grass path towards the house. I asked him if he was a native of Sandbeach. He wasn't. He was an Essex man.

"And what was your regiment?"

"The Norfolks—"

"The Ninth Foot. The Holy Boys."

He stopped.

"You were in them?"

"No," I said. "But I soldiered alongside them. I'm a Suffolk man myself."

"Well I'm damned!" he said. "They say the world's a small place."

We were at the back door. He gave his boots a good rub on the mat.

"My missus is a bit of a stickler for bringing dirt into the house," he told me, and I gave my shoes a rub, too. "We'd better go through to the front room."

"Not for me," I said. "What's wrong with here? Nice and cosy in this kitchen."

"So long as you don't mind, sir."

He said he was going to have a cup of tea. He felt like one though his real tea wouldn't be till his wife got back. While the kettle was boiling on the electric cooker we talked soldiering. By the time we were seated in front of two big cups of black brew, we were buddies.

"How're you actually feeling?" I asked him. "Practically fit again?"

He gave me a blatant wink.

"Never felt better, sir. Never did feel anything much wrong. Only Mr. Sellman, he reckoned I ought to have a day or two off. What would you have done?"

"Taken it like a shot," I said.

He chuckled. Then his face straightened.

"If you see him though, sir, I wouldn't say anything about doing that bit o' digging."

"Wouldn't dream of it. We old sweats have got to stick together. If you like I'll tell him another day or two wouldn't do you any harm."

He laughed.

"Mustn't come it too brown, sir. I'm supposed to be on middle shift this week so I reckon I'll roll along tomorrow."

"And your head is really better?"

"Never much wrong with it." He tipped me another wink. "I had to let on it was pretty bad. A nasty sort of bump, though. That's all there was. Never even broke the skin."

I saw his point. He'd certainly done some quick thinking. My bet was that Hiddon had been asleep when he was struck and that was something he had to conceal. The attack had had to be sudden and ruthless. And the intimacy of that kitchen was telling me that I might learn all sorts of things.

"Strictly between ourselves, this visit of mine is all eye-wash," I told him. "I've already had a report on you from the hotel so I shan't need to make another one out. But just what did happen? As far as you remember, that is."

"To tell you the truth, sir, I'm damned if I know! Everything was just the same as it always was."

What with my unobtrusive prompting and various recapitulations the version was a bit garbled. Sorted out it came to this. That ball, as Sellman had said, had made no difference to the general run of things. He had reported for duty at half-past ten and had made himself generally useful till eleven o'clock when the reception had closed down and the receptionist on duty left. After that the hotel got more and more quiet till just after twelve, when Sellman came in with Mrs. Dovell. Sellman told Hiddon to take her up in the lift to the second floor, but Mrs. Dovell told him it would surely be simpler if he came up himself. So Sellman took her up, and when he came down he went into his office. As I saw it, Mrs. Dovell hadn't wanted Hiddon to bring down the jewel case. It was indeed more convenient for Sellman to accompany her to her room and take over the jewellery direct.

At about half-past one Hiddon was accustomed to have coffee and a snack, and this was provided by the kitchen for whatever porter was on night duty. There was a Thermos of coffee and sandwiches, or it might be the leg of a fowl with a couple of rolls and some cheese. In the full season there were six receptionists, who worked in shifts. In the dull season there were four—two of them women. Only one was on duty from nine o'clock till eleven and what that last receptionist on duty usually did just before coming off duty was to see that the night porter's snack was brought to the reception from the kitchen. That night the Miss Bright on duty had seen to that. As she was leaving she said, "Good-night, Hiddon. You'll find everything here." Hiddon said, "Thank you, Miss. Good-night, Miss," and then locked the swing doors after her.

At half-past twelve the hotel was asleep. Hiddon read the final edition of the Sandbeach *Evening Gazette* and then his stomach warned him that it was time for his snack. He ate the beef sandwiches and the cheese and drank the two cups of coffee that the smallish flask held. He washed out the Thermos as usual in the kitchen scullery and put the sandwich wrappings in the bin, and then settled down in one of the easy chairs. And that's all he knew.

"You mean you didn't feel the blow?"

"Well, that's just between me and you," he said. "But, honest to God, I didn't feel a thing. Not till I came round, and that wasn't till getting on for half-past three."

I told him, still between ourselves, what Sellman had told me about sleeping, and the way we worked it out was that he'd dropped off to sleep and had probably been coshed soon after three. But what neither of us could work out was why, even in his sleep, he hadn't felt the blow. Mind you, that was something again, that no one else knew. There are few situations with which an old sweat can't cope, and Hiddon had had to give the impression that he'd been awake. And that he had felt the blow.

"I'm keeping it to myself, mind you, sir, but damned if I can make it out. When I copped a packet in Normandy—clean through the shoulder here, it was—it knocked me clean out but I knew I'd been hit."

"Just one of those things," I told him. "And what Sellman doesn't know, he won't fret over."

I got to my feet and said I'd have to be going. I thanked him for the tea—real sergeant-major's tea, I told him—and hoped we'd see each other again before I left Sandbeach. Maybe he could slip out for a friendly drink. Then I remembered something.

"I believe that receptionist is one of the people I ought to see." I pulled out my notebook and pretended to check. "Just a lot of red-tape, but there we are. Do you know where she lives?"

"I think it's somewhere near Morley Gardens," he told me, and frowned. "I could always find out. I know she's on the telephone."

"Then I can look her up in the directory. There won't be all that number of Miss Brights."

"Ah, now, wait a minute," he said. "I don't know under what name she'd be. Might be under her married name: Blayde, that is."

For a moment I must have held my breath.

"Blayde? Haven't I heard that name somewhere before?"

"Probably have," he said. "He's a detective, a sergeant. Married her about three years ago and now they've split up. Word went round the hotel that she'd resumed her maiden name, as they call it. Now she's Miss Bright again."

"Was she working in the hotel when she married?"

"Oh, yes. At the desk. Then after they split up she came back. A rare smart-looking woman."

I nodded. I told him that maybe I needn't see her after all. Or perhaps it might be just as well to have something for the records. Not that I was going to work my fingers to the bone on what was a cut-and-dried case.

"Don't blame you, sir," he told me. "Sandbeach for Fun. That's the motto."

He came round the house with me to the front gate. Then he began talking soldiering again and it was another five minutes before I got away. You might say that we parted with mutual winks. There's one thing about us old sweats, we do stick together.

But there wasn't any smile on my face when I'd turned the corner. If there was one thing I no longer had, it was an open mind.

3
ENTER THE PRESS

I ASKED at the desk about Hallows, and he must have arrived just after I'd gone off to that interview with Hiddon. The clerk said he thought he was in the lounge, and there he was, having a late cup of tea.

Hallows is an arson specialist, and he has at his mind's end all the intricacies of the insurance game, but there's little in our line of work that he's not prepared to do. I've always said his best asset, from our point of view, is his inconspicuousness; the absolute opposite, for example, of my far too conspicuous self. Nothing would be more ludicrous than for me to attempt a shadowing job; for Hallows, nothing seems more easy. He's quiet, deceptively soft-spoken but tenacious as a leech. It may seem a strange thing to say, but that early evening when I caught sight of him in the Clarendon lounge I suddenly felt on top of the world, and it wasn't only a case of two heads being better than one. It was all sorts of things: that I'd always liked him, for instance, and that when we were on a job we always slipped somehow into a kind of equality; that he was so utterly reliable and, best of all, that his brain worked in the opposite way from my never too strictly logical own.

I sat in his room while he did his unpacking and he told me what briefing he'd had from Norris. In my room I gave him the copies of reports and the data, and while he looked them through I rang Sellman at the Regency.

"Travers here, Mr. Sellman. Can you tell me offhand what you make that cash claim?"

He said he could tell me exactly. It was three hundred and eighty-five pounds.

"Then let me change my mind," I said. "No need to check. I'll notify the company that it's in order."

"That's very handsome of you," he said.

"Not at all. It's nothing compared with the other claim."

"Well, thanks in any case," he told me. "We shall be seeing you tomorrow night?"

"Looking forward to it. By the way, I might be here for another week. I'm owed a week on last year's holiday and I like it down here."

"That's good," he said. "I hope to be seeing quite a lot of you."

I had a look at the telephone directory. Blayde, J., was there, and the address, Gorse Patch, Lower Churchill Avenue, and he was the only Blayde. There were several Brights, but only two of them a Miss. One was a Miss T. G. Bright of the Old Rectory, Havington. Havington is a suburb, a village that Sandbeach absorbed between the wars. It lies at the west end of Duke Street or the Esplanade, according to which way you take, and you go past a holiday camp and skirt the golf course just before you get to it. The beach rises there to cliffs and Havington sprawls back and merges into the second of those new housing estates. There's a regular service of buses but somehow I didn't think that Regency receptionist would be living out there. The other was more likely— Bright, Miss S., 17b, Wellbrook Gardens. Hiddon had thought she lived in Morley Gardens, but I guessed the other was right. Wellbrook Gardens was the road with the maisonettes, leading into Wellbrook Avenue.

While Hallows was still at those reports I went down to the desk. The clerk gave me a small booklet—all about Sandbeach and a map thrown in. He said there was a new one every fort-night with a complete list of attractions. The local Chamber of Commerce put it out and it cost sixpence. It was far from a dead loss judging by the number of advertisements. There was even a discreetly worded one by Holmes & Co. I bought a second one for Hallows. As I told the clerk, there was something in the air of Sandbeach that made one reckless.

Hallows had finished the reports and was lighting his pipe. Naturally he was non-committal: he knew, none better, that first impressions mean little or nothing, and suspicions are very far from facts. I lit my own pipe and we had a real good talk. He heard what I'd been told and what I'd unearthed and he hadn't a lot to say. The only thing that really interested him was that torch and its prints. I had to draw him a diagram of the reception desk and Sellman's office.

"Let's look at it from a professional's point of view," he said. "No joint is easier to case than a hotel. If I were doing the job I'd have taken a room for a night or maybe two, and so had a good look at the desk and the office, provided I waited, of course, till the door was open. I'd have slipped down in the night and had more than one look at the night porter, but whatever I did, you can bet your life I'd know where that safe was and what it was. So why a torch? You can get to the office by a back way from the kitchens. Once the porter's knocked out you can work at your ease. Draw the blinds, switch on the light, and Bob's your uncle."

I said we'd know more about that in the morning, when I'd seen Overson. If the Yard had the prints, then whatever suspicions we might have to the contrary, the job, as far as we were concerned, was as good as over.

"All the same, you don't think it's all it appears to be," he told me.

I had to smile. He had that trick of virtually reading my thoughts. Or maybe I have far too expressive a face. I wouldn't know. In any case I put my cards on the table.

"Perhaps you're right," I said. "I tried to come to this case with an open mind and everything I've come into contact with so far has a queer sort of smell to it. You heard me ringing Sellman? I'd told him you'd go round and check the cash claim. I didn't mention your name, of course; just that my assistant would be coming round. Now I've told him we'll accept his figures, and that's because I'd rather you stayed under cover. As far as you can, that is."

"Up to you, sir," he said. "But just what kind of smells?"

He was right. I'd had direct contacts. He'd had to form impressions at second-hand.

"We start off with the unusual as noticed by Plygate," I said. "Why Mrs. Dovell decided for the first time not to do a mere twenty-minute drive home on a fine night but to stay in the hotel. Is it fantastic to think it was because she wanted her jewellery to be in that safe? Maybe it is. But take the actual burglary. There's what you just brought up, and the matter of a pro. not using gloves and leaving behind an unnecessary torch. There's the fact that Hiddon didn't even know he'd been hit, and the blow he did get wasn't enough to put him out for more than a very few minutes, if that. Then there's that young sergeant—Blayde: self-assured and all that, but the devil of a way removed from my idea of a detective-sergeant. And by a strange coincidence, the wife from whom he's supposed to be separated was the receptionist on duty that night. Then there's this tough character Garlen, who as good as owns the hotel and pops up just at the right moment and offers me a free dinner. And I've only been here—how long is it? Just over six hours!"

"In fact, you haven't an open mind."

"Exactly. You and I may have to pass the claim, but it'll take me the very devil of a time to admit we've really earned our money. Still, there we are. Tomorrow may be another day."

There wasn't anything we could do that night, unless it were to pay a courtesy call on Plygate. I ought to have rung him before, so I got him at his private address. His house was just as you come into Havington. We spent a quarter of an hour with him but he'd nothing new. He'd never met Mrs. Dovell, but he did show us that day's issue of the Sandbeach *Gazette* which had flash-light pictures taken at the ball. They weren't too good: white, unnatural faces and startled eyes.

"That's Mrs. Dovell. One of my men took her statement and I just missed her, but I made enquiries and this is her. The one in the Indian sort of costume."

It conveyed nothing to us, except that one could just see the ear-rings and the riviere. I asked him if he knew anything else about her. All he did know was that she'd been married to Dovell about four years. She'd been his secretary and he married her a year after his first wife died. He thought she was just over thirty. Dovell, he said, was a gentleman in the best sense of the word.

Dinner at the hotel was from seven till nine-thirty. It was short of seven o'clock so we drove back a very long way round. The road runs back about a hundred yards from Havington cliffs and we stopped the car there where we had a fine view of the town: the lights along the Esplanade that looked, from that distance, like a fallen rainbow or a scattering of those sweets that we children used to call hundreds and thousands, and behind that kaleidoscope, the lights that marked the streets, and, far up the slope to the north, the last tapering off of lights from scattered bungalows.

I didn't know my best way to Wellbrook Avenue but I knew that if I kept due east I must come out somewhere near. What I struck was an almost deserted street in that factory area, but it brought us out past the dirt-track and on to just north of the roundabout. I crossed over into Wellbrook Gardens, drove a fairish way along, and drew the car up. Hallows went to have a look at No. 17. The maisonettes, he said, looked like twin flats. B was the ground-floor one, nearer the car.

We drove on. Wellbrook Avenue was well-lighted and I slowed the car as we passed Wellbrook Lodge, and so on to London Road, back to the roundabout and on to the hotel. After that we had dinner; the table in a near corner which made us reasonably inconspicuous. Hallows said he might drift along to the Regency and have a drink in one of the bars.

We never made it. As we came out to the almost empty foyer a man began making his way across to us. He'd been talking with the clerk at the desk, and somehow I had an idea it was us he was making for, and that's why I watched him as he steered his way round divans and chairs. Hallows was watching him, too.

"I seem to know that chap," he said.

I didn't know him from Adam. He was shortish, stocky and what I'd call casually dressed: sixtyish, red-faced, with a wide, expressive mouth and wrinkles at the corners of his blue eyes. He gave me a look but it was to Hallows that he held out his hand.

"Remember me?"

"Wait a minute," Hallows said. "It's not Bob Quarley?"

"Got it in one." He chuckled. "God-dammit, if you hadn't remembered me I'd have sloshed you."

He was still smiling as he turned to me. "Mr. Travers?"

"Your turn to get it in one," I said. "Slosh me if you like, but I don't know you."

"Well, I know you, sir." He held out a warm hand. "Mind if I sit down?"

"Help yourself," Hallows told him. "What'll you drink?"

"Anything you're having."

"Not in your line," Hallows told him. "We're having coffee."

"And a very good drink, too, so long as you don't make a fetish of it."

Hallows snapped his fingers at a waiter. I sat down wondering what it was all about.

Quarley was evidently what is known as a character. He fascinated me. Under the straggly moustache his lips had a cynical pucker, and yet his general air was that of a man who's enjoying life in his own way and hopes the rest of the world will be of his mind. His linen was spotless and his nails beautifully trimmed, but the hat he'd been wearing was stained round the band and the old tweed jacket, leather reinforced at elbows, cuffs and front, was already in holes elsewhere. The grey flannel trousers had lost all shape and the green necktie was lopsided, and yet the whole get-up was just in keeping; comfortable, easy-going, a sort of don't-give-a-damn. His voice was a fruity baritone with that faint gruffness that comes with age.

"When'd I last see you?" Hallows asked him.

"The first day of the Shepherd trial at the Old Bailey," Quarley said promptly. "Mr. Travers was giving evidence and you weren't due till later, and we slipped round to the Thistle and had a quick one."

"And how long ago'd that be? Seven or eight years?"

"Seven," I said. "And what're you doing here, Mr. Quarley?"

The coffee had come and I poured it out. Quarley said he'd have his as it came.

"What am I doing here, sir?" He chuckled. "A man's a right to be in his own home town. I was born and reared in Havington. My father was the schoolmaster there."

"And now you're on holiday?"

"Yes—and no," he told me reflectively. "But to go back to the secret history of Robert Quarley. I started my meteoric career on the local *Gazette*. After that, blood, sweat and tears—"

"Blood and sweat—my foot," Hallows told him. "You were always a lazy devil. Mind you, I don't say you didn't produce the goods."

"You see?" Quarley told me. "And who's he to cast a stone? But where was I?"

"Bleeding, sweating and sobbing," Hallows said.

Quarley chuckled. He turned to me again. "We're not boring you, sir?"

"Heavens, no!" I said. "I just can't wait to hear the rest."

"And hear it you shall. The *Gazette* at last began to realise it'd been harbouring a genius and it gave me my own column. But Sandbeach couldn't hold me down and the great city was calling. The *Clarion* secured my services, and once more I began at the foot of the ladder. Even lower than that. I became a crime reporter."

"Wait a minute," I said. "I'm beginning to remember. That morning when Mrs. Thompson was executed at Holloway. All that crowd of the morbid and the half-baked lined up outside the prison at eight o'clock, just like the silence on Armistice Day. A wonderful bit of writing. It absolutely haunted me at the time."

"Yes," he said, and the cynicism had suddenly gone. "I doubt if I've ever written anything better. And I was younger in those days, too."

"And what're you doing now, Bob?" Hallows wanted to know. "You're retired?"

"Too much ink in the old veins." The lip drooped again. "You'd better have a look at me. You don't often behold one of the proletariat. Believe it or not, an uncle of mine died six years ago and left me some money. So what did I do? I came back here, bought a little place at Havington near the golf course, and began devoting my talents to humanity."

"God help them," Hallows said. "But your wife, Bob? How is she?"

"Died a year ago," he said. "But I get along. A neighbour comes in and does a bit of cooking and—well, I get along."

"Tough luck," Hallows said. "And what're you really doing, Bob?"

"Free-lancing. And an occasional job for the old *Gazette*. What I call my scandal column."

He caught my questioning look.

"Not what you think, sir. I'm a sort of public scandal exposer. So long as I don't stir up any muck with the big advertisers, I've a free hand. Don Quixote, that's me. Everybody knows me by now. Anybody getting the raw end of a deal. Municipal jobbery. Nepotism. Red-tape. Profiteering. Wastage of public funds. Anything, in fact, with a smell."

"You must have made the devil of a lot of enemies."

"Maybe. And I've made a hell of a lot of friends."

"Yes, there's that," Hallows said.

The coffee had disappeared and I suggested a glass of port. Quarley said if it was all the same to me he'd have beer. A pint of bitter. Hallows had the same and I had a whisky and splash.

"This scandal column of yours," Hallows said. "You wouldn't by any chance be thinking of doing something on that Regency job?"

"Well, now, you've given me an idea," Quarley said slowly. "Not that there'd be anything in it. Unless you've any ideas yourself."

Hallows laughed. "You're a slippery cuss. But how'd you come to spot us? Try and wriggle out of that one."

"Wriggle, he says! The truth is that I was abroad, as I always am, and looking for copy, when I happened to see Mr. Travers having a quick chat with my old friend Sam Garlen outside the Regency." He held up a restraining hand. "Mind you, I don't say that I didn't know that a representative of United Assurance wouldn't be coming down."

"Garlen's pretty tough?" I said.

"You have to be, in his game."

"And the man who was driving the car?"

"That's Len Romsie, his brother-in-law. General handyman. The name convey anything to you? If it doesn't, he was a pretty useful welter-weight. *You* must have seen him, Tom. The old days at Blackfriars. Still a tough character. He's the one who interviews the defaulters. Got himself three months four or five years ago for making the interview too boisterous."

"I must have a look at him some time," Hallows said. "But let's drop all the backchat, Bob, and spread our hands. We trust you and you trust us."

"Sounds fair enough to me," Quarley told him soberly. "You tell me how the investigation's going."

"We might do that," I said. "But let's clear the ground first. You know all about the finding of a torch?"

He didn't reply for a minute. He took a pull at the tankard and wiped his heavy moustache.

"That's as good a start as any. As a matter of fact, I have a good friend at the Regency and I was on the spot as fast as my old Austin could bring me. You know all about that torch?"

"Only that it had prints on it and it was found on the spot."

"Well, Overson found it. He's a Chief Inspector, in charge of the C.I.D. There used to be a superintendent but he retired about three months ago and they haven't replaced him yet. I think Overson's hoping for a general move-up and him getting the rank. I doubt it. He's a pretty smart man, but thirty-six is young for superintendent. By the way, I dropped in at police headquarters just before I came in here. They know whose the prints are but they're not giving anything out. And we weren't allowed to print anything about that torch."

"The idea being to let the burglar think he's got away with it?"

"Maybe." The lip drooped again. "The ways of the police are inscrutable, like Providence. All I'm telling you is that everything's being kept quiet. You saw the safe, Mr. Travers?"

"Saw it this afternoon."

But I didn't know just where the torch was found and he told me. A patrol car reached the Regency first and Blayde was there a few minutes after. Overson arrived about a quarter of an hour later and it was he who found the torch. It was in the space between the safe and the wall; a pencil torch that must have fallen from the top of the safe, and that's why the burglar hadn't missed it. At least, that was the theory.

"More like a raw amateur job on that showing," Hallows said. "Still, they're the ones that make the theories."

I wanted to know what the police force was like. Quarley guessed what I meant. By and large, he said, it was as good a force as any in the country.

"Garlen gets a certain amount of protection, but that's inevitable. Money may pass or not—I've no proof. It may be more a question of keeping eyes shut. And if you want a tip, here's one. There's a little newsagent's and tobacconist's at the end of Carter Street. Salmon's the name. Just keep an eye on it from within an hour after the first edition of the *Evening Gazette* comes out. That'll be at about ten o'clock. I could give you at least half a dozen more."

"I might do that," Hallows told him. "But the Chief Constable—what's he like?"

"Harry Triller? Oh, quite a good man. Retiring in another eighteen months."

"To get back to the case proper," I said, "you haven't done any researches on Mrs. Dovell?"

"No need to," he told us dryly. "You can practically follow her up right through the *Gazette* files. Her people were farmers at Banford. You know Banford, Tom?"

Hallows said he'd heard of it.

"Four miles on from Havington," Quarley said. "The father married pretty late. The sporting type. One of the rip-roarin'-est old hellions about here. Went bankrupt not long after the war and moved to the Midlands somewhere. Died a few years back. Probably from Quarley's disease."

"Cirrhosis of the liver?"

"Right on the mark," Quarley said complacently. "And not a bad death, too. But where was I?"

"Slowly arriving, we hope, at the daughter."

"Ah, yes," he said. "Our Mona. She went to the girls' grammar school here and then on to a secretarial college. Just got a job before the old folks had to move, as secretary-typist at Millbridges, the local brewers. She was there about seven years. There was some juicy scandal about her and young Gerald Millbridge, but what truth was in it I wouldn't know. Then Dovell's secretary got married and she got the job."

"No scandal about *him*!"

Quarley looked horrified.

"Crude, my boy. And it shocks me. Dovell used to be our local Galahad. County magistrate, president of the High Church this and that, public enemy Number One to the race gangs and the bookies. Then his wife died and he went and married Mona. And no funeral baked meats about it."

"And what's she like?"

Quarley chuckled.

"About as snappy a brunette as you're likely to clap eyes on. She'd give ideas to even a worn-out old lecher like you."

"May and December," I said.

"That's about it, sir. Or David and Abishag. Mind you, she's pretty high and mighty these days. Mrs. Charles Dovell is really someone. But still a bit of a tail-swisher, unless I'm a long way wide of the mark. And don't prick your ears, Tom. You're about five years too late."

"Plenty of fish in the sea," Hallows told him. "Anything else fit for us to hear?"

Quarley started to fill his pipe, thought better of it and put it in his pocket.

"I could give you another tip before I hear what you two gents have got to tell me." He slowly emptied the tankard while we waited. "The world's still a very small place. Now and again I get a horse given me and invest a few bob with Garlen. My informant is the woman who does for me, as they say, and she has two brothers. One's odd man at Freddy Martin's racing stable at Banford and the other's a gardener at Laneford Hall."

He sat back and looked at us.

"And that's all?" Hallows said.

"That's all. Just an idea. I haven't the time to make anything of it but you might."

There had been a trickle of people in and out, but just at that minute a man came through the swing doors. It was Garlen's brother-in-law, Romsie, and I swivelled round a bit for a better look at him. Quarley looked round, too. Romsie's eyes rested on us for a moment and he went straight on to the desk. He had a word with the clerk and went through to the bar.

"Talk of the devil," I said, and told Hallows who the man was. Quarley reached for his hat.

"Will I be seeing you in the morning, Tom?"

"Why not?"

"Right," he said. "About eleven. The Waggoners. Just this side of the dog-track in Carter Street. Think I'd like to keep an eye on Romsie."

He gave a nod to Hallows, held out a hand to me, said it had been nice seeing me again, and went out by the swing doors.

"I think we've struck pay-dirt," Hallows told me.

"Quarley's a reliable man?"

"Don't let him kid you," he said. "All that blether and cheap cynicism is just a front. He was always like that. A damn smart man. Nose like a ferret's." He smiled to himself. "Wonder how much that uncle of his left him? Must have been pretty much of a packet for him to have left Fleet Street."

I frowned.

"The problem is, just what are we going to give in exchange for those couple of tips?"

"Leave it to me," Hallows said. "I think I can handle Bob Quarley."

4
OUT AND ABOUT

THE Regency job was hardly mentioned in the morning's Sand-beach *Gazette*. Hallows had ordered it overnight and I'd been looking through it after breakfast while he went on with his meal. There was nothing much he could do until his rendezvous with Quarley, and he thought of having a daylight tour of the town to get himself better acquainted. He was at the toast and marmalade stage when I was called to the telephone. It was Norris.

"Thought I'd better let you know as soon as I could, but I've had two opinions on your Mr. S. I don't think there's any doubt about his being a man of the highest integrity. Also he's very high up in his profession and commands a very big salary."

"Unlikely to lend himself to even a high-class swindle?"

"Absolutely. His reputation's worth far more than eighteen thousand pounds."

So that was that, and my own opinion entirely. But Norris was asking if there was anything else, and it struck me that it might be useful to have an opinion on Triller, the Chief-Constable. Norris is a retired C.I.D. inspector with useful contacts among his old friends.

I left Hallows looking through the papers, went upstairs and prettied myself, and at five minutes short of the half-hour set out for police headquarters. I had only a hundred yards to walk. It was a very large red-brick building; post-war and somewhat incongruous against the Victorian stucco of Henry Street. The main entry was nearer Duke Street; at the sea end was a widish entry to the garage. A black patrol car swung out as I stood watching, and turned up towards the Esplanade. Triller had certainly made a good job of the traffic problem.

I didn't know whether he'd got his ideas from Manhattan, but each of those connecting roads from Duke Street to the Esplanade was a one-way street.

A uniformed constable took me up to the first floor and Overson's room. I waited while he made enquiries and then he ushered me in. It was a nice airy room overlooking Henry Street. The flat-topped desk had an inter-com and a telephone. Steel filing cabinets stood along the walls: a bookcase held quite a lot of books and there were a couple of mahogany cupboards. A few police photographs hung on the walls, and there was a fireplace with an electric fire turned partly on.

The door had hardly closed on me when Overson came in. He was carrying some papers which he put in the tray. He'd already given me a smile and now he held out his hand.

"Mr. Travers? My name's Overson. Very good of you to come round."

Blayde came in. Seen with Overson he looked even more immature. The smart get-up of the previous afternoon had gone and he was wearing a blue serge suit. He gave me a faint smile as he passed.

"Do sit down," Overson told me. "Sure you won't take off your coat?"

I'd had a good look at him. He was tall and athletic-looking, and the rather pale face had plenty of character. His hair was dark and the dark moustache even more closely clipped than my own. Virile was the word for him. He reminded me of a film star whose name I couldn't recall and whom a woman in that particular picture had alluded to as "a gorgeous hunk of man". Not that there was anything glamorous about him. His manner was easy and he spoke quietly. His clothes were quiet, too: a well-worn brown suit of quite good cut and an old-gold tie.

He sat down at the desk and Blayde drew up a chair a little behind and to his right. He took something from a top drawer of the desk and laid it on the blotting-paper in front of him. There was the same quiet smile as he looked up.

"How's the investigation going?"

I shrugged my shoulders. "Almost finished. Unless we have strong suspicions of any irregularities these jobs are more or less routine."

He nodded. "Mind if I ask you a question? Naturally you needn't answer it."

"Go ahead," I told him.

"Have you any suspicion of any irregularities? At the hotel, for instance?"

"None at all," I said frankly. I was going to add a quip to the effect that maybe I was a trusting sort of soul, then kept my mouth shut instead. Overson smiled. He picked up whatever it was he had in front of him.

"This is a copy of the *Police Gazette*. You know it?"

I said I'd heard of it. I could have told him I'd known it even long before the speeding up of printing and distribution, when he was probably taking his meals from a high chair and wearing a bib. He thought it necessary to give me the low-down. It was issued daily to all police forces throughout the country and contained for the benefit of those forces up-to-the-minute information on crimes and criminals. He added that it wasn't available to the general public, which presumably included myself.

"This is the issue for November 17th, 1956," he said, "and you'll soon see why. The prints on that torch we found belong to a Herbert Davitt, and this is his record. Born Coventry, 1930. Left school and worked for a wholesale store and later drove a delivery van. Turned down for military service on account of inclination towards T.B. Next heard of in London. Drove a stolen car with two other men who did a wages hold-up. A big job—over five thousand pounds. At Stepney. Davitt slugged a man who came to the assistance of the cashier and clerk. That was in March, 1953.

Then in January, 1954, he was picked up with two men in the act of bringing off another hold-up. That was at Walthamstow, where he'd been driving a lorry for one of his confederates. He was sentenced at the Old Bailey to five years. Then on the afternoon of 16th November he escaped from Wormwood Scrubs. This is the issue sent out the morning after."

"I think I remember that escape," I said. "And he hasn't been seen or heard of since?"

"Not a word, not a sign, until we were lucky enough to get that torch. Mind you, for all anyone knows, he might have done a score of jobs since he broke out. After all, he had to live."

"Yes," I said. "And what now?"

"What you've been told is in the strictest confidence. The idea is that he should think he's got away with yet another job. But his description and so on has been re-circulated and every force in the country will be on the *qui vive*. He's fairly distinctive. A snub nose, for instance. Five-foot seven and only about nine stone. Inch scar from a cut on his left forearm. Unmarried, by the way, and probably very much of a lone wolf." He leaned back. "So there we are. I don't know how this special information will affect your investigation, but I imagine it'll shorten it."

"It will indeed," I said. "Naturally I have to go through the motions according to the procedure laid down, but I ought to be finished today. The company will be settling the claim in the course of the next few days. And I'm most grateful to you for your co-operation. Your confidences, needless to say, will be absolutely respected."

Quite a speech. Almost like opening a bazaar. Overson nodded, smiled, and got to his feet.

"Then we shan't have the pleasure of seeing much more of you?"

"Not unless I land myself in trouble."

He gave me a quick look. I chuckled.

"What I mean is that I've got a week's holiday owing from last year. I don't think there's anything else in the offing for me and

I'm very comfortable at the hotel and I like it here, so I thought I might stay on. Also, if you don't grab your holidays when you've half a chance, you're likely to get them cut short, as mine was last year."

"That's fine," he said. "You interested in police work?"

"Aren't we all?"

"Then drop in when you feel like it. Things are pretty quiet at the moment but you never know when something interesting might turn up."

He went out with me. He stopped. "Oh, by the way, the Chief would like a word with you if you can spare the time."

"Very good of him."

"This way," he said, and turned back towards the stairs. Just along a short corridor he tapped at a door, looked in, and then drew back for me to enter. I went in—alone.

It was a fine big room, again overlooking Henry Street: more like a library than an office. The floor was well carpeted: the wide desk was reproduction Chippendale; silver cups and trophies were in cases all round the walls and there was a long, reproduction bookcase. For all its size there was something cosy about it, even the smell of tobacco smoke and furniture polish.

Triller was signing papers and a uniformed inspector stood at his elbow. Triller looked up.

"Make yourself comfortable, sir. Shan't keep you a minute."

He was a huge man and looked the sixty I'd been told he was nearing. His shoulders were like the end of a barn, but he'd run a bit to fat, and one of his chins as he bent forward was cascading over the stiff white collar as far as the blue polka-dot tie. Though his badger hair was going bald on top, his eyebrows were about the bushiest I'd ever seen.

But I liked his manner. Now and again when he looked at a paper the inspector put in front of him he would say something, and when he looked up it would be with a nod or a smile. But all that lasted only another three or four minutes; then the inspector gathered up the papers and went out. Triller got to his feet and he looked an even bigger man. He held out his hand.

"Glad to see you, Mr. Travers. You're investigating that Regency job?"

"Yes," I said. "But from what I've just heard in confidence from your people, the investigation is as good as over: except for the red tape."

"There's always that."

He waved me back to the chair and settled himself again. "A cigarette? Personally I hate the damn things. Always smoke a pipe."

He had a quiet, friendly voice. We stoked up our pipes. He got his own well going before he spoke.

"I think we're doing right in holding back on Davitt. It'll be far easier now for him to make a slip."

I said that even to a layman like myself it seemed the only thing to do. Then he asked me how I'd got on with Overson.

"He's up and coming," he told me. "Right on top of his job. He and Blayde make a first-class team. Practically brought up together, those two." He smiled. "Known as David and Jonathan. Dave Overson and John Blayde."

I couldn't think of anything to say, so I just smiled.

"Nothing like a first-class team," he said. "By the way, you'd like some coffee? It ought to be just coming in."

He spoke on the inter-com and almost at once a couple of cups were brought in. He took sugar and so did I. In that brief interval we'd begun to talk about crime.

"Think we've got everything here in hand now," he said. "Between ourselves, a lot depends on the Bench. Far too much namby-pamby stuff these days, but we were lucky. The chairman then was Charles Dovell. It's his wife whose jewellery was taken, by the way, but he was the ideal man. We used to have trouble with the various gangs, most of them coming from town. It took us about four years after the war to stamp all that out." He smiled. "The assizes used to be chock-a-block. Mind you, we still get the wise boys down here, and the wide boys. And an occasional bit of slashing, but compared with the old days—" He chuckled and waved a hand.

"Which reminds me," I said, "I'm paying a red-tape visit there this afternoon. Just a formal check of the wife's statement."

"Give him my best regards," he said. "Poor chap, he rarely drops in on the Bench nowadays. Almost crippled with arthritis." He nodded to himself. "One of the very best. Between ourselves a bit of a crank on religious matters but one of the very best. He's got a fine place there at Laneford. I believe his people have been there for best part of a couple of hundred years."

"Any children?"

"One son. Killed in the last war. Just about to get married, too." He let out a breath. "A bad business. I hate to see the old names die out."

He asked me about my own experiences. I told him the story of the Russian Cross, making a mystery of it and inviting him to find an answer. He chuckled away When he heard that answer and wanted to hear some more. Now and again the inter-com. went and he'd speak a few words, but things seemed quiet and we must have been talking for quite half an hour. It was only the entry of that inspector to remind him of an engagement that made him get to his feet. I told him about the week's holiday and he said he'd certainly be seeing me again. A nice fellow, Triller. I liked him. And beneath that velvet glove I was betting he had an iron hand.

I made my way out and, just as I came to the head of the stairs, Overson appeared.

"Hallo, sir. How'd you get on with the Chief?"

"Had a capital time," I told him. "And now the nose to the grindstone again. Which reminds me. Just a matter of form but I have to have a quick word with the receptionist who was on duty that night. I believe she's a Miss Bright. You don't happen to know where she lives? Or is she in the telephone directory?"

"Wait a moment." He frowned; then he smiled. "I've nothing on in about ten minutes' time, so if you like I'll take you there.

Matter of fact, I want a private word with her myself. Pick you up in, say, ten minutes, outside your hotel?"

"That's very good of you. I'm most grateful. Ten minutes' time and I'll be on the look-out."

I walked quickly back and went up to my room to telephone. Five minutes went before I had John Hill on the line. I said I'd be writing officially that evening but he wasn't to credit any rumours to the effect that everything was aboveboard. As a matter of fact, I was putting out information to that effect myself. The truth was that I was a very long way from satisfied. I also put him wise to that week's holiday and by that time the ten minutes were practically up and I had to ring off.

Overson was only a couple of minutes late. He was driving a Ford Zephyr and he noticed my look of surprise.

"Can't be too careful in this town," he told me. "I always come down in my own car. I even stretch a point in a case like this. There was a bit of scandal about a superintendent here who used a police car a bit too freely."

He'd already turned into the Duke Street traffic.

"Not far to go," he told me. "There's a short cut here that misses the roundabout."

We swung round and then right. It wasn't more than three or four minutes before we were crossing into Wellbrook Gardens. I thought he was going to draw up at No. 17 but he moved out a bit. The wide gate was open and he drove the car slowly in and to within a foot or two of the main door. I saw that just beyond, the narrow drive moved slightly round and back.

"Nice little places," I said. "A natty idea each having a garage."

"Put up just after the war," he said, "when things were cheaper. Anyone owning the pair could make a thousand pounds profit tomorrow. But let's go in."

He didn't ring. With an "Excuse me," he went first, opened the door and walked in.

"Shirley! . . . You there, Shirley?"

We were in a lounge-sitting-room: quite a large room and beautifully furnished. Everything about it was good, from the soft beige carpet to the matching chintzes on easy chairs and the divan. There was a television set in the far corner, a Danish coffee-table and a small reproduction Queen Anne bureau-bookcase. The room was chilly, and Overson walked across and switched on the electric fire.

He listened, gave me a nod and almost at once Shirley Blayde came in, and through the open door I caught a glimpse of an up-to-date kitchen, all stainless steel and gay cupboards. She was a blonde. I don't say I gasped, but I think I blinked my eyes. She was about five-feet six and beautifully built. The trim little bottom fitted to an inch the tight, brown trousers, and the just as tight yellow jumper displayed a bust from which it wasn't too easy to avert one's eyes. Her lips might have been a bit too full, but she was really something when she smiled. But she wasn't smiling as she came in. Her face clouded at the sight of Overson, then she gave me a quick look.

"You here again?"

He shook his head. "Now. Shirley. Don't be like that. I've just brought along Mr. Travers here who wants to ask a question or two about Saturday night. Only a formality." He turned to me, "I'll wait outside."

"No need to go," I said. "Nothing to be alarmed about. Miss Bright. It's only that I have to say I've seen you. For the sake of our records."

"Might as well sit down," she said. "You're not forced to stay, Dave, but if you must—"

She left it like that and sat down on the divan, and she didn't seem somehow to know what to do with her hands. I offered my cigarette case and then held the lighter. Dave Overson, who'd already lit up a cigarette of his own, still stood by the door.

I told her who I was, said I wouldn't keep her more than a couple of minutes, and asked if she'd noticed anything suspicious on that particular night. She hadn't. Did Hiddon seem perfectly normal when she'd left? As far as she remembered, quite normal. A reliable man? She guessed so. Always made himself useful. Admittedly did pretty well out of tips. I gave a quick description of Davitt. Had any such man to her personal knowledge booked a room in the last few days? She frowned in thought and said she didn't remember one.

I got to my feet and smiled down at her.

"That's all, thank you, Miss Bright. Not very terrible, was it?"

She laughed. "I was almost scared when I saw you. Wondered what I'd been doing."

I held out my hand. "Well, thank you again. You'll be relieved to know I shan't be troubling you any more."

Overson and I were through the door when he stopped.

"Just a minute. There's something I have to see her about."

He left the door open. I stood by the car and I couldn't help hearing every word that was said.

"You back again?"

"Look, Shirley, you've got to tell me what you're going to do about Jack."

"Oh?" she said. "Who're you to tell me what I've got to do?"

"God-dammit, will you listen! Are you going to divorce him or aren't you?"

"That's my business."

There was a moment's silence. I could almost see him shaking his head. His voice was quiet again.

"Why don't you go back to him, Shirley? Think of the good times we used to have. And you know what he thinks of you."

She laughed.

"Oh yes: I know. And if he sent you here, tell him I'll slam the door in your face if you ever bother me again. Now get out—and stay out."

He came out. The door slammed behind him and his face was black as thunder. I'd already shot into my seat.

"Women!" he said. "My God, they drive me crazy! Thank God, I always managed to cut loose in time."

He slowly backed the car. Something of the anger went from his voice.

"Did you know she was Jack Blayde's wife?"

"Really?"

"Yes," he said. "Married him three years ago and left him after two years."

He backed the car out, saw the road was clear and then suddenly halted.

"You in any hurry? I'll take you back if you are, but I ought to run up to my place."

"No hurry at all. As a matter of fact, I'd like the ride." He watched the road till we were nearing the Beacon Estate, then he took it more easily.

"A bad business about those two," he told me. "Just like a couple of damn silly children. My place is quite near theirs and we used to have some damn good times together that first year. Then she started to cool off and later she packed up and went."

"Missed the glamour of the Regency reception?"

He grunted.

"Partly, perhaps. But she was always nagging him about money. Why didn't he do this and why didn't he do that. Money's her god. That, and being in the local swim."

The car turned away left, and always uphill. The bungalows were now well spaced, and suddenly he drew the car in at a small-ish one. Homeland was the name on the gate. It had a lean-to garage at the near side and the garden, what I could see of it, was beautifully trim. He drew in at the gravelled drive, then backed out again.

"This is my little place. Shan't keep you a minute."

He went along to the front door and let himself in. In two or three minutes he came out again and a short, plump woman was with him at the door. He turned back for another word with her, and I guessed she was a daily help.

"Nice little place," I told him as he settled at the wheel. "Quite big enough for me," he said. "Don't like living in the town in any case. Jack Blayde's saddled with a place twice the size of this. I think he ought to sell it. As a matter of fact we'll see it if we go back another way. There's a lane we can get through."

He went on about hundred yards and turned left into what was more of an unmetalled track. The car bumped along for another hundred yards and then came out at a good road. He turned right and stopped the car.

"That's his bungalow—the second one along. The garden's gone to pot, but it's not a bad place."

"A fine view."

"Yes," he said. "Shirley used to rave about the view. Then she started to say she hated the sight of it."

"That place of hers a furnished flat?"

"Oh, no. Furnished it herself. Always had the bungalow cluttered up with magazines on homes and decoration. You know the sort of thing."

"Must have cost her a packet."

His lip drooped. "Oh, our Shirley's got money. Had a goodish bit put by when she married, and hung on to it. And he was always far too generous with the housekeeping money, and you bet she did pretty well out of that. Did you notice what she had to bring in about Hiddon ? What he made out of tips ? And she's got social ideas."

He made as if to move the car on, then dropped his hands again.

"You seen Mona Dovell yet?"

"Seeing her this afternoon."

He grunted. "I oughtn't to tell you this, but she's one of the causes of the Blayde's splitting up. Mona used to be a secretary-typist, like Shirley. Did you know that?"

I said I thought I'd heard something of the sort somewhere. "She and Shirley went to the same secretarial college," he went on. "They were very friendly at one time, then Mona caught Dovell on the rebound and she dropped Shirley like a hot potato. That rankled. Shirley hates her like sin. And my idea is that Shirley's got her eye on some man with money. She mayn't give a damn about him, but she'd marry him, just to get even with Mona. By the way, don't even mention Shirley's name this afternoon. I know you won't, but I thought I'd better mention it."

He moved the car on and almost at once he was having to keep his eyes on the road. In under five minutes we were back at police headquarters.

"You don't mind walking the few yards back?"

"Not in the least," I told him. "And thanks for the trip. I've enjoyed it."

"Sorry you had to be bothered with all that other stuff."

"Not at all. Besides, it does one good sometimes to get things off one's chest."

"Maybe you're right. When shall I see you again?"

"One of these times," I said. "Perhaps you'll have a meal with me some day soon."

He said he'd love to. Then he waved a cheerful hand and disappeared in the entry to the garage. According to my watch and my stomach it was nearly time for lunch.

5
LANEFORD HALL

The morning had been such a series of new experiences that I hadn't a mind sufficiently free to assess the real value of what Overson had told me. When Hallows and I came to a cold-blooded appraisal, it looked—when a cursory visit had been paid to Laneford Hall—as if we might as well take an evening ride back to town. What one couldn't easily dismiss was the fact that a man with a record had left his prints on the torch, and even the most melodramatic of suggestions couldn't find a way round evidence like that.

And yet, somehow, neither of us wanted to take that evening trip back to town; in fact, the more open and aboveboard everything appeared, the less we felt inclined to accept it as such. In our game one gets at times such obstinate gnawings: uneasinesses that insist, against all logic, that black isn't always black or white white. And to the original suspicions that everything was far from what it seemed, my morning had added more. It seemed a bit too opportune, for instance, that Overson should have remembered private business with Shirley Blayde at the very moment I told him I wanted to see her. And it seemed to me that she'd been unusually bitter with Overson himself. Was that a deliberate hostility in order to keep him from investigating too closely something in which she and her husband had been concerned? Had that separation business been an elaborate fake?

Hallows didn't see how that could apply to the Regency job. After all, it had been a year since she'd left her husband, and the Regency business couldn't have been planned as far ahead as that. His idea was that she might have been up to the ears in that job, that Blayde might have discovered it, and that he was now covering up. He might even be using it as pressure for a reconciliation. And yet, whatever either of us thought, we always got back to that inescapable fact—that Davitt must have done the actual robbery. You can't simulate finger-prints and superimpose them on a torch. And if Davitt did the job, then why were we hanging on in Sandbeach?

Hallows had had a good morning but what he had learned was no more substantial. He'd met Quarley at the rendezvous and they'd had a couple of quick ones and then Hallows had kept an eye for a few minutes on that newsagent's shop.

"Just what you'd guess," he said. "A trickle of customers leaving bets. Almost blatant, but what good it does us I can't exactly see. The fact that the police don't seem to be worrying their heads over Garlen can't have anything to do with the Regency job." He frowned as he told me that. "And yet Quarley seems to think it has. Close as a clam, that chap. Opens his shell a sixteenth of an inch and snaps it to again."

"Get anything else?" I said.

"Not that we can use. I did gather he's got a contact, or hopes to get one, in Garlen's office." He gave an amused little snort. "And there again, I couldn't get out of him what for. My own idea is that it's something to do with Mrs. Dovell. You remember that vague tip he gave us about her gardener, so if she should have got in a bit deep with Garlen, there's a whole lot explained."

He smiled to himself. "He's a likeable cuss. Always was. Maddening sometimes, but always a chap you couldn't quarrel with. And deep as they make 'em. Always had contacts everywhere. Probably has now. We went along to the *Gazette* morgue and he showed me some of the stuff he's done. Pretty good. Must have meant the devil of a lot of leg work. And that's what's making me think. Either my name's Jones or he's out to make a real big thing out of the Regency job. And he wouldn't have been attracted by it in the first place if he hadn't been sure there was a devil of a lot more in it than the police gave out."

"What'd you give him in exchange?"

"Only about the door being unbolted. I'd have liked to tell him about Hiddon and that gentle crack on the skull, but I daren't. I gather you wouldn't want Hiddon to know you'd done any talking."

I said he was right. Hiddon had told an old buddy things no one else would ever know. But what we'd do—if we stayed on, and I was almost committed to it—would be to have a system of exchange and barter. If Quarley opened up completely, well and good; if not, we'd decide on what to exchange for what.

"One hint he did drop," Hallows said, "and that was about that gardener again. Don't know what you'll gather there this afternoon but I might do worse than drift along tonight or tomorrow morning."

I asked where he'd left Quarley and he said at his bungalow.

"We went back there for a final drink. Quite a nice little place. Remember where we pulled up last night and had a look back at the town? I shouldn't think he's more than two hundred yards from there. Garage and quite a nice garden. Sort of place I wouldn't mind myself. Only one thing against it, a bit too windy for me."

*

March that year had been a weather clerk's display of just what you could do if you really put your mind to it. We'd had snow and frosts, then slush and fog, then dry, biting cold, and now we had the wind blowing half a gale. As we had lunch you could hear it howling, and our waiter said that when it dropped we should get rain. But there was no sign of it and the wind was as strong as ever when I set out for Laneford.

It was a pleasant journey, and snug in the car with the heater on and I didn't regret not bringing an overcoat. About half a mile along the London Road I took a left turn, climbed for a bit up the slope and then dropped down to wooded, undulating country with a farmhouse or two. I went through a village called Narfield, bore right and three miles on was Laneford. It was a smallish village—only about four hundred souls—but as pretty a one as I'd come across for some time. In a way it was too good to be true; the half-timbered houses here and there, the picture-postcard village green and the church tower peering above a clump of leafless oaks. Just near the village end was a pub called the Hare and Hounds, and just beyond that, round a short bend, was a park. It was reasonably well wooded, but a lot of its grassland had been ploughed and just short of the main entrance was a pretty big acreage of winter wheat. A few yards on a gap in the trees showed me the Hall. I turned slowly into the drive, saw by the dashboard clock that I was well on time, and pulled up a hundred yards on. From where I sat the view was curiously evocative, and suddenly I knew why. Had there been a horse in the foreground, held by a groom and bestridden by some eighteenth century squire, I'd have been looking at a picture by Stubbs.

From then on, though the drive wound between trees, the Hall was never out of sight and the white of its front and the blue of its slates stood clear against the grey of woods and a stormy sky. It was early Georgian, with beautiful tall windows and a handsome porch, though that might have been later. I kept left and made the circle to just beyond it, heading for home.

I pushed the bell and it was a minute or two before the door opened.

"My name's Travers and I have an appointment with Mrs. Dovell."

He was the elderly butler to whom I'd spoken the previous day. He drew back to let me in.

"I think madam is out at the moment, sir, but I'm sure the master will see you. May I take your hat?"

The entrance hall was large and lofty. A handsome staircase rose from the back to a wide landing, and there were at least four doors. Pictures were everywhere, and on the polished floor were two Oriental rugs and a Bukhara strip from the door to the foot of the stairs. The butler made for a door at the back and to the left. He tapped, looked in and drew back for me to enter.

"Mr. Travers, sir."

It was a lofty but medium-sized room for a house of that size, the walls panelled in soft wood and hung with oils; family portraits, one guessed, and that of an eighteenth-century judge above the marble mantelpiece most probably a Gainsborough. My collector's eyes went covetously round. The long, twin bookcases were Chippendale, as were the chairs; the marquetry Queen Anne clock was walnut and in the quiet of that room its tick could be plainly heard. A Sheraton cabinet with lattice doors held china in a Worcester green. On the mantelshelf was a French clock, decorated with a Neptune and nymphs. A pair of *famille verte* vases on ebony stands were flanking it. Through the windows I could see a stretch of lawn and behind it a garden with topiary work.

The chair in which Charles Dovell sat, or reclined, was a wing grandfather, and his right leg rested on a cushioned cabriole-legged stool alongside which lay a stout stick with a ferrule of thick rubber. On another stool or side-table to his left was a telephone and the book he'd been reading, and as I went towards him I could already feel the comforting warmth of the fire in the ornate Adam basket.

I could judge only as I saw him in that chair but he must have been about six feet. The hair was still abundant but very white, whiter even than the pointed beard. His cheeks were pale and finely drawn, and there was the first faint yellowing of age. His eyes were a pale and watery blue and the suit he was wearing was grey. His hands were thin and the fingers bony and long.

"Pardon my not getting up," he said, and stirred in the chair. "I'm sorry to say I have a knee which is giving me considerable trouble and it takes me quite a time to settle again. You're the insurance investigator who rang me yesterday?"

"Yes, sir—Travers. Losses like that of your wife's jewellery have to be investigated by headquarters, though it's largely a matter of routine. I'm sure I shan't trouble Mrs. Dovell more than a minute or two."

"I understand. I understand." There was nothing querulous about the way he said it. "But draw that chair up to the fire where I can see you. I'm told it's very cold outside."

"Very windy, sir."

"Yes," he said, in that quiet, rather tired voice of his. "I can see that from the trees. My wife had an unexpected call but she should be back. And this is the first time you've visited Laneford?"

"Yes, sir. It looks a charming place."

"You've seen the church?"

"Only from the road."

"You must see the interior. Ten years ago we were doing some necessary restoration work and were fortunate to uncover a Doom. You're interested in church architecture?"

"Frankly, no, sir. I like to look at old churches, but I doubt if I could do more than tell Saxon from Gothic. I do happen to know what a Doom is."

"This is very fine and remarkably clear. But, let me see. You've come about the loss of the jewellery. I remember when I was a boy there was a fire in the stables—they're pulled down now—and an assessor came down." He smiled quietly. "That would be before you were born, but you see we were quite up to date, even then."

"I'm sure you were. But the jewellery, sir. It was family jewellery?"

"No," he said slowly. "I doubt if you could call it that. We have some admirable silver, but I don't think jewellery was ever a Dovell obsession, if one can call it that. No. This came through my first wife and was intended for my son's wife. Unfortunately, that was not to be."

In the silence one could hear the tick of both clocks. Then there was a sound and he stirred in his chair. The door opened and a woman came bustling in and the quiet of the room was all at once disturbed, as if she'd been a gust of wind. She was wearing a short fur coat over a brown tweed costume, and she came in so quickly and stooped so quickly over the chair that I'd barely time to see her face.

"All right, darling? Sorry I had to be so long."

The voice was just a bit strident.

"I'm quite all right, my dear. Mr. Travers and I were getting along very well."

She must have seen me as she came into the room, and now she allowed herself to become aware of it. I'd long since got to my feet. Her hand rested lightly on the back of the chair and it didn't strike me till afterwards that the pose had been that of a Victorian husband and wife photograph—with variations.

"Of course." She gave a little bow. "As you've probably guessed, I'm Mrs. Dovell."

"How d'you do."

She was a fine-looking woman, a tallish brunette who at that moment looked even younger than her thirty-two years. Her eyes were brown and her cheeks flushed with the wind. That she was trying to impress me was obvious.

"I'm sorry to have had to trouble you," I said.

"No particular trouble. I mean, if these things have to be done, then it's best to get them over. Don't you think?"

I smiled. "You mean on a par with the dentist?"

She didn't quite catch what I'd meant. She bent over the chair again.

"I think we'd better go to my room, darling, then we shan't disturb you."

"As you wish, my dear."

She turned at once. I stopped to say a quick goodbye and a word of thanks to her husband, then followed her through the door and in the wake of some very attractive scent. I don't admit that I have an exceptionally dirty mind, but I was beginning to have ideas. What this room was to which we were going, I didn't know, but I did suddenly wonder if those ridiculous attempts to impress me had been more for the benefit of her husband than for myself. There was sex in every inch of her and maybe in a minute we'd be very good friends.

But things weren't shaping like that. It didn't look as if there was going to be a room of any sort, for she didn't turn towards the stairs but made for the front door, and she stopped by the chair on which the butler had placed my hat. There was a little cough and there he was, coming through the far door.

"You wanted me, Wellard?"

"No, madam. I thought perhaps the gentleman was going."

"It's all right," she said. "I'll see him out."

She waited till the door closed behind him. Her head tilted slightly sideways in a new appraisal of me.

"Let me see, what is your name?"

"Travers."

"Oh, yes. And just what is it you want from me, Mr. Travers? Surely you must know I've already made a very full report?"

There was quite a disapproving look. I didn't answer for a moment. I unhooked my glasses, blinked a bit and replaced them. I'd been wondering what she'd say if I were to ask her what the world had been like in the old secretarial college days, or if there'd been any truth in those rumours about a man named Millbridge, or what sort of times she'd had with Shirley Bright. What I did say was a long way from that.

"As I told your husband, Mrs. Dovell, this is something that has to be done. When a claim is for over a certain amount it automatically has to be checked by headquarters."

She clicked her tongue impatiently. "Then do please hurry. I've some rather important people coming and I haven't much time. Just what is it you want to know?"

From the very first moment there'd been something about her that antagonised me, but if I'd had even the faintest suspicion of only a part of the consequences of what I was about to say, I'd have left it unsaid. What I did say was this, and no wonder it surprised her.

"Nothing at all, Mrs. Dovell. Nothing at all."

She frowned. She stared. "You're settling the claim without any more delay?"

I put a half-apology into my shake of the head.

"I wouldn't say that. What I really meant was that in my experience there's no point in putting questions to someone who mayn't have any intention of being co-operative. Perhaps I'd better find any answers I need elsewhere."

She was hardly believing her ears. For a moment I thought I'd had her badly worried, then she was drawing herself up.

"Just what do you mean by that? You realise, of course, that my husband and I have quite a lot of influence?"

Maybe I was showing the anger I was feeling, for just as suddenly there was a change. Maybe she realised she'd overstepped the mark. She actually smiled.

"Is there any need to argue like this? What is it you want to know?"

"You want me to be frank?"

The smile was far less sure. "I don't know what you mean by frank."

"I think you do," I said. "But there *is* one thing I'd like you to tell me. Shall we say in confidence? Mind you, it's a question I shall probably deny ever having asked."

She was puzzled but she couldn't keep back the sneer. "It's all very mysterious. And what *is* this marvellous question?"

"Only whether in the course of the last few weeks you've had any financial worries?"

Her face flushed. She moistened her lips and then she pulled herself together.

"Of all the impertinence! I shall see you're reported. And at once. My husband will be simply furious."

"I don't think so," I told her quietly. "I doubt if he'll ever know."

I picked up my hat. "A pity you didn't decide to be more co-operative. We might have found out what each of us knew."

I gave her a quick look and turned to the door. I didn't look back but there was no sound of a movement as I closed it behind me.

A smart little red M.G. stood just in front of my car and I had to back before I could move on. I went through the village and I didn't even notice the church. A mile on I stopped the car in a straight stretch and lighted my pipe, and my hands were still shaky.

I smiled somewhat sneeringly to myself. Those last few moments with Mona Dovell had been sheer melodrama arising from a series of false evaluations: that of herself by herself and the just as facile a one of me. It was a long while since I'd let anyone get deeply under my skin, not altogether because I hate snobbery and affection, not because being treated as what she so offensively assumed I was—the probably underpaid and subservient employee of an insurance company. No, it was all sorts of vague but cumulative things: the innate courtesy, gentleness and maybe the frailty of Charles Dovell, the certainty, in my own mind that, in spite of that show of affection she'd staged for my benefit, their individual moral values and private ways were hemispheres apart.

Out of all that had emerged, virtually of its own volition, the challenge I'd thrown out. As I saw it, sitting there in, as it were, cold blood, I knew that what had happened was as near as nothing to a point of no return. In the morning I'd ring John Hill and, if that threat to report me hadn't been a cheap bluff, then I'd have to take stock of where I stood. I might even find it hard to justify that challenge. But if there'd been no complaint surely that would be a sign that what I'd said had struck clean home, and what she'd be fearing was an involvement of her husband. Something would have to be done. She might even be foolish enough to make another false step, though what it might be I hadn't more than a faint idea.

It was after four o'clock when I got back to the hotel. Hallows was having tea in the foyer-lounge and I joined him. He told me he'd only just got in. I guessed something was coming when I caught his quiet smile.

"Had a bit of luck just after you left. Saw that Mrs. Dovell."

He hadn't had a look inside the Regency so he'd thought of slipping along to the bar for a short one before closing time. Just as he came through the swing doors, a man—whom I was able to identify as Sellman—was coming towards them with a woman. He heard him say, "I'll certainly do that, Mrs. Dovell." But Hallows hadn't been too sure about the name, so he put a question at the desk about a certain someone he was supposed to meet and was she the one who'd just gone out. That, it appeared, was a Mrs. Dovell, and Hallows was puzzled. It was then twenty-past two and he knew she was supposed to be meeting me at half-past, so he went out again and was just in time to see her shooting away from the kerb in a smart red M.G.

"How'd she strike you?" I said. "Mrs. D., not the car."

"A smart piece," he said. "Rather be alone with her on a desert island than a dead policeman. And that mink coatee she was wearing must have cost a packet. How'd you make out with her?"

I gave him an account of my afternoon. What I particularly wanted was his reactions to that challenge I'd thrown out. I thought perhaps he'd say I'd rather stuck my neck out, but he didn't. His idea was that she'd planned an attitude and therefore had something to conceal.

"Aren't you having dinner tonight at the Regency?"

For a moment I'd forgotten it.

"Then I might slip along to Laneford," he said. "Don't know if that Dovell gardener frequents that pub you saw. I think I ought to drop in and find out."

I asked him what else he'd done that afternoon besides having a nap and ordering tea. He knew I wasn't serious.

"As a matter of fact, I went along to the *Gazette* office and had a look through some files. Didn't find anything much beyond what Bob Quarley told us. Two things perhaps. Four years ago Blayde's wife was runner-up for Beauty Queen of Sandbeach—"

"Wait a minute," I said. "Don't tell me. Mona won it."

"She didn't even enter," he told me. "Very *infra dig*. She was all out then to hook Dovell. Which brings me to the other thing. That Dovell wedding was very, very quiet. Practically private. Not more than a paragraph except for a longish puff about him and a much shorter one for her. Two photographs, one of each, but not taken on the wedding day. Honeymoon in Italy."

"Well, I think she's wearing the trousers now," I said. "Whether she has any control over the purse-strings remains to be seen, but I very much doubt it. Also she's still playing for very big stakes. He looked to me as if he mightn't last much longer and who's he to leave his money to if not her? I liked him. I think he's a man of very fine character but pretty rigid in his moral outlook. Scandal would be a very severe shock and that's why I'm betting she gave him her own account of this afternoon's interview. If neither of them has complained to Hill, then we ought to be sure she's got the devil of a lot to conceal."

We went upstairs together. He went into his room and I went on to mine. I hadn't been in more than a minute when there was a tap at the door. Hallows handed me a sheet of paper. The perforated edges showed it had been torn from a note-book.

"Found it poked under the door," he said. "Quarley must have come here looking for me."

Saw that contact at lunch and think he's game to act. Promised £10 for the right info so what about your boss making it £20? Expect to be primed first thing in the morning. See you same time, same place, tank empty.

R.Q.

P.S. Just saw Romsie deep in chat with your desk clerk. Just part of the R.Q. service.

That contact, we were pretty sure, was the one in Garlen's office. And that reminded me that I'd never seen those offices, so after I'd had a brush-up I made my way to Warren Street, which is yet another of those shortish roads which connect Duke Street with the Esplanade. They weren't showy and I had some difficulty in finding them, and finally ran them to earth on the two lower floors of a new and solid-looking office building. Nobody came in or out as I walked by.

Just after six Hallows left for Laneford. Just before seven I was going through the Regency doors. Hiddon was attending to some luggage but he spotted me and gave me a wink. I had a delicious Bristol Cream in Sellman's office while he chose my meal, as I'd asked him, from the ordinary menu, and then we went through to the dining-room. I'd put that meal as among the two or three best I've ever had. In the cellar there was even what I think as good a wine as any—a Tavel Rosé—but I refused to have more than a half bottle. A Kümmel with my coffee, a glass of very old Port, and finally a Churchillian cigar which Sellman himself clipped for me. Afterwards I worked it out that that meal would have cost me almost four pounds.

I was savouring that cigar when I heard a voice just behind me. It was Garlen, very natty in a blue suit and blue tie.

"Ah, I thought it was you," he said. "And how did you find the dinner?"

I told him that for well over an hour I'd been leading the life of a millionaire. As for the food, it was even better than he'd said it was.

"Glad to hear it. I think it's good but it's fine to have a second opinion. You're not drinking anything?"

I told him my palate was perfect and I didn't want to disturb it. He actually smiled.

"Well, perhaps we'll see you here again. Or are you going back to town?"

Out came the old story of a week's holiday. I should have had a gramophone record. He didn't bat an eyelid.

"Then we'll almost certainly be seeing you again."

I said I hoped so, but the next time on my own, not that I wasn't most grateful. He just gave a nod and that was that.

I had been sitting at almost the far end of that long room and with my back to the main entrance. When a few minutes later I left, I saw him at a table with Romsie and a couple of other men, but I didn't think they'd seen me.

I was pretty sleepy that night and I didn't wait for Hallows. Just before I dropped off I remembered the morning's fear about going back to town. But I wasn't in town. Maybe it was that somewhat foolish realisation that sent me cosily to sleep.

6
QUARLEY NOT THERE

IN THE morning the wind had died down. The chambermaid who brought in my early tea told me the weather report was sunny intervals with showers, and appreciably warmer—April weather, in fact, rather than March. And not too bad for a man ostensibly beginning a week's holiday.

I'd almost finished breakfast when Hallows turned up. It had been nearly eleven o'clock when he'd got back from Laneford and he'd had what he described as a moist night. From the point of view of an enquiry it couldn't have been much better.

Before setting out the previous evening he'd studied the final edition of the Sandbeach *Evening Gazette*. A filly called Brunette had won the three-fifteen at Lincoln at a hundred to eight, and she came from a smallish northern stable. I know that tucked away in the crossword brain of mine are snippets of information about an awful lot of things, but I wouldn't call racing one of them. I may recognise the name of a past Derby or Grand National winner or that of a famous trainer, but very little more.

Hallows got to the Hare and Hounds when customers were beginning to trickle in. It had one very big room and a much smaller one: a sort of saloon that was very rarely used. Three or four men were in that bigger bar: a nice cosy room, he said, with a roasting fire. He had the usual polite word or two and ordered a pint. Nobody showed any special curiosity but he let it be known he was on his way to Sandbeach for a week's holiday. He'd seen the pub and suddenly felt thirsty. He often came over like that when he saw a pub. The little joke went down well but he didn't make too much of it.

More men and a couple of women came in. The man Hallows hoped to meet was a certain Harry Woods and just before seven o'clock a man came in whose nickname was Woody. He was about forty, pretty well tanned with weather and rather more smartly dressed than some: garrulous, too, and inclined to spread his weight. Hallows decided to take a chance and called for drinks all round. Just a celebration, he said. No, not his birthday. The fact of the matter was he'd had a damn good winner. Pressed to give details he said it'd come home at a hundred to eight and he'd had a quid on for a win and ten bob for a place.

"Pick it yourself or did you have a tip?" the landlord said.

Hallows was being his quietest. The impression he wanted to create was that he was one of themselves: a modest sort of chap who'd had a bit of luck and was making no boast of it. He said diffidently he'd a brother who was head man for the trainer and every now and again he sent him a tip.

"Looks as though they're a damn-sight better than your tips, Woody," someone said. That raised a laugh and quite a lot of chatter. Someone else explained.

"You can't always win," Woods said. "Other horses in a race are trying, aren't they? Ain't that right, sir? Do what tips you get always win?"

Hallows acted as if he didn't want to be drawn in. Only once in a while, he said, did he get a really strong tip and they generally came off. But at a cramped price. The telegram he'd had that morning had simply said, *Brunetta, fear Sundowner*, and that's why he'd hedged on a place bet. Lucky, that's what it had been. Sundowner had come in third, beaten by a neck and a head.

The racing talk petered out and a darts game began. At eight o'clock Hallows reckoned he ought to be getting along, but somehow he still sat on. Later he had a couple of games and always another drink, and still later he found himself watching a four of dominoes. He got up to go but always managed somehow to get into conversation and he was still there when time was called. By then he was very friendly indeed. Didn't matter what the pubs were like in Sandbeach, he'd be coming along again to the Hare and Hounds.

"Believe it or not, I was really popular," he said. "There were the usual protracted goodnights, and when I went to the car two or three were going that way and Woods was one of them, and when the others moved on, he hung behind. The upshot was that we had a sort of pact. If he got a good tip while I was at Sandbeach he'd pass it to me and I was to do the same for him. If mine was a telegram I was to ring Laneford Hall and ask for Mrs. Flint. She was the housekeeper and a bit of a sport. He gave me the Hall number. He told me he was head gardener of two, then I heard about his brother and Fred Martin's stable at Banford, and a couple of certs that had come unstuck: one just before Christmas and the other at the end of January. One had fallen at the last fence, and the other'd broken down. I'd have been there till now if someone hadn't come along who knew him."

"And the next step?"

"You know Jack Mallows of the *Clarion*? I'll ring him at about ten and try to get a tip of some sort for this week. A northern stable if he can. I'll give the pub a miss tonight, but tomorrow morning I'll try to get hold of Woods in the actual gardens. If I can talk to him there I think it should be easy."

But there was one thing which he said had been worrying him. Suppose Mrs. Dovell *had* got in deep with Garlen and he'd done nothing about it for reasons of his own. Those reasons might be that Dovell hadn't been expected to last long.

"I don't know whether you knew that he had a nasty bronchial attack early in February, but he got over it. That seems to tie in. But the point I want to make is, if Garlen decided he had to put the screws on, why couldn't she have raised the money? That Hall seems lousy with stuff that's worth money. Why couldn't she have lifted some of that?"

As I said, it sounded easy, but there was nothing harder. There was nothing I could think of that could be taken without its being missed. Pictures and big stuff were out of the question. Silver, even if it weren't immediately missed, would need a fence. And quite a lot would have had to be taken to raise any sort of sum.

"I'm pretty sure we're on the right track," I said. "Everything we've come up against so far says that Mona Dovell had a lucky break—or so she thought—when that jewellery went. And yet we have to come back to the one fact. *Davitt did that job.* And I can only explain that away like this. Garlen or Romsie must know every crook that frequents this town, so they may have got wind of Davitt's whereabouts and brought him in to do the job."

Hallows didn't like it and he wouldn't tell me why till I pressed him. It was all so unnecessary, he said. Davitt was hot. Any small crook could have done that job, especially if everything was ready for him. So there we were, going round again in circles. Davitt did the job. But Davitt was a pro and doing that job would presumably have been child's-play. So why unbolted doors and a night porter being knocked out with a gentle tap on the head? It beat us and we left it.

Hallows was seeing Quarley. I went out soon after ten o'clock and like a man who's on holiday. There was quite a good antique shop not far on from the Regency in Duke Street and I spent a half-hour having a look round. I had a look at the programmes of the two largest cinemas. One of the theatres was closed till Easter but the other was trying out a new musical intended for town, and I booked a seat for that night. Then, still leisurely, I made my way past Garlen's office but on the opposite side of the road. His car was drawn up by the entrance and I hoped I'd be seen. So through to the Esplanade and along the East Pier. The Pier Pavilion wasn't running a show but I treated myself to coffee in the restaurant. The air was fresh and the sun was shining and quite a few people were there. Next I walked to the pier end and watched the few anglers. I walked back and along the Esplanade to the West Pier. I cut back, crossed Duke Street and headed in the general direction of Wellbrook Gardens. A distant view of No. 17 told me nothing, so I went on to the roundabout and so home.

It was getting on for twelve o'clock so I had a drink in the bar. I got into conversation with a man who said the golf pro. would fix me up with a set of clubs if I wanted to have a round. It was then lunch time. Hallows wasn't about. He and Quarley might be heaven knew where, so I began my meal. It was a quarter-past one when I went into the foyer and there was still no sign of Hallows. I was having coffee when he did come in.

Something was wrong. I knew at once. He gave me a kind of beckoning nod and made for the lift. We went into his room.

"Quarley's disappeared."

"Disappeared?"

"He wasn't at the pub. I waited half an hour and tried the *Gazette* office and he hadn't been there. Went back to the pub and waited a bit, then I came here and got my car in case he was ill or something. Called again at the pub on the way and went on to his place. And what d'you think? He didn't sleep in his bed last night. That woman of his was there and she couldn't make it out either. Never happened before. She's cooked something for him and put it in the oven in case he comes back."

It was queer. I didn't think it more. After all, neither of us was conversant with Quarley's private life.

"That isn't all," he said. "I think someone had had a good look through the living-room and his bedroom. She reckoned she'd never known him leave the place so untidy, but I thought it was more than that. The bureau drawers had definitely been gone through. And his car's still in the garage, by the way."

"The bureau had been broken open?"

"Not at all. Open absolutely normally. His chair was in front of the fire-place and a part bottle of Scotch and a small jug of water on a table alongside it, and he'd taken the dirty glass to the kitchen. Only one glass, so apparently he'd been drinking by himself. The woman's gone home now but I got her to say she'd come back at half-past two. I think we should both go along."

"No," I said. "I'd better keep under cover. You were a pal of his and she knew it. I'll go with you but you can drop me well short and pick me up later—if he hasn't come back." He had a quick wash and went down to lunch. It was after two o'clock and I thought John Hill might be back, so I went to my room and rang from there. I had to wait a bit but I got him. I asked if he'd received my letter. I had posted it just short of seven the previous night. He said it would probably arrive by the afternoon post.

"This is all Greek to you till you read the letter," I said, "but I had to put a very direct question or two to our Mrs. D. She'd been very much riding her high horse and threatened to report me, if you please. I'm guessing it was all bluff, but was it?"

"Haven't heard a thing," he said. "Anything like that would have been passed straight to me."

There was a pause before he asked how things were going and I said the letter would bring him up to date. That was about all. I went down to the foyer and waited for Hallows.

Then I had an idea. I looked up Quarley's number and called him. I heard his bell ringing for a good three minutes before I hung up.

We set off for Havington in Hallows's car and the curious thing was that it was he who was beginning to wonder if we weren't jumping to conclusions. Quarley might have been called away at very short notice. It might have been he who'd been looking for something in a hurry. And he hadn't left a note for Mrs. Sprigg because he'd expected to be back before morning. The car hadn't gone because whoever had rung him or called had had his own car. It was quite comprehensive. Hallows couldn't have been thinking of very much else while he was eating his lunch.

The worries of Hallows and even his wishful thinking were for Quarley himself, and far more than for a loss or hold up of what should have been the likely handing over that morning of vital information. Quarley, I was sure, was far more to Hallows than someone to be used. Evidently they'd seen a lot of each other in the old days and even I, who'd met him for the first time two days before, had found him quite likeable. His cynicism had been a bit laboured and his humour a long way from scintillating, but there's something about a crusader that demands respect. I knew, too, as Hallows must know, that he'd been playing a very dangerous game. Municipal graft and public waste are fair game: tackling a man like Garlen was a vastly different thing.

What I didn't like about that disappearance was that matter of a glass that had been taken to the kitchen. Quarley had been reading or merely thinking in front of his sitting-room fire. The taking of a dirty glass to the kitchen meant the end of the evening, and bed. Why, then, hadn't he put away the whisky bottle and taken the water jug to the kitchen, too? It was the last thing I'd have told Hallows at the moment but it looked to me as if some-one else had taken away that dirty glass.

He was drawing up the car. We'd passed the deserted holi-day camp and were coming to the new roads that lay between it and the golf course, and there was now a choice of roads. One ran slightly inland to the golf course outskirts and on to the west housing estate, and the other was the one we'd taken at night:

the one that rose towards the cliffs and ran some hundred yards back and followed the coast due west.

"That's his bungalow," Hallows was saying. "Just along there. The one with the garage."

It was almost the last before the upward sweep of the road towards the cliffs. I said I'd have a look round and then start walking back. If he didn't overtake me it wouldn't matter. The walk would do me good. I turned sharp left and made my way down to the beach. Just off the foreshore were a few of the original Havington houses, and the boats drawn up on the beach and the nets hung on their poles announced a little colony of fishermen. One or two were working at the nets and further along a man and a boy were caulking a boat. They hardly bothered to look up as I went by. The beach was now petering out and the cliffs rising. Fifty yards on I could go no farther. The base of the cliffs ran out to sea and continued like that for best part of half a mile when the cliffs ended and there was a long stretch of sandy dunes.

What I'd hoped to find, or feared to find, I didn't know. Maybe Quarley had met with an accident. Maybe at night he'd liked to get a breath of air before turning in, and for once, he'd gone too near the cliffs. Maybe he liked the view back to the east and that colourful nocturne that Hallows and I had watched from my car. It had been a dark night and up there the wind must have been blowing a gale. Maybe that was why he hadn't put away the bottle and jug. He'd intended to do that when he came back.

I made my way along the beach well past the spot where I'd left Hallows and then cut back to the road. He overtook me just short of the fork that gave a choice of Duke Street or the Esplanade. Hallows took the right fork. He drew the car up about a hundred yards along.

"Nothing different," he said. "What I don't like is that there isn't a note of any kind in his bureau. It ought to have been lousy with notes."

"Has he any relatives?"

"A son in Australia. I've got his address. No other relatives at all on either side."

"So what now?"

"Well, Mrs. Sprigg—that's his woman—and I talked it over and the only thing seems to be to notify the police. Thought I'd have a word first with the news editor at the *Gazette*. I don't think so, but Bob might have given someone a hint of what he was up to. I mean that Garlen business."

He drove on to the *Gazette* building and parked outside. It was a quarter of an hour before he came back.

"Nothing doing," he told me. "Always very secretive when he was working on one of those exposures of his. They expected him round about midday today. He was supposed to be seeing the editor."

He didn't argue when I said there'd be no harm in waiting a bit before he went to the police. He drove round to the hotel and parked the car and by that time I'd ordered some tea. What I wanted to know was just what kind of approach he'd worked out.

"Quite a good yarn," he said. "Some truth and some not so true. How we'd been pals a few years ago and dropped across each other here, and how I'd finished my job with you and thought of having another day or two down here, and how we'd sort of fixed up a day together."

"And suppose they ask you what your job is? We don't want the Agency brought in."

He hadn't thought of that. The best way out was for me to ring John Hill and rig something up. If I was a chief inspector, Hallows might be an assistant inspector.

"Now let's look ahead. And on the black side," I said. "Quarley was playing a mighty dangerous game. He didn't tell us everything, but he'd obviously thought he'd nobbled someone in Garlen's office who'd pass on a list of debtors. If that someone gave the game away, then he was in a spot. You and I know that. What might have been done to him we can only guess. I don't think they'd have resorted to murder, but you never know and we can't ignore it. Suppose that's what it turns out to be and then the question arises what we're going to do. Mightn't it mean a change of your original story? Or do we still have to lie low?"

It was a problem. Our loyalties had to be to United Assurance: anything we might owe to Quarley was infinitesimal compared with that. All we could hope was that both loyalties might somehow overlap, if it came to that kind of showdown, and that was the last thing we wished to think of. I don't think either of us really believed that we'd ever hear that dry, rasping voice of Bob Quarley's again but we kept that thought to ourselves. All we could decide was to temporise: in other words, that Hallows's original idea should stand.

He was back at half-past five, far earlier than I'd thought. He'd made a brief statement to the man on desk duty, who'd passed him on to a uniformed sergeant. A driver had taken them in a police car to Quarley's bungalow. The sergeant, Hallows said, had been stolid and highly uncommittal, but it had been pretty obvious that his had been a storm-in-a-teapot point of view. Hallows and Mrs. Sprigg had gone back to the station to make formal statements, and the last thing Hallows had been told was that enquiries would be made and, in the event of its being necessary, he'd be informed.

It was all very calm and official, a sort of soothing syrup, but it didn't have that effect on Hallows. There was nothing more we could do, but he wouldn't let me book another theatre seat, and when I left after an early dinner he was still at his meal. I thought the show needed a lot of pulling together before it opened in town but it did pass the evening. I didn't get in till nearly eleven. There was no sign of him anywhere, so I guessed he'd gone to bed. In the morning I'd finished breakfast before he appeared. He seemed his usual self again and when I asked if he'd turned in early, something seemed to amuse him. I smoked my pipe over an extra cup of coffee while he told me about it.

Every time he'd made up his mind to have a good look round the Regency, something had happened, he said, so he'd had another try. For one thing, he wanted to have a good look at Shirley Blayde and he was lucky enough to find her on duty. Apparently she was on the middle shift, from one o'clock till eight, with time off for meals. He thought she was what he called a pretty hard-bitten one; just the girl for the job.

"You know," he said. "All smiles for the clientele. Couldn't be too helpful, and then, almost before the guest had turned his back, off went the smile and she looked hard as nails. I saw your friend, Hiddon, by the way. He was apparently on the middle shift, too.

"Then I went and had a drink. Pretty well crowded in the bar and a bit too high-toned for me, so I went back to the foyer intending to come back here, and just as I was going through, Shirley was coming off duty." He smiled. "I don't know what made me do it, except that I hadn't anything particular to do. At any rate, I did a shadowing job on her. Like following a blind man, except that she went at a devil of a pace for one her size. When she had a look at her wrist-watch for the second time, I guessed she was going somewhere later, or had an appointment. I forgot to say, by the way, it was a quarter-past eight when she left the hotel, so apparently she was late. At any rate, she took a short cut that brought us out just opposite Wellbrook Gardens and she went across and into her flat. I went by just as she was opening the front door."

He poured himself out another cup of coffee and reached for the toast. Something was still amusing him.

"Well, I thought I might as well make a job of it while I was there, so I went along almost to Wellbrook Avenue and kept an eye on the entrance to her flat. The Avenue would be well lighted if it weren't for the trees and that made watching a bit tricky. However, I thought I'd give it till about a quarter-past nine, and as it turned out I didn't have to wait so long. Just after nine o'clock a man came round the corner into Wellbrook Gardens. There'd been other people about, of course, but what struck me about this one was that he went by the flat and I was getting ready to shift my ground when he turned back, and almost before I knew it he was through the gate."

"You had a good view of him?"

"Never a hope. That flat's between two street lights and then there's the shadow of the trees. All I know is he was tallish and was wearing an overcoat and hat. What I thought was it was some boy friend calling for her and they might be going out somewhere, so I kept on the move when anyone came along but still managed to watch that front. I stuck it out till after ten o'clock and then I thought I'd call it a day. Then I thought I might as well be hung for a sheep as for a lamb so I nipped through the gate myself when the coast was clear. There's plenty of grass all round, as you know, but I could only go on the far side because of the light. The whole place was dark as pitch, by the way. Not even a crack of light from a window and not a sound inside, so I moved round to the back, just in front of the garage. A window was a bit open at the top and there was a sort of fitful sound inside, whatever it might be. Then I knew what it was: it was two people talking—well, not talking, sort of just more than whispering. One voice was hers—it must have been—and the other a man's. I couldn't hear a thing, mind you, just that sort of occasional murmur."

"Just a minute," I said, and reached for the breakfast menu and began a rough sketch on the back. "This is a plan of the flat, leaving out what I didn't actually see. Here's the room I was in and here's the kitchen. That makes the room they were in a bedroom."

He nodded. "That's what I thought at the time, but I couldn't stay there, of course. I nipped out when the coast was clear and shifted back towards Wellbrook Avenue. I stuck it out there till nearly eleven and then I told myself, what the hell, they're making a night of it. And that's when I had the damndest idea. I thought I'd try and flush him out."

He laughed.

"You know there's a telephone box on the corner there, near the bus stop? Well, I went along and took a chance. They've the 999 system, so I dialled. Reckoned I'd seen something suspicious at No. 17 Wellbrook Gardens. A suspicious-looking character round at the back, then I rang off before they could ask me my name. Lucky for me there wasn't anybody about so I got the hell out of there and along towards Wellbrook Avenue again. I hadn't been there more than three or four minutes when a squad car rolled in and drew up outside No. 17. A couple of men got out, so I gave them a minute or two and then drifted past, and I was just in time to see them coming out. I heard one say, 'Seems all O.K. there. Perhaps he made a mistake in the number.' I went on till it might be safe to turn back and that's when I knew I'd been wasting my time. I just daren't hang about. For all I knew, that car might be on the prowl there for an hour or two, so I came back here and went to bed."

I had to laugh.

"Fun while it lasted. But the man. I wonder who he was. Too much to expect it was her husband."

"Don't know," he said. "They might be playing a double game. Not that I can see the point of it, not if they separated a year ago."

"Necessity makes strange bedfellows," I said. "There's the devil of a lot more than we've even suspected in this job."

I must have given a little gasp. "Don't look round, but we've got a caller."

Blayde had taken a quick look through the dining-room door and had smiled at the sight of me.

"Looking for me?" I called to him. "Come along in. Just in time for a cup of coffee."

7
QUARLEY COMES BACK

HE WASN'T wearing an overcoat and his grey felt hat was in his hand. His suit was that double-breasted blue serge I'd last seen him in. Tartuffe Travers held out his hand. Blayde shook it, but he was looking at Hallows. I introduced them.

"Mr. Hallows is really the one I want to see," Blayde said, and took the chair I'd moved nearer. "It's about that Quarley business. You knew Quarley, too, didn't you, Mr. Travers?"

"Not till I came down here," I said. "Have some coffee while I tell you about it. Hallows here was his pal. He knew me, though, if I didn't know him."

I expanded that a bit while Hallows poured the coffee. Blayde was good enough to say it was now all very clear. Best to have everything straight.

"You knew him years ago then, Mr. Hallows?"

Hallows did some explaining. Blayde said that was straight enough, too.

"And what was your opinion of him?"

"Bob Quarley?" Hallows smiled. "A bit of a reprobate, like myself. We didn't run across each other all that often, but when we did we had a few drinks and a yarn. Once or twice we went to boxing matches together. I'm Mr. Travers's assistant, as you know. Our investigations run to all sorts of crime: arson, burglary and so on, and that's what Quarley was interested in as a crime reporter. A first-class one, too: make no mistake about that. He couldn't have held down his job on the *Clarion* if he hadn't been."

Blayde was looking a bit uneasy. I was wondering why. "You know he must have made a lot of enemies here?"

Hallows looked at him, face straight. "What's that supposed to lead up to?"

There's something more attractive about most people when they smile. Blayde's smile showed up the weakness in his face.

"Well, we've been making enquiries ever since yesterday afternoon and we don't like things any more than you do. He might have had an accident. The hospitals know nothing, but that isn't quite what I mean."

"You're surely not thinking in terms of murder?" I said. His finger-tips went together and he let himself think. "Well, not exactly. But he might have had a quarrel and there might have been blows and—well, you never know. And there's the possibility of an accident, as I said. We don't want everybody to know this but we're making arrangements straight away to have a look along under the cliffs. I don't say anything'll come of it, but we've got to have a look."

"I don't know his place," I said, "but was there anything there that you thought unusual?"

"Nothing," he said. "He'd obviously had a night indoors. The local system's automatic as you probably know, we can't check if he had any calls. Looks as if he just got up and went out for a breather before turning in. That how it struck you, Mr. Hallows?"

"Yes," Hallows said slowly. "And that's why I think it's a good idea having a look below those cliffs. You noticed his overcoat and hat weren't there?"

Blayde finished his coffee and got up. "Well, I'll be pushing along. If anything should happen I'll let you know. You staying here long?"

Hallows smiled. "Well, the boss here is taking a week and thinks he can fix it for me, too. Doesn't matter to me when I have my holidays and a few days down here suits me all right."

"Be seeing you, then," Blayde said.

I cut in quickly, "Any news yet about that chap Davitt?"

"Not a thing. It's early yet though. We reckon he came here and left by car. Nothing on him at the railway station or the bus depot." He gave a smile that was meant to be tough. "We'll get him. They all slip up in time."

"Well, good luck," I said, and he gave us a wave of the hand as he moved on again. We watched till he'd gone through the door.

"Wonder how much he really knows?"

"Don't have an idea," I said. "I know one thing, though. I wouldn't trust him further than I can throw a battleship."

"Well, it was nice to have met him," Hallows said. "We missed a chance, though. We might have managed to get him to tell us just where he was last night. Still, I'm seeing life. Only got to meet Overson now and I'll have seen everyone."

We went through to the foyer to read our newspapers. I asked when he was going to Laneford. He thought the best time would be at about twelve. That might be Woods's knocking-off time and they could adjourn to the pub.

"One thing I've been thinking of about Quarley," I said. "He should have been seeing the editor of the paper at about noon yesterday and I think I know why. He was so dead sure he'd be getting the information he wanted from that contact in Garlen's office that he could broach the question of another exposure article. He wouldn't want to go any further till he had a lot more, but he didn't want to waste his time. Garlen was a big advertiser in the *Gazette* and the editor might have wanted to think twice. He might even have turned the idea down flat."

Hallows had had that idea, too. No point in Quarley going any further if nothing was ever going to be printed. And that was about all we said. Soon after ten I got up for my morning stroll. A man supposed to be on holiday had to make a public show of enjoying himself. I went to the cloakroom first and it was just as I came out that I was called to the telephone. Norris was on the line.

"That enquiry you wanted," he said. "Triller's a good man. Spoken of most highly up here. A first-class record and the last one to tolerate even a suspicion of anything not on the square. That all you wanted?"

I thanked him and said it was. I didn't feel any particular gratification at that confirmation of the way Harry Triller had struck me. What slight warmth I did feel was because I'd liked him as a man. And it wasn't too bad to feel that if anything really fishy were unearthed, there'd be no covering up.

Hallows wasn't in the foyer when I went through and I didn't see him again till after lunch. I got my car out and went for an exploratory drive. I had another look at Blayde's bungalow and went up that track to where Overson lived. There was no sign of life at either place. The road petered out further up the slope but there was a fine view of the town. I'd brought my glasses but when

I focused them on the distant cliffs there was no sign of activity so I guessed that what exploring was being done was from the sea.

It was a sharp, clear morning and I could even see some golfers on the Havington course. I looked for Quarley's bungalow but it was masked by taller houses. I turned the car and came back by the new park and the grammar school, and down into the old town with its kerbside markets, little restaurants and junk shops. One of the old book shops had gone but the other was still there. So was the old print shop. There was a Baxter print that I liked. You don't see them so often nowadays and this one looked right enough. Paper and colour were good. The subject—Windsor Castle—wasn't too attractive, but I thought it might come in handy, if need be, to bolster up that holiday claim. Also it was pretty cheap at a couple of pounds.

I was just a bit late for lunch but Hallows was later still. It was nearly two o'clock when he got back, and he didn't want any lunch. He'd had some bread and cheese with his beer at the pub. Straight away he wanted to know if there was any news about Quarley. He seemed relieved to hear there wasn't. Then he said he'd had a good morning.

"It's in the bag," he told me. "Everything we wanted and easy as pie."

There'd been a back lane that ran by the kitchen gardens at the Hall and he'd spied out the land from there. Another, younger, gardener was doing some digging and Woods was having a word with him. When he'd finished his chat he went across to a greenhouse and Hallows joined him there. It was a heated greenhouse and the tomato plants were already heavy with young trusses. Woods gave quite a start at an unexpected voice but was all smiles when he recognised the caller.

"Morning, Mr. Green. Come to pay us a visit?"

Hallows explained. His holiday looked like being cut short so he thought he'd drop in with a tip he'd just had. Hallows was taking no chances. The horse wasn't going till a fort-night's time, so from our point of view it didn't matter if it came in last or won by a street. Woods was delighted enough. Even the name—Spring Crop—was a tip in itself.

"What time do you knock off?" Hallows asked him.

It wasn't till half-past twelve. That was why Hallows decided to have a scratch lunch at the pub. Woods said he'd drop in for a quarter of an hour at about one. He liked to keep to time. Too many eyes watching.

"Your boss strict, is he?"

"Well, not the way you mean." He smiled. "A rare one against betting and gambling and that. He'd have a fit if he knew some o' the things that go on round here. Never see much of him nowadays though, 'less he send for me. He's full o' rheumatism and can't get about. He'd a real bad go of pneumonia last February and everyone thought he was a goner, but he weren't."

"And what's his wife like?"

"Madam?" He smiled again. "She's all right. A bit of a sport like her old father was. By the way, we both come from the same parish. Bandon. Do you know it?"

Hallows didn't.

"Well, you know Havington, and all you do is go straight on. Old George Franks—that was her father—used to have the Hill Farm there and his land used to run alongside Freddy Martin's, the one that have the racing stable where my brother is now. A rare sport old George used to be. Heavy drinker, too. Forget what his wife's name was, but she was just the one for George. What I'd call a rare sporting couple." His smile was a bit complacent. "Rather overdid it, though. Got into difficulties and had to sell up. Somewhere in the Midlands they went to. George died there about seven or eight year ago."

Hallows gave him a crafty look.

"The daughter didn't do so badly, though?"

"You're right there," Woods said. "Pity old George isn't still alive. But she's not too bad. Give herself a lot of airs and that sort o' thing. And she's got the devil of a temper. Don't worry me, though."

"You know too much."

Woods gave him a quick look.

"Maybe something in that. If I didn't know more than the boss do, I wouldn't know much, and that's a fact." Then he looked at his watch. "Getting on for time to knock off. Got to go to the house first, though. You know your way to the pub?"

So far so good. Better was to come. Hallows had another approach ready. He was on the lookout for Woods soon after one and went to meet him.

"Something I ought to have mentioned. That tip's strictly confidential so don't go spreading it round. If everybody gets to know about it, down the price'll come, and then it won't be any good to anybody. I don't mind one or two, if they can keep their mouths shut."

"The housekeeper's all right," Woods said. "Don't know about the madam, though. When she bets she really puts it on, judging by what she said when that last tip I give her let us all down. Damned if I didn't think she was going to give me the sack!"

"Well, use your own judgment," Hallows told him.

"Mr. Green," as the pub knew him, stood Woods a drink and stayed on for the look of things when he left.

"I'm staying clear of Laneford from now on," Hallows told me with a chuckle. "In a fortnight's time they'll probably be out for my blood. A lucky morning, though."

"Not all that much luck in it," I told him. Hallows has just that touch of genius: adaptability to any company, the quiet, convincing manner and the gift of making himself liked. I'd never have got that information in a month of Sundays.

"Yes," I said. "It's in the bag, as you said. Everything dovetails in like a piece of first-class cabinet work. That Regency job was a fake. You know it and I know it, and we still can't prove it."

There was a way, of course, but we doubted if it would work. Hill might judge that the evidence we had was sufficient for the company to refuse to pay. That would leave it to the policy-holder to sue. Woods would be a key witness, but no one was more likely to let us down. Quarley, alive, might have clinched the whole thing. What a dead Quarley had told us wasn't evidence.

So there it was. For an action to succeed we had to get far more than we had, and now we had the main picture it looked as if the place to look for evidence was the Regency itself.

We hadn't brought everything out into the open. Hallows and I are like that. We take it for granted that the obvious needs no discussion, and there was plenty about the Regency that was obvious enough. Someone had unbolted that service door. Someone had put sleeping pills into Hiddon's coffee. Whoever had tackled the safe had given him a crack on the skull for the sake of appearances. Maybe the safe hadn't needed manipulation with a bent wire. Doubtless there'd have been opportunities for a copy to have been made of the key: the scratches had been mere eyewash. And all that accumulation of still unproved facts gave us a choice of two persons: Shirley Blayde and Hiddon himself.

Hiddon was crossed off at once. He could hardly have cracked his own skull and what he had told me, and the way he had told it, made his account of things ring true. That left us with Shirley. And what had we got? Hearsay only. That, for instance, she was out for money: susceptible therefore to being bribed to play a minor role. All she'd had to do before she left soon after eleven o'clock that night was prepare the ground. It wasn't she who jemmied the door, gave Hiddon that crack on the skull and all the rest of it. And, if not, then who did? And the answer—and by now it was an infuriating one—could only be Davitt.

"Davitt," I said. "Ever since we've been here he's been round in my mind like a teetotum. No professional could ever have been as careless as he was."

Hallows gave his quiet smile.

"Why not take what we've got? Concentrate on Shirley. That man, for instance, who was there last night. He might turn up again and I might have a look at him. If he should be that husband of hers we might spread the net a bit wider."

There was an interruption. We'd been in the far corner of the foyer and talking very quietly, and yet I hadn't heard the telephone ring at the desk. The call was for Hallows. He said he'd take it there.

I watched him. He didn't seem to be doing much talking and there was nothing to be judged from his face. I guessed the call was about Quarley, and I was right. He stood there for just a moment and there was a quick shake of the head before he came over.

"Bob Quarley," he said. "They found him all right. Wondered if I wanted to see him before they began the p.m."

As a rule I'm squeamish about corpses. To the police they're just pieces of evidence, but not to me. Sometimes they're not the most pleasant of sights, and even when there's only a similarity with sleep, there's always that grim finality. And my job has usually begun only when a post-mortem's ended.

But Quarley had a nice temporary home. That morgue was better than most. White tiling was everywhere and the disinfectant wasn't too strong. The main room had the usual porcelain slab with a drain at one end and a water pipe below. Overson was in the refrigeration room.

"A bad business," he told me and had a quick look at Hallows. I introduced him, and Overson held out his hand.

"You were the one who knew him. He doesn't look very different. I may be speaking out of my turn, but he must have had a very quick end."

The uniformed sergeant pulled out the tray and drew back the cover. I had one look, then turned away.

"He was in a little break between the rocks," Overson was saying quietly. "The tide must have hammered him a good deal. About sixty feet up to where he fell, so he must have been dead in a tick. See this wound in the skull?"

"Yes," Hallows said. "Looks as if he couldn't have felt a thing." He shook his head. "Well, we've all got to come to it."

"Not that way though. Not my idea of passing out."

The tray slid back. For a moment or two Hallows didn't move. When he did it was to ask a question.

"Any chance of having a look at what you found on him? I'll tell you why." He smiled. "Mind you, I don't expect anything to happen now, but the last time I saw him I was admiring a little meerschaum cigarette-holder he had. He nearly always smoked a pipe so I told him he might as well sell it to me. He said I could have it, but somehow we were talking and I forgot about it and— well, if you like to take my word, it would be a bit of a souvenir. Sentimental, perhaps, but I'd like to have something of his."

"I think something might be done," Overson told him. "Let's have a look in any case. Through here."

Just off the main room was a smallish laboratory. Overson took a cellophane bag from a drawer and began emptying it on the porcelain-topped table.

"Can't say I remember a cigarette-holder, but here's what he had."

Hallows had a look. It certainly wasn't there. Maybe it was at the bungalow. If it wasn't in the wallet.

The wallet was soggy with sea-water and it was empty. The contents had been put in an envelope: three pound notes, a ten-shilling one, a Press card, a snapshot of Quarley's wife and another of a youngish man, a woman and a small boy.

"That's the son and his family," Overson said. "He's in Australia, but Mrs. Sprigg had seen it." He let out a breath. "Well, no sign of the cigarette-holder. Maybe in the bungalow, as you said."

We went out by a side door and along a corridor to the main entrance hall.

"The doctor'll be along at any time now," Overson told us. "I don't expect he'll find anything unusual. The way I see it is that he"—Quarley, of course, he meant—"went out for a bit of fresh air along the cliffs and that wind suddenly caught him. It's a bit ironical in a way. I don't know if Quarley was behind it at all, but there's been a lot of agitation to have those cliffs fenced. This is the second accident there's been in twelve months."

He shook hands with me and then with Hallows.

"Nice to have met you, Mr. Hallows. Only wish it had been to do with something more cheerful. If there should be anything unusual I'll ring you at the hotel. That be all right?"

We went down the steps and along Henry Street towards the hotel. Hallows was quiet and I didn't feel much like talking. What I couldn't get out of my mind's eye was that quick sight I'd had of Quarley. It was Hallows who spoke first, just as we turned into Duke Street.

"Quite a nice chap, Overson."

"That's how he's always struck me," I said. "That ciga-rette-holder, by the way. There never was one?"

"That's right," he said. "All I wanted to do was have a look at what they found on him."

We went into the hotel and to me it was all at once queerly different. The foyer had its usual smell of stale tobacco smoke and ancient meals but to me it was suddenly frowsty and unbearable.

"Let's go up," I said, and stopped at the desk to order a couple of teas.

"A cup of tea is just what I want," Hallows said as the lift moved up. "The last half-hour hasn't been all that good."

He went into his own room. I gave a knock on the wall when tea came up. We neither of us felt like eating much and it wasn't long before we were lighting our pipes.

"About Overson," he said. "Looks a smart man at his job. That's why I've been wondering why he said nothing about the keys."

There hadn't been any keys. I suddenly remembered that. All sorts of oddments that a man usually carries, but no keys.

"Back door and front both have Yale locks," he said. "So if Bob went out, how the hell was he going to let himself back in?"

"They couldn't have dropped out of his pocket when he fell?"

"Never a hope. He carried 'em on a chain in his trouser pocket. The usual little leather loop at the other end to put round a trou-ser button. Then there's the wallet. The last time I saw him he had some papers in it. And what about his note-book? You never saw Bob without his notebook. Always carried it in his inside breast pocket."

I thought it over while I poured myself a second cup of tea.

"Take it as read," I said. "And then what?"

He looked surprised. To him it was all so obvious. And why should I so suddenly be so obtuse?

"It's just unanswerable," he said. "Somebody else wanted the keys to get back into the house and do a search. How that somebody got into the house originally I don't know, but he did get in. Might have just knocked at the door and been let in."

"Quarley couldn't have been lured outside by a telephone message? There's a call-box just at the end of the road."

"Don't think so," he said. "He had to be searched and you couldn't very well do that in the dark. The way I see it is that he was knocked out as soon as whoever it was entered the room. He was searched in double-quick time and the lights put out, and then he was dumped over the cliffs. After putting his rain-coat on him and chucking his hat after him. Any bump or wound would be put down to the fall."

"Wonder what time it was," I said. "I had dinner that night at the Regency and when I was leaving the dining-room I saw Garlen with Romsie and a couple of other men. Prosperous-looking types. That'd be just after nine o'clock."

"Garlen didn't do it." He waved a contemptuous hand. "He was behind it: you can bet your life on that. Once that contact ratted on Bob Quarley and Garlen knew what the game was, he just had to do something. But you can bet your life he's got himself well covered up. My bet is that Romsie did it, and if so, it's a cert he's got an alibi."

He drank the last of what must have been almost cold tea and got up.

"Sounds a funny thing to do but I'd like to go to the pictures. There's a pretty good one on at the Odeon."

I said I'd join him. He wasn't the only one who felt a need to get that afternoon out of his mind.

It was a fine picture. There were quite long spells when I forgot all about Bob Quarley. Dinner was on when we got back, and it was just after we'd finished that Hallows was called to the telephone. I think he'd gone to the cloakroom, but I guessed who was ringing and took the call myself. It was young Blayde. He said I'd do just as well as Hallows.

Quarley's death was solely due to a fractured skull, he said. No water whatever in the lungs. I asked him if the time of death had been established.

"As a matter of fact we had some luck," he said. "You know the Feathers? Just past the holiday camp? Well, he dropped in there at about eight o'clock and had a drink and a couple of the Welsh rarebits they serve there. He often used to do it, probably to save himself cooking supper: at any rate, that establishes the time of death at about half-past ten to eleven."

I thanked him. I just had time before he rang off to ask about the funeral. He said the *Gazette* had expressed the wish to take charge of everything. I felt relieved at that. Hallows might have wanted to handle things himself and something had told me it wouldn't be too wise to stick out our necks quite as far as that.

8
ODDS AND ENDS

THE inquest was at eleven o'clock. Hallows was not being called but he told me at breakfast that he'd like to attend.

I didn't want to go myself, and because it didn't seem good policy to have my name connected with Quarley's. Some spy of Garlen's would almost certainly be there.

As a matter of fact I didn't feel like going anywhere or doing anything: what I did feel was a futility in it all. One gets those moments of depression and I certainly had one then. What brought it on was the realisation that Hallows and I were alone. In most of our cases the police had been natural allies; here, in Sandbeach, the police might as well not have been functioning at all. If we went to them with what we had, all we'd get would be a polite but incredulous smile. The very things that were beginning to build up our case were precisely the ones that in their view were outside all questioning. The Regency job was a Davitt job and that's all there was to it. Quarley had been blown over the cliff on a windy night—regrettable, maybe, but a hard fact. What would happen if we asked them to investigate Mona Dovell? I had to laugh ruefully at the mere thought of it. And if we suggested something similar in the case of Shirley Blayde? I could imagine Overson listening to that and reminding us in a dry, official voice that there were such things as laws of libel.

"What is it about local police forces that can make one so furious?" I said to Hallows. "There's always a kind of live and let live. Mona Franks wouldn't have been sacrosanct, but Mona Dovell is. All that kind of thing."

"We're just passers through," he said. "They live in the place. They've got to mind whose toes they tread on and be ready to turn a blind eye. Take Garlen, for instance. I think the betting laws are damn silly, but they're laws. The police can't help knowing there're half a dozen spots in the town where ready-money bets are handed in, but they don't do anything about it. If there was a bank robbery you'd hear the sirens screaming in a couple of seconds. That'd be different."

"Talking of Garlen, you think he's got that jewellery?"

"Wouldn't like to guess," he said. "It's all too complicated. The police are cocksure this Davitt did the job. That makes him have the jewellery. If Garlen had him on tap and brought him in, then he'd only get so much."

"What'd the break-up value be?"

Hallows is a good valuer. The settings were all good, solid late-Victorian eighteen-carat gold. The stones were up to four carats, and good. Even a fence, he thought, would spring as much as six or seven thousand pounds. Out of that Davitt might have got five hundred or less. That left Garlen with Mona Dovell's debt cleared and a nice profit, even after a pretty good present to Shirley Blayde.

"And if the company pays, Mrs. Dovell gets the whole eighteen thousand?"

"She'd have to," he said. "Her husband would feel himself involved. He'd have to see the cheque and have a hand in what was done with it. After all, it was his first wife's jewellery."

He was right, not that that prospect made me feel any happier. Nor was it any good indulging in mental fireworks and telling oneself that, sooner than that should happen, I'd do this and I'd do that. The fact of the matter was that we seemed to be at a dead end, and you can't Coué yourself out of an impasse like that.

"We've still got Shirley," Hallows reminded. "I thought of putting in an evening or two on her, if it's all the same to you."

I remembered something. I'd had it on my mind just before I went to sleep and now it had come back. That mention of Shirley Blayde, perhaps.

"Remember something Woods said to you yesterday? Two things, in fact. One was that Dovell would have a fit if he knew what was going on at the Hall. Then he said he wasn't worried when Mona Dovell flew into a temper and you hinted it was because he knew too much about her, and he didn't disagree. Just what ought we to read into that? Only that Dovell didn't know she was betting heavily?"

"Don't know," he said. "There might be more."

Probably I was clutching at a straw, but I thought there was more. "Things that were going on at the Hall." That wasn't the sort of phrase to apply even to heavy betting.

"Look," I said, "we've got to take a chance. Wash out what you said about not going back to Laneford. Is Woods married, by the way?"

"Married and three grown-up children."

"Right," I said. "Try to get your nose in at his house. Get on Christian names terms with him. Invite him up to some mythical place of yours in town. If you can work it, get in with that house-keeper at the Hall. Don't be afraid of throwing your money about."

"All right with me," he said. "I've had my own ideas, too. Thinking of Bob Quarley reminded me of what he said about her and her husband. David and Abishag. I doubt if even that's right. I don't think she even keeps the old man's bed warm. And according to all reports she's about as sexy as most. There's one thing that's going to be awkward, though. If we're going to watch Shirley we can't watch Mona."

"I'll get another man down," I told him. "French is a good man if Norris can spare him. Perhaps we can put him on to Shirley. Depends what you find out about Mona."

I felt a whole lot better. In fact I went upstairs at once and rang Norris. He thought French could be spared and we arranged for him to come on the three o'clock from town. Hallows went out to fix a room for him at one of the smaller hotels. I wrote a long letter to John Hill bringing him bang up to date. I also remembered that I owed a letter to my wife. Hallows came in when I was still in the middle of it. He'd got French fixed up at the Lumley, about three hundred yards from the roundabout, in Duke Street, and now he was off to the inquest.

I posted my letters in the hotel box and went out. The sun was shining, the wind had gone and it was more like a day in June. That depression of mine had gone, too.

I walked a few yards along Duke Street with no particular route in mind, then I stopped for a moment, wondering just where I should go. Later on I was to think about that indecisive pause. I might have gone anywhere on the whim of the moment, and then something or other put into my mind the junk shops that I'd seen the day before. Most of my collector's life I've heard of fabulous finds in junk shops, but that kind of luck had never come my way. Hope springs eternal and I told myself that that morning might be a first time.

It took me well over ten minutes to get to Cooper Street, even taking the short cut by the football stadium, and as I was turning into it I saw a couple of police cars drawn up just beyond the Swan. More people than usual were hanging about on the opposite pavement and a uniformed constable was trying to move them on. I was about fifty yards away and, as I slowed down, three or four plain-clothes men came out of a general store, stood for a moment talking, then entered the cars. As they moved off, I moved on. Curiosity is one of my few remaining vices, so I moved over to where the cars had been, and just as I was passing that store and craning up for a look inside, who should come out but Overson. We practically collided.

"Hallo, sir," he said. "What're you doing down here?"

I told him the truth. I mentioned that Baxter print.

"You're an authority on all that sort of thing, are you?"

"Well, in a modest way," I said. "Can't afford to invest heavily. That's why I'm looking for bargains."

"Not a bad way to spend a holiday either." He looked at his watch. "They're open, so what about a drink? Say in a quarter of an hour? I've got one or two things to clear up."

"The Swan, then, in a quarter of an hour."

I went on to the nearest junk shop. The plump, elderly woman in charge asked if there was anything particular I was looking for, but seemed quite happy to have me look round. The place was chock-a-block, and I hadn't time for more than a general browse before I was due to meet Overson. He came out of the Swan just as I got there.

"The saloon bar," he said. "A bit too crowded in the other. What'll you have?"

I said if the bitter was good, I'd have that. We'd gone through to quite a pleasant room, deserted but for ourselves. There was a serving hatch and quite a lot of noise was coming through from the other bar. Overson rapped on the shelf. A middle-aged man in shirt-sleeves was soon framed in the hatchway.

"Yes, sir?"

"Two pints of bitter. In tankards."

Overson felt for some small change. The tankards came through.

"How much?"

The barman smiled.

"That's all right, sir. Only too happy to oblige the police." Overson frowned. "I see. And what police are you in the habit of obliging?"

The barman looked confused. "I didn't say I did, sir. Just being friendly, that's all."

"Well, don't be friendly with me—not if you don't want to lose your licence."

"No, sir. I'm sorry, sir."

"Sorry, be damned. You just opened that big mouth too far. Wouldn't be a bad idea if we had a little chat."

The barman spread his palms. "Look, sir: I didn't mean anything. It was the first time you'd come in—"

"How much?"

The barman shrugged his shoulders. "Three and five, sir."

Overson paid, picked up the tankards, and brought them to where I was sitting. His face was a thundercloud.

"Let's move over to the corner," he said. I followed him to a table facing the street.

"You've got to watch these chaps," he told me. "No end of that sort of thing goes on, but you just can't stop it. This one happened to choose the wrong man."

We wished each other good health. The bitter was cold and better than good. I said I didn't suppose the barman was altogether to blame. He must have had orders from his boss. Overson gave a dry smile.

"That *was* the boss. Harry Oakley. An old professional footballer here. I saw him earlier this morning about what'd been happening."

There'd been a couple of burglaries, one at the store, the other at the bakery next door. What was missing hadn't been assessed yet, but a safe had been removed from the store. There was a back entry and the thieves had almost certainly used a van. He said it would probably be found abandoned, and the busted safe too.

"Much of that sort of thing here?"

"About the usual," he said, and passed me his cigarette case. "On the whole I think we're just about the average for a town of this size."

"Any hold-ups?"

He smiled.

"Not recently. We had a small crop of 'em two or three years back. The usual thing: wages snatched, escorts coshed. Then we had the idea of a staggered system; you know, getting firms to draw from the banks at odd times instead of the usual Friday and Saturday mornings."

"It did the trick?"

"Yes," he said. "In a rather unusual way. We did have one more case of the kind but it told us just what we wanted. Since no one could have known till just beforehand when the money was being drawn, it had to be an inside job. We got the whole four who'd been in it."

We emptied our tankards and I asked if he'd have another. He said he wouldn't. He ought to be getting back to head-quarters. There'd be another time, though. There was something of a question about that last remark. I said there definitely would; that holiday of mine had hardly begun.

He asked if he could drop me anywhere, and the upshot was that he set me down at the hotel. It was twelve o'clock in any case and I hadn't been in the mind for another junk shop.

Hallows wasn't back and I didn't feel like another drink, so I just sat in the foyer till it was time for lunch, and suddenly I had a very queer idea. I was going over the events of that morning and all at once there was something that struck me in quite a different light. I've said that I'm abnormally curious: a natural corollary is that I'm also suspicious, and that's why I began wondering about that scene between Overson and the landlord of the Swan.

Hadn't it been too drawn-out? Couldn't Overson have said, "Thanks all the same but I'd rather pay?" Hadn't he thrown his weight about too much and been unnecessarily severe?

Give me an inch of evidence and I'll supply the rest of the ell. Hadn't he put off that drink for a quarter of an hour when we could just as well have had it then? Was it something he'd rigged up with the landlord? Something on the lines of, "A friend of mine's coming in, Harry, and I'd like to pull his leg"? If so, why was Overson trying to convince me of his incorruptibility? Was he venal? If so he had no need to be. A bachelor drawing his money wasn't surely in need of graft. Not that we all don't like a little bit more tacked on to what we have.

Having got that far I came reluctantly back to earth. Blayde might be susceptible to bribery but surely not Overson? Overson had far too much to lose if a whisper got out. And, if it came to that, why should Overson think of me as someone who had to be convinced? In fact, it suddenly wasn't making sense. There are times, we all know, when to abandon logic is the most logical thing to do, but this, at the moment, didn't seem one of them. In any case, Hallows was just coming in and the whole thing went from my mind.

The verdict had been what we knew it would be—Death from Misadventure. All our quarrelling with that had been done long ago: what Hallows hadn't liked had been certain insinuations. Too much emphasis had been laid on two pieces of evidence by the landlord of the pub where Quarley had eaten the two welsh rarebits—that Quarley had obviously had a drink or two when he came in, and later had one or two more. Add to that Mrs. Sprigg's evidence about the whisky, and Quarley had been as good as drunk when he fell. Hallows said the point hadn't been laboured but few could have had any doubts. Previously there'd been just a hint at the possibility of suicide. Had the deceased been depressed? Had there been financial worries? The sergeant who had been in charge of the case disproved at least that. Evidence in possession of the police was that he'd been in possession of ample funds.

It left a nasty taste in the mouth, as Hallows said. I read all about it later in an afternoon edition of the *Evening Gazette*. Hallows had gone up to have a nap in view of a definitely late night at Laneford Hare and Hounds. I also read the special leading article, which was an obituary notice evidently written after the inquest. I don't think I've ever read a finer piece of writing in a provincial paper. I read it twice. It gave the highlights of Quarley's career, listed and appraised his services to the town and to the paper and gave a quote or two to remind one of the saltiness of the man. It disposed in a few ironical words of those insinuations at the inquest, and its final appraisal was trenchant enough. The crooks, the jobbers, the grafters could let out a breath and get back to business. The under-dog and the victimised had lost a champion and a friend. That was what it amounted to, and I kept that paper for Hallows in case he'd like to cut that leader out.

I was looking through the rest of the paper and had got to the back page when something caught my eye in the Stop Press.

SUDDEN ILLNESS OF CHARLES DOVELL
Mr. Charles Dovell of Laneford Hall suffered a cerebral haemorrhage during the night. His condition is said to be serious and at the time of going to press he had not recovered consciousness. A specialist is in attendance.

It was so sudden, so startling that it hit me like a blow. I looked at the words again but I don't think I really saw them. I leaned back in the chair and the thoughts were still confused. It was Dovell himself that I kept seeing: a frail old man, a gentleman, as the easily embracing term has it, who'd treated me with a quiet courtesy. But he was nothing more. What was I to Hecuba or Hecuba to me? Just nothing, except that Dovell had a wife. That was the question: just what would happen at Laneford Hall if Dovell were to die?

I went upstairs. Hallows would soon be meeting French, and he was having a wash at the bedroom basin. I waited till he'd hung up the towel before I showed him that news. He read it, gave me a quick look and read it again.

"Looks bad," he said. "If it's as bad as it reads, I wonder what'll happen there now."

"She can't possibly withdraw her claim," I said. "That'd be an absolutely damning admission, no matter how much she might come in for."

Hallows smiled wryly. "You never know. I've known women do some queer things."

"But what about tonight? Any point in going there now?"

He thought for a moment. "Far as that's concerned it might be all to the good. What we're after is what she may have done, not what she's going to do. Besides, it'll be all the talk at the pub. Won't seem odd to Woods if I ask him some questions."

He was right. It was good to have one level head in the firm. I gave him the newspaper and we went down for a quick cup of tea. From the railway station, I said, he could drive French round by way of Wellbrook Gardens. As soon as he was settled in at the hotel, it might be a good idea to take him to the Regency for a quick look at Shirley Blayde.

Hallows left. I stoked my pipe and went upstairs to do some more thinking. After stagnation, the investigation was beginning to stir. Cases are often like a log jam. There's a pile-up but once there's a sign of movement it's folly to sit back and hope. Keep the jam moving. Set off, if necessary, a few more sticks of dynamite.

That's what I was trying to find; something I could get busy with, some immediate contribution I could make. I couldn't help thinking how different everything might have been if Quarley were still alive, and it was that that gave me an idea. Whoever had written that leader in the *Evening Gazette* would surely have been on Quarley's side. And now Quarley had gone, what we needed was someone with sources of information that we'd never even suspect. We wanted a sort of listening-post, an ear to the ground.

For once I didn't wait to argue the pros and cons. I looked up the *Gazette* number and asked for the Editorial. A woman's voice came on the line. I asked if I could be put through to the news editor.

"Sorry, but he's not here. Would you like to leave a message?"

"What time will he be in?"

"Not before eight o'clock."

"Then do me a favour," I said. "Who was it wrote that leader on the late Mr. Quarley?"

"Oh, that was the editor."

"Is *he* in?"

"Afraid not," she told me. "He's been here most of the day and I don't think he'll be in again."

"Could you give me his name and address?"

She made no bones about that: a Mr. P. Trowton, of Westacre, Sydenham Avenue. I thanked her and rang off before she could ask my name.

I looked up the number and rang. This time it was a man's voice, a middle-aged voice, but brisk and lively.

"Sandbeach four-two-one."

"Mr. Trowton?"

"Speaking."

"You won't know my name, Mr. Trowton, but it's Travers—"

"Wait a minute," he said. "Aren't you conducting an investigation into a certain jewel robbery?"

"Yes," I said, just a bit taken aback. "But if you know that much about me, perhaps you know a whole lot more. Perhaps you'd let me come and see you."

"Well, I've had rather a heavy day. Just what was it you wished to see me about?"

"I think I have some information that you'd give your ears for. At the moment it would have to be strictly confidential."

"What sort of information?"

"All sorts," I said. "It might even include some light on the death of Bob Quarley."

I heard a grunt at the other end of the line.

"I see," he said, and grunted again. "I have a minor engagement at eight. It wouldn't be inconvenient for you to see me now?"

Nothing could have been better. I looked up Sydenham Avenue and it was where I thought it would be: parallel to and north of Wellbrook Avenue. There was time to drive round to the public library in Hanway Road and find out all I could about the *Gazette*. As it happened I couldn't find either of the reference books I was looking for, but a third one did tell me that the paper was owned by a private company, and independent of the big combines. That wasn't by any means all I wanted. What I'd have liked to know were the names of the principal stockholders, but the little I had would do.

Five minutes later I was in Sydenham Avenue and on the look-out for Westacre. I was lucky to find it about a third of the way along; a smallish but pleasant-looking detached house in Edwardian Tudor with a drive and a built-in garage. As I nosed my way through the gate, the front door opened and it wasn't hard to guess that the man who stood there was Trowton. As I drew the car to a halt and fiddled with the controls, I had a good look at him.

He looked about sixty. His clean-shaven face was rather pink, his lower jaw jutting, and his long, almost white hair swept back to give him something of the look of a concert pianist. The mouth was wide and expressive. The smile was friendliness itself as he held out his hand.

"Mr. Travers?"

"Yes," I said. "Nice of you to see me, Mr. Trowton."

"You've had tea?"

I said I had.

"Then we've all the more time to talk," he told me. "Let's dig ourselves in in the study."

9

TWO LUCKY BREAKS

WE HAD a minute or two of general talk. He was a married man with a couple of children, and much of his earlier life had been spent in London. He'd held his present job for about ten years. A busy life, he said, but he enjoyed it.

"What about your Board? You find them co-operative?"

"On the whole—yes." He smiled. "We had a tussle or two when I took over. Pretty conservative then. Rather resented any modernisations."

"I think that's going to help," I said. "But about myself. I'd like to put a few cards on the table."

I told him about the Agency, our connection with United Assurance and certain personal work at New Scotland Yard.

And I gave him references. He said it was good of me but he was pretty sure he wouldn't have to make use of them.

That brought us to the difficulties. He agreed that what was said in that room should go no further. I said I was sure of that: the trouble was that what I had to tell him was wholly conjecture. Not a single thing could be proved. What I was hoping was that that situation would be altered. There might be things that he could contribute.

I told him everything, though for the moment I left Quarley out. I began with Plygate's private report, went on to Hallows and myself and what we'd suspected, and ended bang up to date with what Woods had let slip. Trowton didn't say a word till I'd finished, but it wasn't in his nature to be impassive and his fingers kept intertwining and untwining, and he'd give me a quick nod as I made this point and that.

"An extraordinary story," he said. "But it's going to be awkward. Charles Dovell is a member of our Board. But about poor Quarley. Where does he come in?"

I told him, and in detail. It shook him. I asked him if he'd any idea that Quarley had been planning a new campaign.

"No," he said slowly. "I'd known him for years, of course. He was with the *Clarion* and I with the *Record*, but I'd run across him from time to time. I'd have liked him on the staff here, but he preferred to go his own way. You know what made him start that particular line of his? It was on account of his father. An excellent man, I believe, and when a new school was built here everyone expected him to get the headmastership. It actually went to a nephew of the chairman of the selection board. A flagrant piece of nepotism, and with Bob it had evidently rankled for years. But about what you've told me. The pattern's plain, as you say."

"Suppose we do happen to pin something on Garlen," I said. "What'd be the attitude of your Board?"

"It depends," he said. "Everything I've heard from you is logical and I'm sure in my own mind it's true. What has to be done is to get the whole thing supported by facts. Incontrovertible evidence, if you like. Once we have that there'll be no question of not printing. The immediate question is, just what can I do to help?"

"Frankly, I don't know. I know what I'd like, and that's information about Blayde and his wife. To start with, what's the rent of that flat of hers?"

"Pretty big," he said. "I can find out, though. If you'll excuse me a minute, I'll have a word with my wife. She'll know."

He was back in a couple of minutes. "Flats with a garage—£250 a year: those without—£200."

"And her salary at the hotel?"

He didn't know. He thought for a minute, checked a number and reached for the telephone. He got Sellman on the line. A little general talk and he was mentioning a niece of his who was applying for a job as receptionist at some imaginary hotel and he thought they weren't offering enough. After that all he had to do was say a yes or two, add a word of thanks and hang up.

"Averages eight pounds a week," he told me. "Depends on the shift. Practically no chance of tips."

Something was wrong. That flat of hers was expensively furnished, and I couldn't see Shirley Blayde keeping herself on three pounds a week.

"What about her husband? Any chance of finding out what his bank balance is? Anything biggish paid in, say, just about the time of the burglary?"

He thought it impossible. Nor could there be an approach to the inspector of taxes. If the information was essential, Triller might be approached as a last resort. He'd every confidence in Triller. It was Quarley who'd uncovered that information about a certain superintendent and in less than a fortnight he was out on his elbows.

"As a last resort, possibly yes," I said, "but I'd like to dig a bit deeper first. The fewer who're in the know, the better."

"I'll still think it over," he told me. "Anything else?"

In detail, no, I said: in general, yes. Now he had the facts he might put wholly new interpretations on anything that reached his ears. In the meanwhile, as I'd said, I and my team would go on digging. Time was a factor, of course. That supposed holiday couldn't go on for ever. Within a week I just had to have enough to make John Hill repudiate the claim. "Well, I'll do my best," he said, as I rose to go. "You can always communicate with me here. If you do have to ring the office, you ought to have another name."

"Haire," I said. "It's my wife's maiden name. I've used it before."

"Fine," he said. "And that reminds me. I'd have liked you to meet my wife, but perhaps we'd better leave that for the time being."

We'd actually gone through the door and into the hall when his telephone went.

"Thought I wouldn't be left in peace much longer," he told me. "Still, it may be for my wife."

I went on through the front door and stood on the drive by the car. He was with me almost at once.

"Bad news about Dovell," he said quietly. "He died about an hour ago."

I didn't speak for a moment. Everything was wide open again, but he'd been generous of his time and I couldn't very well hint at any new discussion.

"A fine character," was what I said. "I only saw him the once, but I liked him. I wonder what's going to happen there now."

"Don't know," he said slowly. "Big changes, I'm afraid."

I held out my hand and his smile was warm as he took it.

"Good luck," he told me. "And don't forget. I'll be doing what I can."

I moved the car on. When I turned at the gate he was still where I'd left him and I thought I saw a wave of the hand.

Long before I was back at the hotel I was feeling a different man. In Trowton I felt we had a sound ally: quick-thinking, even nervy perhaps, but one we were more than lucky to have. It gave a new confidence, the feeling that between us something was bound to be unearthed. But for the moment I decided to keep that visit to myself. What had happened could affect neither Hallows nor French.

Hallows must have left for Laneford when I got back, for his car was still out. It was not long to dinner and after it I began to feel restless. Now that things seemed to be moving again, I wanted to make my contribution, and all at once I made up my mind to go to Laneford. I don't know why, except that it was the only place that came into my mind. It wasn't a cold night for the time of year, so I went out as I was to the garage and brought out the car. There wasn't much traffic about, and practically none once I was through the town. I didn't drive fast but in twenty minutes I was on the village outskirts.

I drew the car up and tried to remember what Hallows had told me, then I drove slowly on. I spotted Hallows's car drawn up outside the Hare and Hounds and then I drove on more slowly still, looking for that side road that skirted the Hall gardens. I found it about a couple of hundred yards past the main entrance. It was a narrow, unmetalled lane, but the surface was fairly good and after a minute I shut off my lights.

It wasn't a really dark night. I think there must have been a moon but it was behind the clouds: at any rate I could see a few yards ahead once I got accustomed to the dark. I even saw the field gate on my near side, but I wanted to be heading for home so I drove slowly on, hoping for a place to turn. I must have gone another couple of hundred yards before I found another gate, but there wasn't much room on the verges and it took quite a time to turn round. Then, luckily as it turned out, I misjudged the distance back to the field gate, and when I pulled up on what verge there was, I had a good fifty yards to walk.

The gate was sagging on a loose hinge and I had to lift it to go through. A track went away to my left and another towards the house, and I realised that if I'd brought the car through I could have turned it with no trouble at all. I chose the track that went on, and in a few yards it was only a wideish grass path. On my left I could just see a greenhouse. A few yards on, the bulk of the house loomed dark against the sky and I moved on more warily. A more immediate darkness came up suddenly as the path turned, and when I went carefully forward I knew it was only a tall clipped hedge. The path went on. Just beyond the hedge I stopped and made my way back. I stood in the hedge shadow and looked towards the house.

It was not more than fifty yards away and it was still nothing but a kind of lighter blackness against the intense black of the trees. In a moment or two I could just discern the nearer windows, but there was never a crack of light. There was a sweet smell in the air and I thought that the lighter patch not far ahead of me must be a bed of hyacinths or narcissi. There was something nostalgic about it, and then all at once, as I remembered a dead man in that house, a something almost funereal like the scent of lilies or wreaths that cover a just-filled-in grave.

I stood there, I don't know why. It was a still night with no wind and far from cold: better than a frowsty foyer or a frowstier cinema, and I must have stood there for the best part of half an hour before I decided to move. For a moment I wondered if I should go on towards the house and round it and so back, and then I thought I might lose my way, and then, just as I went back through the hedge opening, I saw the lights of a car. For just a moment they turned towards the track by which I'd come and then, as suddenly, there were no lights at all.

I drew back and listened but could hear nothing. Then I did seem to hear a sound away at the field gate, and almost at once I knew it for the sound of a car in low gear. It stopped and the night was still again. There was another sound, faint like a gentle swishing through grass, and my heart was in my mouth as I nipped back through the opening and just along it, and stood erect with shoulders tight against the resisting hedge. Something was suddenly in sight: a receding blackness that made never a sound on the turf, but which I knew for a man.

I drew slowly out and stopped, but the line of faint light was too high and there was nothing against it but the dark mass of the trees. Then all at once there *was* a light. It wasn't even that. It was merely a kind of quick lightness as a door towards my end of the house opened and shut. Then everything was dark again and very still, and the scent of the flowers was all at once more strong.

Something told me to get back to the track and my car, and I began making a careful way along the path. Just as it ended or widened I saw another strange shape immediately ahead. I stopped in my tracks and my heart must have missed a couple of beats. Then I could see it was a car: the one I had heard coming in at the gate and then reversing in low gear. A man had left it but another might still be there.

I stooped, listened, and felt out with my fingers till they closed on some cinders. I threw them. They rattled against the car and that was the only sound. I moved slowly forward, stopped almost at the rear door and listened again. There was no one in that car. There was no sound from behind me but I squatted again in case a something moving should show itself against the light. Then I took a chance, covered the rear number plate as best I could, and flicked on my lighter. Then I moved on. It was a biggish car but it was too dark and I was too near it to see its make.

I climbed over the gate and made a careful way back to my own car. From where I sat at the wheel the field gate would have been invisible even in daylight on account of the sharpish bend, but I daren't move the car nearer in case it should be seen. So what I did was drive slowly on to the main road. I drew into it and back on the verge some ten yards away. My sidelights were invisible except to an oncoming driver and all I had to do was to wait till that other driver emerged from the lane. I doubted if that car would be as fast as mine and, with any luck at all, I ought to be able to follow.

When I had stood by that hedge and, later, when I'd been making a careful way back, all my anxieties had been for myself. I'm only too easy to identify and to have been caught loitering on private property might have led to all sorts of things, and probably unpleasant. But now I was sitting in my own car, none daring lawfully, as the Book has it, to make me afraid, and I could begin thinking about that other man.

He, too, had entered the Hall grounds surreptitiously: on the other hand, he'd been both expected and admitted. That quick light I'd seen was proof of that. No argument: a tap at the door and admittance at once. And wasn't the very quickness a kind of surreptitiousness? Why hadn't he driven along the main drive to the front, and, if his business really lay at that back door at the far left corner, why hadn't he simply walked the few yards round?

I remembered the dead man in the house and wondered for a quick moment if the man I'd seen could have come on business connected with the funeral? But that couldn't be right. Even an undertaker's man would have driven to the front of the house and been admitted on his lawful occasions.

I had another idea. I didn't know what staff was in the Hall beyond the housekeeper and butler, but that surreptitious caller might have been a friend. Even that didn't seem right. These are democratic days but a friend of, say, housekeeper or maid would hardly be driving what even in the dark I'd known to be a large and probably expensive car.

It was just after ten o'clock. I lighted my pipe and almost at once heard the distant sound of voices—closing time probably at the Hare and Hounds. Hallows would be there and I wondered if I should overtake him just beyond the village and have a quick talk. But Hallows mightn't be going home at once, so I just sat on. Another ten minutes and the village was dead quiet.

The time went slowly on. More than once I was tempted to make a careful way back on foot to the field gate and the car, and then I'd know it was too risky and I'd just go on sitting and listening. From somewhere came that lone sound I'd often heard as a boy—a dog barking somewhere in the night. From the direction of the Hall there was never a sound.

The night was still, with not even a sough of trees in a gentle wind. There was just nothing, and I was alone in a world of my own: a world of no more than ten yards radius beyond which was darkness and nothing more.

It was half-past eleven when I knew I had to go. The hotel would be closed at midnight, and I didn't want to call attention to myself by being specially admitted, so I moved the car reluctantly on. The whole world, except myself, was asleep and I didn't see a car or a living soul till I was nearing the roundabout. Hallows must have been back long since. I listened at his door and thought I could hear the sound of his breathing. For me it had been a longish day and by the time my head had warmed the pillow I was asleep.

I woke early. I was actually shaved and dressed when early tea came in. I smoked a pipe, saw it was almost eight o'clock and decided to take a chance on getting Trowton. It was his wife who came on the line. I gave her my name and said it was rather urgent, and she asked me to hold the line. She was back in a minute. Trowton was just out of bed but he'd be down almost at once. I heard him clearing his throat almost before she'd finished speaking.

"This is Haire," I said. "Sorry to drag you down like this."

He said that usually he was earlier but the previous night he'd had to go back to the office after all. That news that had come in just after I'd left.

"Something happened to me, too," I said. "You know Laneford Hall pretty well?"

He said he did. He was even aware of that semi-private back lane, so it was easier to tell him what had happened.

"Queer, as you say. You couldn't identify the car?"

"No," I said, "but I have the number. What I want you to do is try to find the name of the owner."

He took the number down. A local registration, he said, and it shouldn't be too hard. I said I'd stay in the hotel till he gave me a ring.

Breakfast was from eight onwards. I'd finished mine, and the long obituary of Charles Dovell in the *Gazette* before Hallows appeared. He didn't go straight through to the dining-room but came over to me and pulled in a chair.

"Have a good night?"

"Couldn't have been better." He treated himself to a sideways nod and a smile. "In fact, I think I've got the whole thing." The pub had been practically normal, he said; at least, no air of general depression. Dovell's name had naturally been mentioned and there'd been speculation about what would happen next. Some seemed to think the Hall would be sold. It was the landlord who thought there was no point in speculation. As soon as Dovell was buried they'd know what had been in his will.

Woods had said very little. He'd been appealed to once or twice and had refused to commit himself. Even if the Hall were sold there'd still be the garden and he didn't see himself out of a job; a sound point of view and one that seemed to be accepted. But in general the Hare and Hounds was as usual: darts, dominoes, beery good-fellowship till the clock hands had moved round to ten.

"Got a little present for you, Woody," Hallows said when they came out. "Meant to give it to you the other morning and forgot all about it."

It was a bottle of Scotch. Woods was delighted.

"Tell you what, Tom. My missus hasn't been so well lately and she'll be in bed, so what about sampling it?"

Hallows drove them to the lodge cottage by the main gates and parked the car in the drive. Woods stirred up the fire in the little living-room and the Scotch was duly sampled. Hallows brought the conversation round.

"You really think your madam'll stay on in the Hall?"

"Depend on the will."

"That's right," Hallows said. "An attractive woman, from what I hear, so why shouldn't she marry again? If so, there might still be some alterations."

"Not to me, there won't. Not while she's there." He smiled knowingly. "Mind you, I wouldn't say she wouldn't like to give me the sack."

That was when things began gradually to come out. One night in February—it was actually while Dovell was seriously ill—Woods had remembered after leaving the pub that he'd left some cold frames open and it felt like a frost. He'd gone round by the house and was just in time to see a man going across the lawn towards the small drawing-room; the one known as Mrs. Dovell's room. It had french windows that opened on that lawn and when he'd made his own way round, the man had disappeared.

Later on he'd noticed one morning the marks of car tyres in the usual winter mud that always lies by a field gate, and it so happened that he saw Mrs. Dovell that very morning and mentioned it. She knew nothing about it, but later on the whole area was made up with clinker and rolled down hard.

"You could tell from her face when I sprung it on her, it was all lies. And I bet she knew I didn't believe her."

"Who do you think was calling, Woody? A gentleman friend?"

Woods gave a wink. That was all it could be. Easy as pie to have someone in that drawing-room. Only Wellard, Mrs. Flint and old Maggie, the housemaid, in the place, and their quarters were at the far end. And they always went to bed at ten. The master, he'd always gone up at about nine of recent months.

"You didn't say anything to the others?"

Woods winked again. "What d'you think I am? When you drop on something like that, best to keep it under your hat."

Breakfasts were supposed to be off at half-past nine so I went with Hallows to the dining-room, and I didn't know if what I had to tell him would be climax or anti-climax. I told him all the same.

"A lucky brainwave," he said. Far more than that, I told him. I'd been at a loose end and I might have gone anywhere, just to spend an hour or two. And on just that night the surreptitious caller had turned up.

"Must have been something to do with Dovell's death," he said. "If he was a man she'd been regularly seeing, he might want to know just where he now stood."

If so, it showed her in a pretty callous light, I said. That affectionate scene she'd staged for me hadn't been worth either the little gestures or the breath she'd wasted on it.

"Lucky you got the car number," he said. "How long, do you think, before you'll know whose it was?"

He looked at his watch. At ten o'clock he had an appointment with French and he didn't think a local taxation office would open before half-past nine. I had to prevaricate. I didn't want to tell him about Trowton. It wasn't that I didn't trust him, far from it: just that it had been more or less implied between Trowton and me that no one should know of our association but our two selves.

"I'm trying a short cut," I said. "Ran across someone who has the usual friend."

We went back to the foyer. He looked at his watch again, said he had another ten minutes and began looking through the *Gazette*. It wasn't a couple of minutes later when the desk telephone rang. I held my breath. I think my heart began to beat more quickly when the clerk called to me.

A few seconds later I was back.

"You know?"

"Give you ten guesses," I said, "and you won't be right."

"You win," he said. "Whose car was it?"

"A black Ford Zephyr," I told him. "Overson's."

10

SATURDAY AFTERNOON

WHEN Hallows had gone I moved to my usual seat in the foyer corner, the swing doors well in view. Saturday would be a busy day at the hotel and already there was more movement in and out than there had been all the week, but that kind of movement doesn't distract me and I settled down to a spell of hard thinking. And the curious thing was that almost at once I began to feel far less elated.

Four people, I'd told myself, all from more or less the same social background and all moving in the same closed circle: Overson and his friend and protégée, Blayde; Shirley Bright whom Blayde had subsequently married, and Mona Franks: the two girls at the same secretarial college and the men their boy friends. In each case the friendships had been those of opposites: Overson, for instance, must always have been a far stronger character than Blayde, and from what I had gathered, Shirley the careful, calculating one, and Mona the one whose aim had been to have a good time. And if Blayde had ultimately been attracted to Shirley, surely it wasn't unreasonable to assume that there had also been something between the other two.

How intimate the association had been I didn't know, though I was prepared to guess. But nothing had come of it. Overson, as he had told me and as his unmarried state still showed, hadn't been the marrying kind, but that was no reason why whatever association there had been shouldn't have been subsequently renewed. And especially when Mona had found that to be Mrs. Charles Dovell wasn't a satisfying bargain for a life of celibacy;

and, when Dovell became so much of an invalid, that life could have its compensating hours with few attendant risks.

And who was I to cast a stone? I'd never been subject to the same temptations, nor was I shaped, perhaps, in the same mould. Much as I loathed the Mona Dovell type, I had at least to try to see her point of view. As for Overson, doubtless his life had been a series of philanderings, and to renew an old intimacy with one so physically attractive as Mona, would have been something at which he wouldn't have balked. All that would have been needed was careful planning.

So, to get down to brass tacks, was what we'd discovered of any use to the investigation? I didn't know. If Overson was the lover of Mona Dovell, then the least he could have done was to make that Regency job a cut-and-dried one. Her anxiety would be for the claim to be promptly met; everything mere formality and then a quick payment, and it was a thousand to one that within a very few hours of the discovery of the burglary, he'd known precisely what her ideas had been. But by that time the case *was* cut and dried. The torch with Davitt's prints had already been found.

What would happen now that Dovell was dead was quite a different matter. Was there the possibility that she'd marry Overson? Somehow I doubted it. A first-class catch for him, but surely not for her. With Dovell she'd been a somebody, and, however hectic had been her past, it had been profitable for people to forget. But now the same people would begin to remember. And a marriage to Overson would be a definite slipping back, and somehow I was sure that she was the kind who'd never yield an inch of what she'd consider had been so dearly won. There was, of course, one complication. If she were really infatuated with Overson, then she might take a kind of gambler's risk, and if she did, then that was no business of mine. In fact, all that emerged from that spell of thinking was only one certainty: that if ever the investigation needed the active co-operation of Overson, it would have as much chance of getting it as it would that of Sam Garlen.

Hallows came back. French, he said, had had an easy night. He'd followed Shirley from the Regency to the flat and she hadn't stirred till just before half-past nine. Then she'd taken out her car and French was helpless. On most nights he could have had Hallows's car and I hadn't thought to let him have mine. At any rate, she'd backed the car out and was away before he could even nip along to see if there was a handy bus.

"He thought he'd pack up," Hallows said. "He hadn't the foggiest idea where she'd gone, and then he thought he'd hang on for a bit in case she came back, and the funny thing is, she did come back. He reckons it wasn't more than a quarter of an hour. She drove right into the garage, came back and closed the front gate and then closed the garage and went in the back door."

"Wait a minute," I said. "I don't remember a back door."

"You wouldn't, unless you'd been round to the back. It's a tradesmen's entrance, round by the kitchen. The garage sort of masks it. At any rate, she didn't stir out again, so he gave it till eleven o'clock and then packed up."

"Could you work out roughly where she went?"

"Well, she swung across and turned right and then due north. Couldn't have been going anywhere except to the housing estate. Probably to that bungalow where she used to live. My guess is she was looking for her husband and he wasn't in, so she came back."

It was possible, though why she should risk a fruitless visit when she could have rung beforehand, we couldn't exactly see.

"What about the car?" I said. "Did French get the make, and so on?"

He'd got the whole thing: a Morris Minor 4-door Saloon de luxe. Pale blue. And newish. The tyres didn't look as if they'd been driven a lot of miles.

"You know what it cost?"

"I do now," he said. "I asked at that garage, just this side of the roundabout. Call it seven hundred net."

I let out an exasperated breath. A pity it would be too risky to find out where she'd bought it, and on what terms.

"Something's pretty badly wrong," I said. "I happen to know how much she earns and what that flat costs her, and if Blayde isn't paying her anything, and I don't see why he should, she's got only three pounds a week to live on. I saw only one room and caught a glimpse of the kitchen, but you can take it from me that it cost her a packet to furnish the place."

"Yes," he said. "Even if she bought everything on the never-never, the payments would more than swallow that three pounds. And she's a smart dresser."

He had an idea.

"What about Garlen? Could she be on his books?"

There was a chance, of course. You had to have money to patronise the Regency, and mightn't a friendly receptionist advise a sporting guest on how to have a flutter? Might there even be games of chance by night? With, of course, always changing venues. For all we knew, Sandbeach might even have its call girls.

But what could we do? Conjecture was no good and an anti-vice campaign a hopeless proposition. And suppose by some amazing stroke of luck we did prove that Shirley Blayde was in the pay of Garlen, would that be sufficient for Hill to repudiate the claim? We doubted it. And we hadn't the time. Nor did we feel somehow that miracles were in the air.

There was just one thing that did occur to me: that after what I'd discovered the previous night I might do worse than have a real good look at Overson. After all, I'd asked him to have lunch with me some time, and who knew what might emerge from a free-and-easy hour. I could bring the talk round to Shirley Blayde. Or what easier than to talk about Dovell and what might happen now at Laneford Hall. Mind you, I wouldn't expect him to hand me information on a silver platter. But you never knew. Truth is often merely the obvious, and there's more to be learned from the recognition of a calculated lie.

I rang police headquarters and found Overson there, and he said he'd be delighted. I proposed half-past twelve and a drink beforehand.

"We might go on to the football match," he said. "You interested at all?"

I admitted I wasn't.

"Then tonight," he said, "there's that big boxing promotion at the ice rink."

That was more in my line and I said we could talk it over. And that, again, was that. Hallows was due for an easy day and he thought he'd spend it with French. Maybe they'd put in an afternoon at the football stadium. He had a look at the *Gazette* and thought the game ought to be good. Then, as he got up, he passed me the paper.

"All about the big fight," he told me, and indicated the place.

Nowadays I know only the big names in boxing, but in my Cambridge days I was a bit of an amateur scrapper myself; in fact it was a mauling I got from a heavyweight who went berserk in a charity contest that upset some optic nerve or other and doomed me to glasses for the rest of my days. But when I'd had the chance I'd always listened to anything in the boxing line that had happened to be on the air. And, according to the *Gazette*, the big bout of the evening looked really good.

It was the final eliminator for the lightweight championship and the capacity crowd would be rooting for the local boy, Arty Stone. He'd switched from amateur to pro about three years before and had rocketed up with fourteen wins and a draw in his fifteen fights. His opponent was a coloured man, Kid Walters, a Jamaican who'd come up the hard way. He'd lost only five of some eighty fights, the last on account of a badly cut eye. I read the whole two columns; in fact I was so engrossed that I didn't even see Hallows leave the hotel. It didn't say who'd win: that would have been too much to expect, but out of the usual *ifs* and *provided thats* I gathered that Stone would be out at the first clang of the bell and making for that damaged eye. I liked the look of the coloured boy, I don't know why. Maybe he didn't look so cocksure as Stone.

I glanced at the clock above the desk and it was already after twelve, and it took me a moment or two to realise that I ought to go up and smarten myself for Overson.

As it turned out I was sorry I'd taken the trouble, for he was wearing a tweed jacket that looked like an old friend, a dark blue and gold tie, a fawn pullover and grey flannel trousers. He couldn't help giving a little start at the sight of my brown ensemble. I had to laugh when he began explaining that it was really his day off. Still, if any ice needed breaking, that broke it. By the time we'd had a couple of short ones, we might have known each other for years.

I'd been rather dubious about the meal but it wasn't too bad. He thought it was pretty good. As he said, most of his meals were pretty scratch ones, and if he hadn't had the digestion of a horse he'd probably have had out-sized ulcers.

I said I was lucky that way, too.

"Do you know," he said suddenly, "I think I was all wrong about you."

"How do you mean?"

"Well, I thought you were one of those serious, too-damn-conscientious sort of chaps. Take boxing, for instance. I'd never have guessed you'd ever had a pair of gloves on."

I smiled. I hoped it was roguishly.

"Even insurance investigators have their moments. In fact you'd be surprised."

He laughed. "I'll bet. It just shows you, though."

Then he leaned forward. "That reminds me. Something I wondered at the time and never thought I'd know. When you saw Mona Dovell, what line did she take with you?"

I had to think quickly. That was the first time we'd either of us mentioned anything even faintly connected with the investigation.

"What line?" I said. "You mean she has several lines?"

"Only two. The who-the-hell-are-you and the come-hither."

I smiled. "You're not serious?"

He leaned forward again. There were a couple of unoccupied tables between us and the next diners, but his voice lowered.

"Let me tell you something. Your job's over now, so it won't make a damn of difference either way, but if you'd asked me anything about the lady even a couple of days ago you'd have had a very short answer, and I'll tell you why: because then she was Mrs. Charles Dovell. He was still somebody, you know, even behind the scenes. A word from him in the right spot and you could be either up here or down there. You go to Laneford next Tuesday at the funeral and you'll see the kind of influence he had."

The waiter came up to clear the table. Coffee there, or in the lounge? Overson said he was happy where he was. I told the waiter to bring kümmels, too.

"I get you," I said. "But today's different."

He smiled. "You bet it's different. From now on she's Mona Franks. Yes," he said, and passed his cigarette case. "And if anyone knows our Mona, it's me."

"Funny you should say that," I told him. "You know that newspaperman Quarley—the one who met with that accident? I happened to overhear him talking to my assistant one morning and I'll bet now it was Mrs. Dovell he was talking about. According to him she'd been a pretty fast piece in her time."

"Fast," he said, and his lip drooped, and then that waiter had to come with the coffee and kümmels. But it didn't happen to make any difference. Overson had something on his mind and he had to get it off. He sugared his coffee, took a sip at the liqueur and went on as if there'd been no break.

"Fast," he said again. "She was about the hottest thing in Sandbeach, and that's saying something, believe me." The cynical smile was there again. "Do you know I nearly married her?"

"No-o-o!"

"Yes," he said. "Every time I've thought of it since I've gone all hot and cold. It was after one of those nice little intimate moments and I came over all moral and it was on the tip of my tongue to start talking about getting married, and then I didn't."

"She'd have had you?"

He frowned. "Damned if I know. What I didn't know then was that she was after a bit bigger game. Son of a big local brewer."

"And what happened with him?"

"Don't know," he said, "but there was a lot of talk at the time. Then her father was supposed to be ill, somewhere up in the Midlands, and she was away for quite a spell, and when she came back she worked in another department."

Once more he leaned forward.

"Know what I think, only for God's sake don't let this go any further. I've an idea he put her in the family way and that was all bunkum about her father. Couldn't prove anything, of course, but one or two others thought the same."

"She's certainly seen life."

"Yes," he said. "And from something she let fall, I think Shirley—you remember, Blayde's wife—thought so, too. That was when that girlish friendship fell through, after Mona came back. But about what she said, which was when Mona married Dovell. I forget what the exact words were, but it was about Mona being nothing but a trollop and look what she'd got for it, whereas she'd only got Jack Blayde. I always reckoned that was why they split up. Shirley was always one of the proper kind."

"Yes," I said, and refilled his cup. "But I've got an idea. Mona played her cards right and married Dovell. Now, from what you've been telling me, you've got a chance to do like-wise, so why can't you play your cards right and marry Mona?"

He looked aghast.

"Sorry," I said. "I didn't mean to drop a brick."

"You didn't." He smiled. "It was just the idea of it. Good God! I wouldn't marry her if she was the last woman in the world. Mona's all right for a bit of fun, if you've got an easy conscience but—" He broke off. "What on earth made you think of that?"

I made the smile sheepish. "Oh, you know. Just trying to do a friend a good turn."

"No," he said. "I'm used to reading faces and there was more in it than that."

"Well—" I broke off again. "No, honestly, it was just an idea."

"Well, what idea?"

"Look," I said, "you're not going to like this, but a funny thing happened last night. I was going to Chemworth to see an old friend and just before Laneford I was tucked in behind another car. Not too close, but near enough to see the rear plate and I was dead sure it was your car."

Once again he leaned forward.

"And what happened?"

I laughed. "To tell the honest truth, I don't know. I remember going by some lodge gates and then all at once it wasn't there!"

"This is interesting," he said, and he was looking quite pleased. "What do you mean, it wasn't there?"

"Well, it wasn't! My car's pretty fast and I never saw it again. What I thought later on was that there must be a side road I'd missed, so when I came back round about midnight, I kept a look out and there wasn't a side road, not that I could see. There was what looked like a narrow track, but the car couldn't have gone up there. I'd have seen its lights."

He laughed, and I really mean laughed.

"The funniest thing I've heard for years." He went on laughing. "Wish I could tell you just how funny it is."

I looked bewildered. "You mean there wasn't a car?"

"There was a car all right." The laugh dwindled to a smile. "The funny thing is that it *was* my car. Only I wasn't driving it."

I stared.

"And it went up that track. I ought to know. I've been up there a few times myself."

Overson's face was slightly flushed and every now and again he didn't quite hit a word square on the head. He wasn't tight. Perhaps he wasn't a great way from it. I'd never thought of him as someone who couldn't carry his liquor, so maybe it was the unusual that had loosened his tongue and made into a confidant one so unlikely as myself. The two martinis, for instance, had been pretty potent, so much so that I'd taken care not to drink more than a quarter of the bottle of Châteauneuf du Pape we'd had with the meal. There'd been the two quite generous kümmels to top it, and even an old stager like myself had for some time been choosing his words with a certain amount of care.

"You know who was in that car?" he asked me. I just shook my head.

"Jack Blayde."

I stared. It had been a surprise and I still couldn't fit Blayde in.

"That's who it was," he assured me. "His car was in dry dock—clutch trouble—so he borrowed mine. And I'll tell you something else."

He pushed aside the coffee cup and leaned forward once more, arms on the table. It was all so confidential that I had to lean forward, too, to hear what he said.

"A certain lady gave me a ring about seven o'clock. No names, no pack-drill."

"Quite right," I said. "Always keep a lady's name out of it."

He nodded. It was good, apparently, to talk to someone who really understood.

"Rang me and reckoned she was going crazy. Nothing but the telephone going and people jabbering, and she couldn't stand it, and what about me coming along. I said what for?—and you know what the bitch did? She giggled. What d'you think of that? And the old man lying up there dead. I tell you, if I'd been there I'd have hit her across the mouth. But you know what I did? I just played along. 'All right,' I said. 'Which door, front or back?' and she said, 'Back, you fool,' and I said, 'You know what you are? You're nothing but a common little bitch,' and she said, 'And you're a cheap bastard,' and I told her to go to hell and I hung up on her, just like that."

"Horrible," I said. "You'd never believe a woman'd want a man as badly as that. But why the hell did he marry her?"

"You've met her," he said. "When she likes she can put on an act that'd take in Old Nick himself. Besides, it was the old lady, the first wife, who took a fancy to her. Made an absolute fool of her. All she had to do was play her cards right. And why'd she ring Jack Blayde? It couldn't have been more than a few minutes before he was wanting to borrow the car. And he didn't bring it back till breakfast time."

"Blayde," I said. "What the devil could she see in Blayde?"

He sneered.

"He wears trousers, doesn't he? And he's not all that bad looking." His voice lowered still further. "I'll tell you something else. It's not the first time he's been there. I can put two and two together. The first few months after Shirley left him he'd have gone down on his hands and knees to get her back. But not the last two or three months. He suddenly turned all cocky. You know—let her stew in her own juice, and she's made her bed and let her lie on it. All that sort of claptrap. And that silly smile of his."

He picked up the liqueur glass, saw it was empty and set it down again. I asked if he'd have another.

"Thank you, no," he said. "About time I was going. But it's funny, don't you think? Him kidding himself he was clever and me not guessing a thing till you told me just now what happened last night." He laughed. "Wonder if the poor bloody fool thinks he's got a chance of marrying her."

He got to his feet. "Think I'll slip along to the cloakroom. You coming, too?"

He sluiced his face and neck with cold water. He squinted at himself in the mirror and combed back his hair.

"That's better. That was too good a lunch, you know. Don't often have a meal like that these days." There was almost a wink in the look he was giving me. "About what we were talking about. Strictly between ourselves, eh?"

"Don't worry about me," I told him, and tapped my skull. "I've got enough secrets inside here to start my own confidential magazine."

His laugh had a certain approval. "I'll bet you have. But about tonight. The big fight won't be on till after nine, so what about dropping in about half-past eight. If I'm not there, Blayde will take you. I'll be seeing you there in any case."

I said that'd be fine. We went out to the foyer.

"Sure you won't change your mind and come along to the match?"

"If you don't mind I'd rather not," I said. "To tell the truth, I thought about having a nap."

"Maybe you're right," he said. "You always think these matches are going to be good and nine times out of ten they aren't worth a damn."

He held out his hand. "Well, thanks again for a wonderful meal. You're leaving Tuesday?"

"That's right. Probably Tuesday afternoon."

"Well, see you tonight in any case."

A final smile and he went jauntily through the swing doors.

11
SATURDAY NIGHT

I WENT straight up to my room. Saturday afternoon, I thought, and a newspaperman's holiday. But not the *Evening Gazette*. Would Trowton edit both evening and daily? I doubted it, and that's why I tried him at his home. I thought at first he was out, but after about a minute he was on the line.

"Haire, here," I said. "Sorry if I've disturbed you."

He chuckled.

"Just having a nap in the next room. And how are things with you?"

"Been having lunch with Overson and think I've unearthed something. You ever know the Franks people who used to live at Bandon?"

He grunted.

"No," he said. "I knew *of* them, of course."

"The point is this: they had financial troubles and moved to the Midlands, where he died. No one seems to know exactly where."

"I see," he said. "You've tried Bandon?"

"No," I said. "For one thing, I didn't need the information till just this minute. Also Quarley spoke as if he didn't know either."

"Yes. Sounds as if it might be difficult. There *is* a man of ours who used to live at Bandon." He thought for a moment. "Look, here, will you leave it to me?"

I said I'd be grateful. And someone would be near the hotel telephone from then on.

It was a quarter to three. If Hallows dropped in after the football match it couldn't be till best part of five, so I rang the desk for calls to be passed to the room, then took off shoes and jacket and lay on the bed beneath the eiderdown. I guessed I'd be in for a late night and I was genuinely sleepy. It isn't once in a blue moon that I sleep by day, but I did drop off and it was after four when I woke. By the time I'd had tea I was in the foyer looking out for Hallows.

It was just about five when he came in. He said the game hadn't been bad and the locals had won, so everybody was happy. And what about that evening?

I told him just the one thing I'd learned from Overson and he pricked his ears at once.

"If it's true, you think we might put a little pressure on the lady?"

"Don't know," I said. "It sounds a bit too much like third-degree, or blackmail. All we'll consider it at the moment is a possible ace up our sleeves. And we haven't even got the mother's address."

There was no use any longer in holding back Trowton and I suddenly felt I'd like his opinion. He thought it had been a good move. Quarley, he said, had had a high opinion of Trowton. And so that was settled. If by any chance the address we wanted came through, Hallows would be away first thing in the morning. If not, then Hallows would have to do some digging himself at Bandon. Meanwhile, he could tell French as much as was necessary and

I'd hold the telephone fort till dinner. He left me the *Evening Gazette* he'd bought. It had the Grand National result in the Stop Press and more news about the big fight. The house had been sold out for a couple of days and there was a warning against touts who might try to foist tickets. The same pictures were there and I still liked the look of the coloured boy. The betting, it was said, was five to four on Stone.

Hallows came back and I went out to stretch my legs. The streets seemed to be packed, and when I went by the Regency garage, the big, open yard looked pretty full of cars. The football match, I guessed, and the big fight. I wondered if Garlen would be there and what he stood to make or lose. I wondered if I should have a little flutter myself.

Dinner was from half-past six that night and Hallows went in first. About ten minutes later there was a call for me.

"Haire? . . . Thought I'd report progress. Our man hasn't what you wanted but he thinks he has something else. He knows the firm who moved some furniture and he thinks he knows the actual man."

I said that was fine.

"Don't expect results," he said. "I mean, not all that soon. It's Saturday and the man may take some finding. Still, I thought you'd like to know."

Hallows was back soon after seven and I went in. I'd had my meal and was dollying myself up for the evening when he came into the room.

"Got it," he said, and gave me his notebook. "The chap was gardening all the afternoon and hadn't been out."

"Wayside," Moreby, Nr. Kettering, was what I read.

"How far from Kettering?"

"About seven miles this side," he said. "I just looked it up. So what about making a start tonight? I could be seventy or eighty miles on the road before I need pull up."

He said he liked driving at night, and we hadn't all that much time, so he went to pack a bag. When I went down I called at the desk but he'd already left word.

Blayde was in Overson's room and waiting for me. It was a bit early, he said, but we might as well start off. He took his time for all that. And I was seeing him with somewhat new eyes. He seemed to be wearing the same clothes he'd had on that afternoon when he'd called at the hotel, but to me he wasn't the same man. Overson and Mona Dovell—yes: Blayde and the same lady—well, as Overson had said, he wore trousers. I wondered if the lady was a blabbermouth. Was that cockiness the knowledge that he, Blayde, had actually supplanted the great lover, Overson?

"We'll take my car," Blayde was saying as he unhooked his overcoat. "Had a bit of clutch trouble, but it's all right now. What's your car, by the way?"

I told him, stressing the old model.

"Always wanted to have a Bentley myself," he said. "Wouldn't do in our game, though. People might wonder where the money came from."

His car was just outside the garage and we moved off.

"No great hurry," he told me. "Those supporting bouts aren't worth a damn."

I asked him whom he fancied and he said he had just a small bet on Stone. I asked if he could put a small bet on for me—just a quid—and when I passed him the note he laughed when I said it was on the other boy. Then he began telling me about the fight. A Johnny Price was the promoter and Garlen had a big piece of Stone. He, Blayde, had seen Stone at his training camp at Chemworth, and he'd certainly looked good, and was I sure I wanted that bet. I said it might just as well ride. After all, I'd always been a sucker for the underdog.

We turned into Cooper Street. There wasn't all that traffic but quite a few uniformed police were about. A smallish crowd was milling around but nothing the police couldn't handle. Blayde drew the car in and a uniformed sergeant was on us at once.

"See to the car, Fred, will you?" Blayde said. "Dave inside?"

"Saw him a minute or two ago."

"Right. Put the car handy, will you? Don't want a mix-up when we come out."

We moved on through the doors. Blayde was known, and we went across the foyer and down a corridor to the right. There was a fug even there, and we could hear the noise of the crowd. We stopped just short of a wider corridor with three or four doors.

"Wait just a second," Blayde told me. "Dave may be in here."

He tapped at the first door and went in, and I could hear the sound of voices. He was out again inside a minute and Overson with him. Overson gave me a smile.

"You made it just right. The first fight only went a couple of rounds and the second's just about over. If I were you, Jack, I'd wait till the lights are on."

Blayde moved on.

"It's all right," Overson told me. "Be seeing you later."

We went up a short flight of stairs. A muscular-looking attendant stood by a door, and all at once there came through it a tremendous roar.

"How's it going, George?"

"Sheer murder," George said, and gave me a look. "Ginger never had a hope."

"This gentleman's with me," Blayde told him. "Using Dave's seat."

"O.K. by me," George said and opened the door. The lights were on and we went through.

We were half-way up a kind of two-tiered gallery, our seats at the near end of a row: good seats, because there was a break between the two tiers and room to stretch your legs. I don't know how many people were in that improvised stadium, but it looked jammed to the doors. The air was grey with smoke and you felt at once the sour, damp warmth. From where we sat the view of the ring was clear, but everywhere there was movement and an indescribable din. Down in the ring-side seats was the white of boiled shirts and colour from women's wraps and dresses. Harry Triller was there, and Garlen with a woman each side of him. If Romsie was there I couldn't see him. And the lights were beginning to dim.

"What was that about Overson's seat?" I said to Blayde.

"These are really complimentary ones," he said. "But don't you worry about Dave. He's probably wangled a ringside seat by now."

Only the ring was lighted and the din was little more than a murmur. A spotlight swung across to somewhere in the far corner. They were doing things in style that night. We might have been at Harringay or the White City, what with the fanfare and the light trailing the little group that moved towards the ring. There was a cheer as the coloured boy climbed through the ropes and raised his clasped hands and showed his teeth in a smile. He did a quick shuffle and moved lazily to his corner, and sat with arms along the ropes. The second fanfare sounded. There was a roar as the spotlight picked up Stone and it followed him into the ring.

Another few minutes and the preliminaries were over. Stone was the shorter man, beautifully made and quick on his feet. The Kid had the edge in height and reach, and by comparison almost looked frail. When he moved at the sound of the gong he looked almost slow. The two circled and dodged and then Stone came in. The Kid moved that vital inch and the glove went by, but there was no counter. And that's how that first round went: Stone carrying the fight to his man and the Kid using the ring, with now and again a lightning left that checked Stone for a moment before he came boring in again.

"Stone's round," Blayde said. "If he keeps that up it's money for jam."

I didn't know. I said the Kid might be weighing his man up, but I didn't know. I did know that so far it wasn't much of a fight, but first rounds are apt to be just that. Stone looked happy enough and the coloured boy's skin showed nothing of the blows he'd taken on forearms and body. When he came out at the gong his face was still deadpan and soon it was the first round over again: swerving, ducking, an occasional clinch and always moving back and around. And then all at once Stone caught him with a looping swing to the side of the head that stopped him dead, and I wondered if he was in trouble. The crowd roared. Someone behind us yelled, "Kill him, Arty!" but when Stone came in, the Kid wasn't there. Then Stone caught him with a left and they clinched. The Kid swerved out of range as they broke and then the gong went, and the Kid moved to his corner like a tired man.

He took a drink from the bottle and spat it out, and his seconds gently massaged his back and shoulders. At the gong he moved almost lethargically out, gloves held high. Stone must have had his orders. He came out like a tiger. There seemed no great punch in the lefts that now and again stopped him, and the crowd was roaring with one huge mad voice as Stone kept boring in. And then it happened. Stone swung a wild right. Had it landed, the fight would have been over, but it didn't. The Kid swayed almost imperceptibly. In that split second of off-balance his right caught Stone's chin with an uppercut that hardly seemed to move. Stone's head went back and you heard the quick gasp. A left caught him and then the Kid almost contemptuously measured him, and another left cracked him to the floor.

The referee was at three before I really knew what had happened. The whole thing couldn't have taken ten seconds, so quickly had the coloured boy moved. And seven seconds later Stone was still on the floor and the crowd couldn't believe it. Then as the Kid's arm was held up there was a roar—an angry roar. Then it was pandemonium: boos, whistles, cat-calls, and pennies hurtling down to the ring. Somewhere beyond us a fight had broken out among the crowd. Attendants were moving in and you could hardly hear the voice at the microphone appealing for quiet. The lights went on and people round us were moving out, and you couldn't see a thing.

"Let's get out of here," Blayde told me, but it was pretty hopeless, and I'd no mind to be swept along with my vulnerable glasses in the crowd that was surging from up below. It was a good five minutes before we could make our way to the door by which we'd come in, and if George hadn't recognised us as we came near we'd never have got through. He shut the door after us and put his weight against it. It was strange to be in that sudden quiet.

"Gawd, what a ruddy fiasco!"

"Yeah," Blayde said. "That bloody fool Stone chucked it away. Anyone could see the other bloke was foxing."

A voice was calling from below the stairs. "That you, Jack? You're wanted in the office."

Blayde moved on and I followed. I waited just beyond the office in the corridor but it wasn't a minute before he was out.

"Back here," he told me and I followed him round to another door. An attendant let us through to a big car park.

"A job on," Blayde told me. "Might be only a false alarm—and then I'll run you back to the hotel."

That sergeant—Fred—was there and three or four of his men were trying to keep the exit clear. We were lucky. Blayde's car was near the exit and heading out, and then when we inched to the road the crowd was still milling around and it took us a couple of minutes before we were partly clear.

"Better try another way," Blayde said annoyedly, and took a turning to the right. It was one of those narrowish streets of little shops, and as soon as we turned left again I knew we were in Cooper Street at the lower end.

"Where're we making for?"

"Another couple of hundred yards. Mortimer's. Carter Street. Someone reported something suspicious."

The car was slowing already. He switched off the engine and the lights and let her coast. Another forty yards and he trod on the brake. We'd taken, as they say, half an hour to do two minutes. The ice rink couldn't have been much more than three hundred yards away and now we were in lower Carter Street, just in that warehouse-factory area: a grimy enough place by day, but now an eerie pattern of dim light and deep shadow.

"Where the devil's that squad car? Ought to've been here by now."

He muttered to himself as he peered from the lowered window. "You stay here. I'll have a quick look-see."

He took a torch from the locker, eased himself out and quietly pushed the door to. He stood for just a moment, head sideways as he listened, and then he moved off and I lost him at once in the darkness of a gap between the buildings. I slid across to the wheel and looked out, too. The building that rose sheer beyond the kerb was only two storied, no door that I could see and windows barred. Then I heard the whine of brakes and a car came round the corner. It drew in just ahead, a few yards beyond the pool of light from a street lamp. Two men got out. One of them must have thought I was Blayde. His voice was a kind of dramatic whisper as he stooped to the window.

"A bit late, Jack. All that blasted traffic."

I began easing myself quietly out and that's when we heard the sound: a quick sound like the slap of a board against a wall, or the crack of a whip.

"What's that?"

"Sergeant Blayde just went that way," I said. "I was with him—"

I might not have been there. "You stay here, Jim. I'll have a look."

He disappeared into the same darkness and the other man stood there, straining to listen. A car was coming from somewhere ahead. It went by. There was the sound of feet somewhere on a near-by pavement and, somewhere beyond, the duller sound of traffic, and yet the night seemed curiously still.

"Who're you?" I had tried to speak softly but my voice seemed far too loud.

"Turner," he said. "And that was Sergeant Bull. And what was that about you being with Jack Blayde?"

"We were at the fight together—"

His hand went out as if to push me back. An urgent voice was coming from somewhere at the far back.

"Jim! . . . Jim!"

He didn't even tell me to stay put. One moment he was there and then he was away into the same darkness of that narrow opening. I moved cautiously a few yards back. The opening was a narrowish entry for lorries. Ten yards from the kerb it was as black as hell's mouth. I moved to the car and waited.

About two minutes and he was back at the squad car and he didn't say a word as he passed. I heard him making a call and there seemed to be an urgency. I couldn't catch a word, but there seemed to be more than one call. I got back into the car and waited. I looked at my watch and it was just after ten o'clock. Somehow it seemed half a life-time.

Turner got out. He seemed to wonder for a moment where I'd gone, and then he spotted me in the car. "What's your name?"

I told him. I said I'd been Overson's guest at the fight and before I could tell him where Blayde came in, he stopped me short.

"Right. You sit here. The first car comes along, you tell 'em round at the back."

I sat on. A car or two came by and a pedestrian or two. Minutes seemed to go by, but it wasn't more than a couple when a squad car rolled quietly in. Two more men got out and I got out, too, and they'd moved down that opening before I'd finished my piece. A minute or two and Turner came back and another squad car drew in. Three men got out and one was Overson.

Turner was talking to them as they moved towards the opening. They stopped for a moment and seemed to be looking back at me, then they disappeared. Turner came back and stood by the kerb. A minute or two and an ambulance drew up. A dark saloon car pulled out just ahead of it and a man got out. It was Triller, still in his black-tie clothes. I could see the white muffler round his neck against the dark of his overcoat. He had a word with Turner but he didn't look my way. A minute later, except for the row of cars, the street was once more empty.

I got into the car again, the windows still down. From some-where at the back of that building I could hear faint sounds and a man calling to another from almost far away. It was like being in a darkened theatre, with the curtain down and the murmur of a play that still went on. One thing only I knew. Something must have happened to Blayde. That sound we'd heard might have have been a shot. And there was the ambulance.

It was twenty-past ten. As I looked at the dark of the opening a man emerged. It was Turner. He stooped at the window. "The Chief says I'm to run you back to your hotel, sir. . . . This way, sir."

We went on to that dark saloon car. He took the wheel and I got in beside him.

"What's been happening?"

He backed the car and drew out. "Something pretty nasty. Sergeant Blayde got shot."

"Badly?"

"Well, yes. Point-blank range. Couldn't have known a thing."

We stopped for a moment at the far traffic lights, then turned up towards Brewers Lane and Duke Street.

"Must have been two of 'em," he said, "though keep that to yourself. One of 'em was getting out a van and the other'd got in through the office. That's the one that shot Blayde."

"What were they after?"

He grunted. "Wholesale tobacconists. A van load of cigarettes."

We swung round into Duke Street. A couple of hundred yards and we were at the Clarendon.

"There you are, sir," he told me. "Got to get back now. And remember what I said. All this is between you and me. We don't want anything to get out—not yet."

The bar had shut down long since, and only a couple of people were in the foyer. I went straight up to my room. I stood for a moment, thinking: then I dialled Trowton's number. I had to wait quite a time before he came on the line.

"Haire," I said. "Sorry if I got you up."

He laughed. "Not a bit of it. I'm a pretty late bird, especially on Saturdays. Something special on your mind?"

There was, I said. In the morning he'd probably know it, but now it was highly confidential.

"My God!" he said when I'd told him. "That's a nasty business. And that other affair. What effect's it going to have on that?"

I told him that was one of the things that was worrying me. Perhaps it was why I'd rung him, so that he'd be ahead of the news and able to give the whole thing some thought.

"Yes," he said. "I'll do that. I don't know that it'll help. You're nearer to everything than I am."

I thanked him and rang off. I might be nearer to things, as he said, but that didn't mean clearer thinking. All I knew at the moment was that a dead Blayde couldn't talk. And that everybody but myself would now be sitting pretty. What Blayde knew about that Regency job had gone with the shot that had killed him.

And the last things I thought just before I finally got to sleep had each a touch of the ironical. It was just a week, almost to an hour, since that job at the Regency. And the shot that had killed Blayde had ended his marital differences. No need to worry now about who was to divorce whom. Whom God had joined, that shot had definitely put asunder.

12

PRIVATE INQUEST

I woke next morning with that mental heaviness that at once reminds one of disaster or foretells it, and in the same second I remembered the previous night, and Blayde. Even if I'd been admonished or upbraided by the massed bishops of a Lambeth Conference I couldn't have been induced to feel any grief. I hadn't liked him, I hadn't trusted him. I'd known him guilty of things which, even in my unregenerate days, I doubt if I'd have resorted to, and I'd suspected him of even more.

All the same, the loss of him in the game we'd been playing was as bad as the loss of a queen—and without exchange—at a vital moment of chess. Although we hadn't formulated it openly, both Hallows and I had had that one theory—that Blayde and his wife had been up to the ears in that Regency job, and the tantalising, maddening thing was that within a few hours of Overson's revelations about the Blayde-Mona liaison, it had suddenly ceased to matter. So what was to be done? What was the point in any further surveillance of Shirley Blayde? Why not send Steve French back to town?

Yet I didn't like to do it. Something might turn up to make him still useful. If it happened suddenly we might miss something vital. On the other hand, Shirley herself, as I all at once realised, was going to be affected. I doubted, for instance, if she'd be back at the Regency till after the funeral, and perhaps not then. And if her time—at least till the funeral—was going to be spent at the flat, that would mean daylight watching. Then again I pulled myself up with a jerk. Watching for what?

Of course I found an answer. When you want one badly enough you can always find something, and what I went back to was Hallows's idea of Shirley being in Garlen's pay. Maybe French could help us there, though exactly how I didn't even remotely know, but it was all a kind of boiling down to the fact that I still liked the thought of French staying on in Sandbeach. It wasn't a hunch. I don't know what it was except a clutching at a straw.

I was a bit later than usual for breakfast, and I'd only just finished when I was called to the telephone. Triller was on the line. His voice had its usual heavy placidity.

"Do you think you could see me here this morning? Say at about ten?"

"About last night?" I ventured.

"Well, yes," he said. "As bad a business as we've had here for years. Any help anyone can give we're only too grateful for."

I said I'd be there, though what help I could give I couldn't see. I didn't tell him that, or that I was itching to know more about what had happened. At any rate, I hadn't a lot of time if I was going to see French.

I got the car out and drove to the Lumley. French had long since finished breakfast and was reading a Sunday paper in the smoking-room. He told me he'd had a quiet night. Shirley had had a visit from a girl friend who'd stayed till after ten, and then he'd trailed the friend to a semi-detached house just off the London Road. He had an idea she was a fellow receptionist at the Regency, and, if I thought it worth while, he'd find out. I didn't. I told him about Blayde. It left him, as it had left me, well up a gum tree, and all we settled was that he might as well take things easy till Hallows got back from his Midlands trip. That might be early next morning. At the latest it ought to be on the Monday night.

I had time to spare before that call on Triller, so I took a chance and drove to the ice rink. The streets were absolutely empty and the whole place had that drowsy, Sunday morning feel. The only trace of the previous night's crowds was the litter in the street—programmes mostly—and I drove slowly on, trying to follow the route that Blayde had taken. I halted at the telephone kiosk just at the back of Cooper Street because of a choice of ways, and then I remembered a left turn and almost at once I was in Lower Carter Street. It didn't look the same by day. The sun happened to be shining and the grime of gaunt walls was merely colour.

Not a soul was to be seen but a solitary policeman, who seemed to be patrolling a beat of only a few yards, and I guessed that he was at Mortimer's. I kept the car at under thirty, glanced up at the building I'd only faintly seen in the eerie light of the street lamps, and went on. In that side entrance a couple of cars were drawn up, and at the side of them I just had a glimpse of an open space and the backs of buildings beyond.

I drove on and took a left turn, which I thought would bring me to the front of those other buildings. Another left turn and I was at the near end of Carter Street proper, with the deserted fun fair on my far right and the buildings I was looking for on my left. I waited till a couple of men exercising a leash of greyhounds had gone by, then I moved on till I came to a lorry entrance. I got out and walked the few yards back and made a cautious way along that short track. Another second and I was scuttling back. In that open space between me and the back of Mortimer's at least a dozen men were searching among the weeds and debris, and if I'd taken another step I'd have been within a few yards of one.

It was getting on for ten. I drove on and round and it was two minutes short of the hour when I got to Henry Street.

I was shown into Triller's room. He looked his massive, unruffled, usual self. Overson was there, too. His face was pale, and the dark hollows under his eyes told of little or no sleep. His hand was hot. Triller's was so huge that it enveloped my own like a soft plaster.

"Sorry to drag you out like this," he said, "but you'll appreciate the position. You never know just what might help."

I told him everything that had happened to Blayde and myself. Maybe I was thinking that if I didn't miss a single detail I might hear as much in return. Neither said a word till I'd finished.

"Yes," Triller said. "An extraordinary combination of circumstances. If poor Blayde had waited just that one more minute, he'd be alive at this moment."

"Yes," Overson said. "And but for that traffic jam, he wouldn't have had to wait."

"Why was he there at all?"

Triller looked surprised.

"Normal procedure," he told me. "He was on call and we knew where he was. The squad car should have been there to reconnoitre, so to speak, and he'd have had to make any decisions. Like getting in touch with us, or calling more cars. But about yourself. You saw nothing at all during that minute or so after you heard the shot? Or what turned out to be a shot?"

I told him I'd seen nothing and heard nothing. I was just someone sitting or standing in the comparative dark.

He grunted. He picked up the paper-knife, looked at it and laid it carefully down. He looked at me, the massive head just a bit sideways.

"Just something personal," he said gently. "The world's a small place, as we all know. I was at the fight myself last night and I had an old friend as a guest. A Chief Inspector Ranger. Do you know him?"

"Ranger?" I said. "The name seems familiar. What's his home town?"

"At the Yard," he said, and I felt just a sudden prickle up my spine. "He wasn't staying the night, though I wanted him to. As a matter of fact, he left just before I heard about poor Blayde. And you don't know him?"

"In a way, yes," I said. "I know of him. I can't say I remember a personal contact."

"Yes," he said. "The Yard's a big place. You can't remember everybody. I, for instance, ought to have remembered you. As soon as I met you there was something that told me I'd seen you somewhere before." He smiled just a bit too gently. "My brain doesn't work as quickly as it did, but it stayed at the back of my mind. Maybe that's why I mentioned it to Arthur Ranger."

I don't think a smile of mine was ever more feeble. "He gave you a sort of history?"

"Well, yes. It made me wonder why you should pose here as a chief inspector for an insurance company."

There was a question in it. I answered it. I came clean, as they say: absolutely clean.

"No prevarication at all. For the purposes of an investigation I *am* what I said I was."

"Yes," he said. It was a word he ought to have had on a record. "But why didn't you see fit to confide in us?"

That was easier. My eyebrows lifted in astonishment.

"Surely you don't mean that? You people knew what I was here for? You could have checked my bona fides. What else was necessary? A dossier?"

"Now, now, now," he told me gently. "It was only that I thought perhaps you might have been a little more—well, friendly." He picked up that paper-knife again and put it quietly down. "But about last night. I imagine you're interested as what one might call professionally?"

"I can't help but be," I told him. "Blayde was virtually acting as my host. I was practically on the spot when he was killed."

"Yes," he said, as if it had only just struck him. "It was a well-planned job. A lot of our men on duty at that fight and everyone's attention focused on it, so to speak." He paused for a moment. "Two men at least. One had been hack-sawing at the padlock of the garage while the other made an entry through the office. Just jemmied the door. Blayde disturbed him. Probably was about to close with him. At any rate, he was shot point-blank through the heart. The scorch marks show that."

"An easy place for a getaway?"

"Yes. Couldn't have been easier. A regular maze round at the back. We're trying to find something to help us, but I'm not too sanguine. The gun, perhaps, if he threw it away."

"You know the kind it was?"

"Yes," he said. "We rushed the bullet up to the Yard late last night. A point-three-eight. Might be a Smith and Wesson."

"And the informer, the one who sent in the report of something suspicious. What'd he actually see?"

"Just two men acting suspiciously. He gave a false name and address, by the way." He saw my quick look and smiled a bit wryly. "Nothing special about that. We get false—say mischievous—calls and we get false names or no names. People just dial and hang up. They just don't want to be drawn in. A hopeless attitude and one we've tried to combat, but there you are. I suppose you could call it human nature."

There was a little silence, and I was thinking it might be a sign that the interview was over when Overson spoke. His voice was as tired as he looked.

"I owe you an apology for last night—really."

"Nothing of the sort," I told him. "I thought it was extraordinarily good of you to let me have your seat."

"Oh, that," he said. "That was nothing. As a matter of fact I knew they'd find me another. And I was just coming up to squat down for a minute with you and Jack Blayde when the fight ended." He shrugged his shoulders. "After that you know how it was. Matter of fact, I'd have gone home to bed if I hadn't wondered if you two had come back here. That's how I heard about it."

"Yes," Triller said, and got to his feet. "A muddled business, all round." He held out his hand. "Sorry you couldn't help us."

I told him he wasn't more sorry than I was myself. "Yes," he said, and he gave me that slow, quizzical look again. "And this holiday of yours—when's it come to an end?"

And that was the moment when I had an idea. Tuesday was just two days away, but by hook or crook I had to stay on. What made me say what I did I'll never know, unless that far too agile brain of mine was suddenly two paces ahead of me. But there it was: Blayde, the investigation, the murder, Hallows not back, the end of the holiday, everything a jumble of ideas out of which I suddenly found myself speaking.

"That reminds me. There's something I ought to report. At first I thought I'd better not. Now I'm not so sure."

"You mean something about last night?"

"No," I said. "Not even indirectly. Also I can't divulge it unless I have both your words that it goes no further."

"Very mysterious," Triller said. "Something you say we ought to know?"

"That'll be for you to judge," I told him. "I'll tell you this much: as a result of it I'm cancelling the holiday and staying on here till I'm satisfied."

The two men looked at each other. Overson shrugged his shoulders.

"Well, we'd like to hear it," Triller said. "And we give you our word." He sat down again. I stayed on my feet. Overson, after an indecisive moment, sat down again, too.

"Let me tell it in my own way," I said. "On the way to the rink last night Blayde and I were talking about cars and I mentioned my old Bentley. He said he'd always had an ambition to own a Bentley. He didn't say it too seriously, mind you. It was more like one of those dreams we all have, but I think now it stuck in his mind. At any rate, this is what he said to me as we were making our way out."

I paused.

"You're not going to like this. It isn't smirching a dead man because it isn't going any farther, but you won't like it."

"Leave us to judge." I'd never heard Triller speak so sharply.

"Right," I said. "He sort of leaned over and asked me what my company would pay for information about that Regency job."

Triller stared. "He must have been pulling your leg."

"Wait a minute. I haven't finished. It was a bit of a startler, so I asked him point-blank what he meant. 'You mean you've got the information yourself?' 'Could be,' he said. 'But you're not getting it till I know what you're prepared to pay.' And that was all there was time for. Things happened, as you know."

"I can't believe it," Overson said. "No, no, no; don't get me wrong. I'm not questioning you: I'm questioning him."

"Yes," Triller said. He leaned forward on the desk, head between his hands. It was a moment or two before he looked up. "We haven't *your* word, you know: I mean about this not getting out."

"I thought it was implicit," I told him. "But why should I mention it? The only difference is that I stay on here till I know whether he was right or wrong. I haven't got to give excuses to anyone. I just tell my company that I'd like to make a few more enquiries, and they'll take my word."

"What enquiries?"

I looked Triller clean in the eye. "How do I know? All I can do is review the whole thing. It may even be that I have to approach you people later on. In confidence, of course. But I don't know."

"Yes," Triller said, and hoisted himself up from his seat. "That seems eminently fair. It was good of you to tell us."

"It might even be that we may have to dig a bit deeper ourselves," Overson said. "How and when and where, I don't know. It depends on you, Chief."

I knew Triller would say yes, and he did. We were moving towards the door. Overson drew back and Triller went with me down the stairs. He held out his hand again.

"I'm glad you came. A bit of a shock, some of it, but I'm glad you came. See me personally if you should happen to think it's necessary."

I thanked him and said I'd do just that. As I went through the door he was already going heavily back up the stairs.

The bar wasn't open. As a resident I could have had a drink but I felt more like coffee. A waiter brought it to the foyer. That Sunday morning it was even quieter there than usual. Another week and it would be different: Easter, and the hotels crowded.

Have you ever had thoughts in your mind and deliberately kept them back? I sipped the hot coffee and lighted my pipe before I let mine come right up to the surface. It wasn't that disclosure of his knowledge of me that Triller had so suavely made that was worrying me, though maybe I'd been just a bit too clever and cocksure, and it's never too pleasant to be caught out. No, what was clouding my mind was that accusation I'd made against Blayde.

Was it what one calls ethical? I wasn't so sure, though some said that means were justified by ends. But if that was a sound argument, then the third-degree ought to be routine, let alone thumb-screws and the rack. So put it another way. Had I smeared the dead Blayde's memory? I didn't think so: in fact I was sure that I hadn't. For one thing, what had been said had been in confidence. And there was something else. If Blayde *had* been involved in that Regency job and I could prove it, then what I'd said was true in substance if not in fact. If I couldn't prove it, then what I'd said would remain the private knowledge of only the three of us.

So I began to assure myself that I'd been right. And already the means seemed to have been justified. I had reasons now for staying on in Sandbeach, and, what was more, I could now count, if necessary, on the co-operation of Triller. I admit it made me a bit uneasy to recall how shocked he had been, but if I'd told him what Overson already knew—about that night visit to Laneford Hall—I guessed he'd have been shocked almost as much. As for my own conscience, I could tell myself far more blithely that it was a Sunday morning, the time when consciences, like ghosts at midnight, creep furtively out.

After lunch I wrote to John Hill. I read a newspaper or two, but after tea the day began to drag. Crosswords didn't hold me. What I wanted was a change of scene, and the only place I could think of was Laneford Hare and Hounds. There wasn't anything I expected to unearth. It would just be a change. And I wasn't known. So I had an early meal and set out, and it was just after eight o'clock when I drew up at the pub.

I'd backed the car so as to be heading for home and was just getting out when I saw a man approaching from further beyond. As he came into the light from the projecting lamp above the inn sign, I recognised him. I'd put his age at about seventy, but he was walking with the upright carriage and the swing of a much younger man. I got out and was practically heading him off.

"Mr. Wellard?"

"Yes, sir." He gave me a look. "Do I know you, sir?"

"We've met," I said. "My name's Travers, chief inspector for the insurance company."

He smiled. "I remember, sir. It was about the jewellery."

"You drop in here often?"

"Occasionally, sir. It makes a change. And tonight I happen to be particularly free. The madam's in London and won't be back till tomorrow."

"Then perhaps I can offer you a drink?"

We'd been slowly moving towards the door. He opened it for me to go through. Things were quiet in the bar-room, only five customers, all men. Wellard was known, and respected. An elderly man flicked a finger to his hat. It reminded me of my boyhood days when a butler was a man of standing in a village. Now, but for the big houses and the nouveaux riches, they're rarer than great auks.

I ordered two double Black and Whites and a Schweppes.

"Is it right that you're leaving us, sir?" the landlord asked Wellard. The four dominoes players stopped their game.

"Well, yes," Wellard said quietly. "The last of the old family's gone and it's time for me to go, too. Going to live with my daughter."

"Sorry to hear it, sir. But we'll be seeing you again?"

"Oh, yes. It'll be at least another week."

I took the tray to a table nicely in range of the open fire. It had been a warmish day, but the night was quite cold. We wished each other good health, and Wellard asked if I played dominoes. I said I could always make a start, so the landlord brought a box and a pegging board. We had two or three games. I was hopeless, but he seemed to enjoy it. He insisted on my having another drink. A few more people dropped in and one or two came over to watch. Wellard knew them all by name.

It was half-past nine when he got up to go. I went out with him and asked if I could drive him back to the Hall. He said that was very good of me, and it was pretty dark along the drive. Just short of the Hall I drew the car up.

"Mr. Wellard, may I take you into my confidence?"

He looked surprised. It was a moment or two before he said he'd be honoured.

"What we say will never be repeated by me," I told him. "All I want to do is confirm certain impressions. But about your retirement. Is it really because of the reasons you gave back there in the pub?"

"Well, mainly yes, sir. I have reason to know that the late master has left me an annuity. And I'm not so young as I was."

"But if he'd been alive, you'd have stayed on?"

"Yes," he said slowly. "We grew up together, so to speak. I don't think I could have left him. And, if I may presume, I don't think he'd have wished it."

"But now things are going to be different? At the Hall, I mean."

"Yes, sir. Very different."

"Any other staff leaving?"

"Yes, sir. The housemaid who's been with us many years."

I told him that so far, instead of taking him into my confidence, he'd taken me into his own. I told him, perfectly frankly, of certain suspicions we'd had about that jewellery. It was something in which, he said, he couldn't help.

"In fact, sir, if there was anything I knew, I wouldn't help. Madam mayn't be what the late madam was, but I couldn't help to bring disgrace on the name."

I said it did him credit. I said I'd add something else. In the course of my investigation I'd discovered many things about life at the Hall. I said I didn't want him to affirm it or deny it, but I was sure that in the course of the last two or three years there were many things he'd succeeded in keeping from the knowledge of the late master. For instance, certain surreptitious visits by night.

He didn't affirm or deny, unless the shake of the head was an affirmation.

"She'll sell the Hall?"

"No, sir," he told me quickly. "I don't think the will allows that."

"She'll remarry?"

He thought for a moment.

"No, sir. I don't think so. I don't think madam is the marrying kind."

I moved the car on. As I drove towards Sandbeach I knew it had been a pleasant, if unremunerative night. I'd learned nothing that I didn't already know or suspect. But what I didn't know was that just one little thing had been let fall that was to come back to me later.

EVEN the London papers had that murder. The *Gazette* had it spread clean across the front page with pictures of both back and front of that wholesale tobacconists and one of the dead Blayde. There was little that I didn't already know. As for the appeal by the police for the reporting of any suspicious characters seen in the neighbourhood of the crime, that struck me as the faintest of hopes. There'd been the football crowd and the fight crowd, and a couple of strangers in Sandbeach would be as uncommon as two more pebbles on the beach.

Just after nine o'clock I was called to the telephone. Hallows's voice came through so clearly that he might have been speaking from the foyer itself.

"Don't expect to get back much before ten tonight," he said. "I got held up. The lady had shifted and I've only just picked up the trail again."

"Where're you speaking from?"

"A village called Yaxham. A few miles south of Northampton. Only just got here. Been waiting for the post office to open."

"No other news?"

"Only that we may be on the right track. Anything from your end?"

"You've seen a morning paper?"

"Haven't had a chance. Why?"

I told him he'd see why. Then I rang off. I didn't want to hold him up at the job.

After that I waited till nearly ten o'clock, then I made my way to Garlen's offices. I stepped into a smallish lobby across which was a room with a frosted glass window—ENQUIRIES. Things were busy already. From somewhere beyond was the click-clacking of typewriters and voices speaking into telephones.

I went into the room. A smart-looking brunette was sitting at a roll-top desk sorting some papers. She showed me some nice teeth.

"Good morning. Can I help you?"

I carry as many cards as a con man. I gave her a private one. "I'd like to see Mr. Garlen."

She frowned. "I don't know if he's in. I might see."

There was a small switch-board to her left and she plugged in. She read from my card. At the end of the line must have been some intermediary, for she asked if I'd mind waiting a moment. I waited a couple of minutes before the all clear came.

"Up the stairs," she said, "and across the corridor. The door marked PRIVATE. You can't miss it."

I thanked her, returned the smile and went up. At my tap I was told to go in. The voice had been Garlen's.

It was a very pleasant room, overlooking the street. There was a thick red carpet up to the walls, and the walls themselves a kaleidoscope of sport: photographs of horses, jockeys, fighters and a biggish one of a couple of billiard players. The desk was mahogany, flat-topped, with an inter-com and a couple of telephones. Garlen had only to reach and there was a caseful of what looked like reference books. He was wearing glasses, and that made a difference. You couldn't see his eyes.

He'd got up as I came in and was as near as he'd ever get to a smile. He laid down the cigarette, flicked some ash from the dark waistcoat and held out his hand.

"Mr. Travers. Nice to see you again."

"And you," I said. "But you won't be pleased when I leave. I hope you'll be a poorer man."

The thin lips clamped together for a minute and I'd have liked to see his eyes.

"Take a seat. . . . Excuse me for a moment."

He pressed a button on the inter-com. "Miss, no more calls for a minute. . . . Yes, I'll let you know."

He sat back in the chair. "Now, sir, what was this about me being a poorer man?"

I told him about my night at the rink and the bet I'd had through Blayde. I said I thought he'd put it on and, if so, I ought to have over two pounds coming to me.

"You say he went into the office?"

I said he'd gone in and I'd waited.

"Might be a bit hard to check," he said, and his fingers went together as he thought. Then he pulled open a drawer.

"I wouldn't doubt your word. One pound note and a pound note and five bob. There you are, sir."

He pushed the money towards me across the desk.

"No, no," I said. "I couldn't do that. It isn't fair to you."

"You take it," he told me. "A dissatisfied client is a book-maker's bugbear. Or leave it like this: we'll check and unless you hear to the contrary it's okay."

"That's very good of you."

I pocketed the money. "You had a bad fight—if it's the sort of thing to ask?"

He shrugged his shoulders.

"You know how it is. You've got to take the swings with the roundabouts. And so you were there with young Blayde." He waved a hand at the paper on the desk. "A nasty business. Just been reading about it."

"Yes," I said. "A young fellow like that, cut off in the prime of life."

"What d'you think of it yourself? I mean professionally."

"Professionally?"

"Yes," he said. "They tell me you're connected yourself with the police."

"And who's 'they'?"

He shrugged his shoulders again. "You know how it is. Things get around."

I smiled. "You haven't by any chance been making enquiries about me yourself?"

"Me, sir? Why should I do that?"

"Don't know," I said. "Just an idea."

He got to his feet. "Well, a pleasure to have had your business. Bring some more our way. You staying any longer, or is your holiday up?"

"Can't say," I told him. "I have an idea the company aren't any too satisfied with what I've done. They may want me to stay."

"Ah, well," he said. "That's how it is. Len, see Mr. Travers out."

Garlen must have pressed a button. I hadn't even heard the door open, but Romsie was there. He was wearing riding breeches and a black-and-white check jacket.

"Well, thanks again."

Garlen nodded. I went out, Romsie closed the door. There was a strong smell of tobacco about him.

"It's all right," I said. "I know my way out."

He mightn't have heard me.

"You're that insurance inspector. Enjoying your holiday?" His voice had a faint croak. Maybe at some time in his fighting career he'd taken a nasty one on the larynx.

"Yes," I said. "The weather's helped."

We were at that lobby; he didn't speak till I was at the door. "Come again," he said. "And next time don't stay so long."

Before I could ask him what he meant, he'd turned and gone, but if I hadn't been half-way through the door I'd have gone after him. There are still a few things I don't take lying down, and a crack like that was one of them. And it was annoying to me all the more because I couldn't see what had prompted it. Come again, he'd said, but to where? Just Sandbeach generally, or that office? Had he been waiting to see Garlen, and was that why I shouldn't have stayed so long? Or had the whole thing been a kind of warning?

I went straight up to my room and rang Garlen. It took me so long to get him that I might have been ringing a Cabinet Minister. When he did come on the line I didn't waste time on preliminaries.

"You must have misunderstood him," he told me.

"I don't think so," I said. "It sounded plain enough to me."

"Len's just a bit touchy at times," he said. "It could be, you know, that he doesn't like you."

"You mean the way he didn't like Bob Quarley?"

I waited for an answer, but the line was suddenly dead. There was another call I wanted to pay, but that was reserved for the afternoon. It was just short of three o'clock when I rang the bell at the front door of Shirley Blayde's flat. I could hear the low sound of a wireless set, so she had to be in and I rang again. The set was turned off and I could hear her humming the same lively tune as she came to the door.

"Sorry to trouble you, Miss Bright, but could you spare me a minute? Only a personal matter."

She hadn't looked all that surprised to see me. There was only a moment's hesitation before she drew back.

"Come in. You're that insurance inspector, aren't you?" She'd known who I was. As I've said before, once I've been seen it's not too easy to forget me, so why the hesitation? Or was that her idea of a polite reserve?

We were in the room which I'd been in before. She wasn't wearing black and she was still about as good as they make 'em in blondes. No tight slacks this time: a brown skirt and open-necked jumper, and a wispy bit of something round her neck, with the ends tucked inside.

"It's really unpardonable of me to have come," I told her. "I mean, in view of your trouble."

"Trouble?" Her lip dropped slightly. "Oh, you mean my husband? My late husband."

I sat down in one of the over-stuffed chairs. She was on the same divan, skirt smoothed across the nyloned knees.

"You can't tell people," she said. "They just couldn't understand. But what do you think I left him for? Just for fun?"

"Don't know," I said. "It isn't the place of an outsider to start airing views about a husband and wife."

"Well, he's dead. I'm sorry, but I don't have to be crying my eyes out all the time."

"You're right," I said. "There's far too much hypocrisy in the world. But about why I came. A niece of mine is coming to Sandbeach to live; her husband is taking up an appointment here, and they wanted me to enquire about a flat. To come to the point, I liked what I saw of this flat when I called that day with Inspector Overson, so I did make some enquiries and I believe there's a flat available in the near future."

"Top or bottom?" She was looking quite interested. "If they have a car it'd have to be a bottom. The top ones don't have garages."

"Yes," I said. "I understood that. But would you do me a great favour and let me see the rooms?" I smiled. "Don't worry about anything being untidy. I'm a married man, as you can guess."

She didn't hesitate. She was proud of that flat. And she had good reason to be. It was very much smaller than my own, but everything about it was attractive. I liked the small kitchen with its dining recess, and the way it was fitted up.

"That door's the back door?"

"That's right," she said, and opened it. It had a paved approach and I had a good view of the garage. Just nicely big enough, I said, for my niece's small car.

There was a compact little bathroom with lavatory and a couple of bedrooms, one only about ten by eight, but the other much larger. That was the one at the north-east corner, taking in the angle past the front door and round half-way to the garage. It had a four-foot bed with a silk spread.

We went back to what she called the lounge, and I was wishing I could have brought with me someone in the furnishing trade. But even the little I knew confirmed what I'd already thought— that the furnishing of that flat must have cost the very devil of a lot of money.

"You've got a lovely place here," I told her. "You're going to stay on?"

She hesitated. "You mean, go on living here?"

What else could I have meant?

"Well," I said, "if you don't mind my being personal, you're a very attractive young woman, so why shouldn't you marry again?"

The laugh was more of a sneer. I didn't think the bitterness was real, or the droop of the lip.

"Marry? Once bitten, twice shy. I know all the answers—I ought to."

"You can't judge by one experience," I said pontifically. "Some of us aren't all that bad, you know."

"I know," she said. "And your trumpeter's dead. That's how you all are. Stick together: you can lie your way out of anything."

Her eyes suddenly popped a bit. "Sorry. I didn't mean you. You know what I meant."

We'd been moving towards the door. Her hand just touched my arm. "No offence?"

"Heavens, no," I said. "You may even be right."

"I'm damn sure I'm right."

I held out my hand. "I'd better get away before we start having a fight. Thanks for letting me see your lovely flat. You think my niece might drop in on you when she gets here?"

The smile left her face, and I wondered just what it was that I'd said.

"When would she be coming? I mean to Sandbeach?"

"Probably not till the early autumn."

"That'd be nice," she said. "Young, is she?"

"Just about your age, I'd say. Full of fun, too."

I turned for just a last word.

"I ought to warn you, though. She wouldn't hear a word against her husband."

If she laughed I didn't hear her. When I looked back from the gate the door was closed. I waited a moment before turning back, and as I stood by the door again I could hear her telephoning. Through the window I could see her back towards me so I didn't make an excuse about leaving my gloves but went quietly and quickly back through the gate.

As I walked to the hotel I didn't let myself be so precipitate as to assume that that telephoning had been a report on my visit. It might have been all sorts of things: to the Regency, to a friend, to a tradesman. All I did think was that it had been somehow apt. After the comparative friendliness of the last few minutes in the flat I'd have expected her to extend that friendliness to at least a wave from the door to me at the gate. As it was she'd lost no time.

I'd lost no time either. I had what I'd come for—the exact lay-out of that flat. I'd wanted it because of certain vague ideas that had ceased floating in my mind and had only just begun to coalesce. Now they were far less vague. I knew for a certainty that this and that *could* have been done. What I still didn't know was the identity of the second party. I had an idea, mind you, but it ran so contrary to all the known facts that I'd have been a fool to have worked at it seriously. But there was another thing I did know—that I must have had some extraordinary prescience to have kept Steve French in Sandbeach.

It was time for tea when I got back, and as I sat there, taking my time over it, I was thinking of two other things. Why was it that Shirley Blayde had shown no great surprise at the sight of me? I'd paid her just that one quick business visit and I'd told her I wouldn't be seeing her again. That was almost a week since, and there I'd suddenly popped up on her doorstep and she'd taken me almost for granted.

And how was it that Sam Garlen had known that I had a connection with the police? Who were the particular *they* who'd been talking? I'd been assuming that only Triller and Overson knew that much about me. Triller had acquired the information on the Saturday night and thirty-six hours later Garlen had it, or something of it, too. But was it that much of a mystery? Considering how much Garlen had at stake, wouldn't he have made his own enquiries about me? After all, he had his sources of information. Maybe he'd known quite a lot about me as early as that afternoon in Sellman's office. Maybe it had been behind that offer of a dinner at the Regency.

The afternoon post brought two letters: one from my wife, the other from John Hill, who must have answered my overnight one in double quick time He told me to go on digging. There were always means of dealing with an impatient claimant. He'd had a letter from certain solicitors and was taking his time about answering it; all the same, he'd have to be more positive in, say, another week.

From where I sat in that foyer, a week seemed a pretty long time; far more, in fact, than I'd hoped to get. That's the kind of optimism that generally comes when you begin to get a few ideas. If it did nothing else it reminded me of French, so I rang him at once. I was lucky to find him in. He's a phlegmatic sort and didn't sound surprised when I asked him to keep an eye that night on the Shirley Blayde flat. He did ask about a car.

"I can't tell you why, not at the moment, but I don't think a car matters. Just take up your stance after dusk and report what happens. If everything's still quiet at, say, eleven, then sign off."

I went for another walk, just to kill time, had a bath and changed my clothes just to kill more time, and went in to dinner before seven. I'd just got to the main course when someone slid into the seat opposite me. It was Hallows.

"Good Lord!" I said. "Didn't expect you back for a long time yet."

"Had a lot of luck," he said. "Couldn't have gone better if I'd planned it myself."

He'd stayed the night near Oxford and had reached Moreby at about ten on the Sunday morning, the worst of all days for making enquiries. He'd waited till midday when the pub opened, and had learned that Mrs. Franks had left the village years before. No one seemed to know her present whereabouts.

"Don't know what you've been told before," he said, "but these are the facts, dates and all. Franks died in Moreby in the spring of nineteen-fifty and Mona was at the funeral. A month after that, Mrs. Franks moved, and how it ties in I think you'll see later. But about finding where she'd gone to."

He'd followed the same procedure as in the matter of the Franks's move from Bandon, and that's where he'd had the luck.

The rest had been brains and the fact that Hallows was Hallows. Someone had remembered the firm who'd removed the furniture, and as a result Hallows stayed the night at Kettering. At eight o'clock he was at that removal firm and had got into touch with the right man.

He went straight to Yaxham and rang me, then he had a look at the electoral roll. Franks, Mrs. Eva, lived at "The Nook". Next, he buttonholed a postman, still the Canadian on holiday and looking for an aunt. Was there a Mrs. Franklin in the village? There wasn't: only a Mrs. Franks. Had she got a little son? The postman laughed. This Mrs. Franks was a grandmother, a widow with a grand-daughter, Doris.

Hallows located the house—a largish bungalow that he'd passed on the way in—almost as soon as he'd entered the village. He drove on and back to Northampton.

"Lucky I brought my camera with me, otherwise I couldn't have worked the stunt I did. Went into a photographer's and bought some film and asked if he'd any odd photos of children he could spare as I was writing an illustrated book. Ended up by buying over a dozen prints and then I went back to Yaxham and waited till the children came out of the local school. When a little girl went into the bungalow I waited a minute and knocked at the front door."

Mrs. Franks, a thin-faced, stringy woman, he called her, looked at him suspiciously, but she thawed as he told her the tale. He wasn't selling anything. All he wanted was a favour. He was a photographer on the staff of *Picture Weekly*, and they were running a feature to which prizes would ultimately be attached. Just pictures of children: not studio photographs necessarily, but taken quite naturally. He let her just see his samples and asked about the little girl he'd seen going through the bungalow gate. Would it be a grand-daughter? It was. Her son's daughter. He and his wife had been killed in an accident and she'd brought her up.

Within ten minutes Hallows had taken a couple of pictures: one of Doris holding her pet rabbit, and the other squatting down and tickling the ears of the cat.

"A really nice little girl. Nine, and tall for her age. Be a good-looker when she gets a bit older. Not a bit shy, either. I gave her a ten-bob note and told the grandmother I'd let her know if and when the prints were going to be published. Then I beat it out of the village and didn't stop till I got to Reading. Found one of those quick passport photographers and got him to develop the prints while I had a scratch lunch. Told him not to worry about there being only two. Didn't get them till after four o'clock."

He took out his wallet and gave me the two prints. They were quite good work. A professional wouldn't have been ashamed of them. Doris looked as charming as Hallows had said. In both cases she was almost full-faced and I couldn't for the life of me see any resemblance to Mona Dovell, except maybe the dark hair.

"Work everything out from the dates," Hallows told me. "Mona was at her father's funeral at Moreby ten years ago and the way I see it is that she knew she was pregnant then. That's why the mother left Moreby. Mona might have been known in Moreby. In Yaxham she became a daughter-in-law, so that the child could have the Franks name. Who paid for the upkeep is anybody's guess. Mona? Or whoever was the father?"

"They looked well enough off?"

"The bungalow was in good order. And the garden. Furniture a bit old-fashioned but that's nothing. Doris was nicely dressed. I'd say a cut above the village ordinary. Mind you, once Mona was Mrs. Dovell there'd always be enough money. One thing is pretty certain: I bet Mona hasn't been back there since Doris was born. She couldn't very well, not if that yarn about the parents being dead was to hold water."

"Yes," I said. "Wonder what's going to happen to Doris now, though. I don't think somehow that Mona's the maternal kind."

That was when I remembered what Wellard had said about her not being the marrying kind.

"Wish I could have a look at that chap Millbridge," I said. "Let me have a look at those prints again."

I thought about Blayde, and Overson, and there might have been others besides Millbridge. Blayde, surely, was out of the question since he subsequently married Shirley. And I doubted if he could have contributed to a second home without her knowing. Then as I moved one of the prints to catch a different light I thought I saw something.

"Have a look," I said. "Don't you think she has something of Overson?"

He had a good look. He looked at both prints.

"I haven't seen him all that often, but there might be something. Wouldn't like to swear to it, though."

"Better let me have the prints," I told him. "If I go on looking at them long enough the resemblance might be a bit more strong."

He didn't see what I was driving at.

"You mean you *want* him to be the father?"

I said that personally I didn't care one way or the other. It wasn't a question of my being convinced but what it might come to, if we were ever going to crack the case, was the need to convince someone else. He didn't ask me whom. Hallows knows me. Maybe he thought I was away up in the clouds again.

14
TRILLER PROVES HIS CASE

I DIDN'T get down very early that Tuesday morning—the day, as I remembered, of Charles Dovell's funeral. There'd been a lot of things to tell Hallows and we'd sat arguing and theorising till pretty late. At any rate, I was reading the *Gazette* and wondering if I should attend the funeral that afternoon, when I was called to the telephone. I'd never have guessed it was Tiller. He wanted to know if I were likely to be busy that morning. I said I wasn't.

"Could you be outside the Regency in, say, ten minutes? I'll pick you up there."

"I'll be there," I said. "Anything special in the way of clothes or anything?"

"Oh, no," he said, and didn't give even a formal chuckle. "Nothing like that. Just as you happen to be."

He was dead on time and driving the sleek, black police car himself. He leaned across and opened the door for me, and moved the car on as soon as the door was shut. We were heading east.

"You're going to be a sorry man in a few minutes," he told me. "A very sorry man."

As a conversational opening that was a bit of a shock. I think I gasped as I swivelled round to look at him. He wasn't smiling.

"Sorry? In what way?"

"Just have patience," he told me gently. "Another minute or two and you'll know."

We were circling the roundabout and moving with the traffic into the London Road. We passed the last straggle of shops and a garage or two and were nearing the area of strung-out bungalows and small houses when he slowed the car and turned into an opening on his near side. It was a metalled road, now overgrown with grass and weeds, and ahead of us was an area of desolation: a huge car cemetery with rusting bodies piled high, some old railway carriages and what had once been a Georgian house with its slated roof almost stripped and the walls a mass of ivy. He pulled the car up.

I'd been looking out to the left. On the right, well back from the track, was a double garage with what looked like an occupied flat above it. I could see curtains at the windows, and in the desolation around it the place looked well cared for. The paintwork was clean and the weeds and tallish grass had been cut to make an approach. The garage doors were open and I could see a smallish car that looked like a Morris.

"Used to be a small stabling for the house there," Triller told me, "and then an office. The man we're going to see bought it and spent a bit of money on it."

He turned towards the steps that ran up from the left of the garage to the flat. Two men came into sight from just behind. Plainclothes men, and methodically looking for something.

"Something's been happening here?"

He shrugged his shoulders. A wave of the hand directed me up that outdoor flight of stairs.

"Go right in," he told me.

I went in. It was a fair-sized living-room. As soon as I'd opened the door there'd been a strong smell of paint, but it wasn't that that made me stop dead. The room had a central table and a couple of kitchen chairs. There was an oldish settee and an easy chair drawn up to an electric fire. There was an old bureau with a radio on the top and the flap down. Between the table and the bureau lay the body of a man. I couldn't see his face. Someone had taken off his jacket and placed it carefully over the head and shoulders.

"Morning, Mr. Travers."

Overson was at my elbow. He must have been sitting in the old leather chair in the corner on the left.

"A murder?" I said. "Or a suicide?"

"Murder," he said. "No weapon, so it couldn't have been suicide."

"Know who he is?"

"Oh, yes." He smiled dryly. "We know who he is all right. Like to have a look at him?"

I moved round the table. He stooped and drew back the jacket.

The dead man lay with arms loosely by his head, face upwards as if he'd fallen sideways from that chair by the fire. The wound was in his left temple and the blood had congealed down the cheek to below the chin. He was a man of about thirty, or maybe younger; the heavy, dark moustache made it hard to tell. He looked fairly short and slimly built. His pullover was dark green and the oldish grey flannel trousers had here and there a slight smear of paint. The pale green sports shirt was spotless, but the clip-on bow tie was askew.

"Look at his arms," Overson told me.

I knelt on the rumpled rug. Both forearms were tattooed. The designs matched: clusters of red roses and foliage about seven inches by three. I took out my glass. "Do you mind?"

"Not at all. Have a good look."

It was there—a thin, whitish scar on the left forearm. The design had been something special, but the curl of a rose petal didn't quite hide it, not when you looked for it as I did.

I got up again. I mechanically brushed my knees. "No need to ask if it's Davitt."

"It's Davitt all right," Triller said. "The inspector here spotted him almost at once. What's more, we wanted to make dead sure, so the prints were rushed to the Yard. A minute before I rang you they rang me and confirmed."

His head went sideways as if he'd heard a noise. There was the sound of a car. Overson went to the door and looked down. He called something I didn't hear. A minute or two and a couple of ambulance men came in with a stretcher. With them was that Sergeant Bull whom I'd seen on the Saturday night. He helped get the body on the stretcher.

"Let the doctor know as soon as you get him in," Triller told him. "I want that bullet there when I get back."

Overson stood by the door till the sound of feet had gone from the steps. He closed the door and came back. There were chalk marks where the body had been.

"You've been here a long time?" I asked Overson. It was Triller who answered.

"Since just after eight. A lot of work's been done here in the last couple of hours."

"You've found the gun?"

"Oh, yes," he said. "We found the gun. Stuck beneath a clump of young nettles just along the track. A Smith and Wesson point-three-eight."

I didn't get it for a moment: too many things to wonder in too short a time.

"Yes," I said. "You must have been pleased."

He grunted. "You get all sorts of luck. You know that. This was the good kind. Still, we'd have known from the bullet."

"You'd like to tell me how you work things out?"

He looked surprised, and no wonder. It was all so obvious that a child should have worked it out.

"Plain as the nose on your face," he said. "Davitt had a confederate, the one who shot Blayde. When they bolted they came up here. The confederate was the one who was certain to swing, and his only danger was Davitt. Davitt had been living here. Also he might panic, so he was shot. And five pounds to a penny with the gun that was used on Blayde."

There were too many questions to ask.

"Seems to go back to someone who worked with Davitt on one of the earlier jobs."

"Yes," Triller said. "The Yard are working on it at this very moment. Too big a job for us. But about why I asked you to come here. I wanted you to see things for yourself. Now there's something else: the last time we three were together you made a serious accusation against one of my men."

"Well?"

"Well be damned," he said, and his face suddenly flushed. "Is that the best you can say?"

"What do you want me to do?" I asked him. "Deny a fact?"

"What fact?"

"That Blayde told me what he did?"

"Look," he said, all mildness again, "let's be reasonable about this. Let's accept that he said what he did. But not why he said it. He must have been pulling your leg. I told you so and now it's proved. It's plain as the nose on your face. He pretended to have private information about' that burglary. Is that right?"

"Yes—so far."

"But he couldn't have had. Davitt did the job, as we knew at the time. Blayde knew it, and this morning proves it, if proof was needed."

"Very well," I said. "Blayde was pulling my leg and I'm willing to accept it. All I would add is that it was a stupid sort of thing for a man in his position to do."

"Not Jack Blayde," Overson cut in. "There were times when he was little more than an overgrown boy. Maybe he thought he was just being clever."

"No hard feelings?" I said to Triller.

"None at all." He held out his hand. "Far as we're concerned the whole thing's washed out. But it'll make a difference to you, though."

"Yes," I said. "No need for any further investigation. Some time today I'll get in touch with the company."

Triller smiled. "Don't get the idea we want to hurry you away. If you can wangle a day or two's holiday, good luck to you." He turned to Overson. "Did you take Jarrett's statement?"

"Only formally."

"Then I'll have a word with him myself. You get back and see about the bullet and the gun. The papers are on my desk."

He turned to me. "Jarrett's the one Davitt was working for. If you've nothing better to do you might as well come along."

At the end of the track Triller turned left. A couple of hundred yards on he turned left again into what must have been the last side road before the Laneford turn. It was a road with a few terraced houses running north up the gradual slope and just inside it on the right was a small garage. It was flush with the kerb and all it had was a couple of pumps with long filling arms set high in the brick wall, and an entry for cars. Triller drew in his car a little way beyond and we walked the few yards back.

It was darkish inside in spite of a couple of overhead lights. Three or four cars were there. One was jacked up and a man was working at it. He came forward at the first sight of us.

He was in dungarees, his hands and forearms smeared with grease; a shortish, stout man in the early fifties.

"Mr. Jarrett?" Triller said. "I'm Harry Triller, the Chief Constable. I gather you've seen Inspector Overson, but I'm wondering if you'd mind going over things with me. Anywhere we can talk?"

"Yes, sir," Jarrett said, and he was looking a bit nervous. "There's the office. By the door there, sir."

We went in. There was no room for the three of us to sit, so we just stood. Jarrett didn't wait to be questioned.

"I just couldn't believe it, sir. I still can't."

"I know," Triller said. "But start at the beginning. How'd you first come into contact with George Wilson, as he called himself?"

"Well, it was like this, sir. I'm a good mechanic, though I say so, and I was getting more business than I could handle, so I thought I could expand a bit, see? So about eighteen months ago I put an advertisement in a couple of the trade journals for a working partner and George was the first one I saw. He didn't write or anything; came down himself. I showed him the books and he had a good look round the place, and the long and short was we agreed on four hundred; sixty per cent of the profits to me and forty to him. We didn't have any proper contract drawn up. Sort of just took each other's word."

"Wasn't that risky?"

"Not when you're paid spot cash," he said. "He just took out the notes—fivers mostly—and paid me on the spot, and I give him a receipt saying what it was for."

"Did he give any reason for wanting to come here?"

"Yes, sir. He'd had a nasty attack of pneumonia and the doctor had recommended sea air. And I must say it did him good, sir. He hadn't been here long before he was putting on weight."

"You got on all right together?"

"Never a cross word. I won't say he was as good at the job as I was, but he picked up a lot as we went along. The nicest fellow in the world to get along with. And we was doing pretty well."

"That place of his—how'd he get it?"

Jarrett smiled for the first time.

"Funny about that, sir. It was a fortnight before he could come and when he got here I asked what about diggings. I knew he wasn't married, and then he told me he'd been down a few days before, having a look round, and he'd spotted that old garage. Used to belong to the ones who had that wrecked-car place, so he'd fixed up a lease. Little or nothing it cost him. Mind you, he had to do a lot to it."

"He kept himself to himself? Didn't like company?"

"Well, not more than most, sir. He'd come round to my place and have a meal on a Sunday sometimes, and he used to go to the pictures. Sometimes I'd go round to his place and we'd have a bottle of beer."

"I get you. And what about Saturday night?"

Jarrett shook his head.

"Don't know a thing, sir, except he said something about painting his living-room. We closed down at five and we hadn't anything fixed up, so what he did with himself I don't know. I told the inspector that. We don't open Sundays, so I didn't expect to see him till yesterday morning. Then he didn't turn up and I kept expecting to see him at any minute, and when he hadn't turned up at dinner-time I got my car out and went round, and I didn't know what'd happened. You can't see into the windows from the top o' them steps, and the garage doors were locked, so I went home to dinner and thought he'd be along in the afternoon. When he wasn't I went round again later, but there wasn't a light or anything, so I thought I'd give it till the morning. I went along about half-past seven and two milk bottles were there and some papers, and then I happened to see a policeman so I talked to him about it, and he come along here and rang up about making an entry."

"And what you saw was a bit of a shock?"

He moistened his lips.

"It was that, sir. Made me come over all queer. I wouldn't have been working just now only I wanted to get it out of my mind. I still can't believe it, though. I keep looking round expecting to see him on a job."

He gave a slow shake of the head.

"And then when the inspector let on that he was wanted for robbery—well, sir, you could have knocked me down with a feather. I just couldn't believe it: I still don't."

"Afraid it's only too true. But about last Saturday week. Inspector Overson say anything to you about that?"

"Yes, sir, but I didn't know a thing. A Saturday night's a Saturday night, if you know what I mean. All I thought I did remember was something about George having gone to the pictures, but I wouldn't be sure."

"He never had a day off?"

"Never. Always here on the job. Except yesterday."

"Well, we're much obliged to you." Triller held out his hand. "Some time this evening after you've closed we shall want a formal statement from you. We'll let you know about that."

We went out to the car. Triller drove straight on for a bit, then took a left-hand turn. A minute or two and we were at the far end of Wellbrook Avenue, and he let the car idle.

"An extraordinary fellow that Davitt must have been," he said. "Wonder why he was such a damn fool as to go back to crime again? Safe from us, you'd have thought, and a nice little business."

"I doubt if he wanted to," I said. "Everything seems to indicate that one of his old pals recognised him. All the world comes to Sandbeach, or so they claim."

"Yes," he said as we turned into the roundabout. "I think you've hit the nail clean on the head. Someone put pressure on him and he had to do the jobs whether he wanted to or not. And that we shan't know—not unless they get the swine who killed young Blayde."

"Shouldn't be too hard," I said. "It isn't as if they didn't know the ones he'd worked with before."

The car drew in at the Clarendon.

"Thanks for taking me into your confidence," I said to him. "It's been a very instructive morning."

"Well, don't take it too hard," he said. "Look me up again before you finally go."

"I will," I said. "And if you like to keep me informed—well, I'd be grateful."

He smiled, waved an affirmative hand, and moved the car on.

It was just after midday. Hallows wasn't in the foyer, so I went straight upstairs. I wondered if the *Gazette*'s morning conference were over and I guessed it was. No harm in any case in trying the house first.

Trowton must have been in his study; the receiver was picked up at once.

"This is Haire," I said. "Any sensational news reach you this morning?"

His voice instinctively lowered. "If you mean about another murder—yes. Only in confidence, though. The big official hand-out isn't till two o'clock."

"You going to be there?"

"No. There's the funeral at Laneford. But how'd you get to know about it?"

"Been on a conducted tour," I said. "Just to show how wrong I was to have suspicions about a certain job."

"You're out of my depth," he said. "I'm not all that wise yet."

"You will be by the time you get back from Laneford," I told him. "It's possible I might want to see you tomorrow."

"Well, you know where to find me," he said, and that was that.

I hadn't a lot of time. If anything in Sandbeach was a certainty, it was that from the moment he made his formal statement Jarrett would be warned to keep his mouth shut, if he hadn't been warned already. I went down at the double without waiting for the lift and got out the car. I didn't turn into Acland Road but went a little way on, drew the car in at the kerb and walked some fifty yards back.

Jarrett recognised me at once. I told him I thought I'd left my gloves in his office, so we had a look.

"Probably dropped them somewhere," I told him. "What're you going to do about a new partner, by the way?"

"Nothing at the moment, sir. We had to take on a youngish fellow who's coming along nicely. This business shook me, I'm telling you."

"I'll bet it did. The sort of thing you won't get over in a hurry. Might be a lot of publicity for you, though, and bring in some business."

"I'd rather not have it, sir. I'd give—well, practically anything to go back as we were. George might have been a crook, sir, but he was fair and square with me. Never robbed either of us of a penny." He let out a breath. "What I'm going to say to my missus I don't know. I haven't told her yet."

"Yes," I said. "You've certainly had a rough morning. How'd you get on with the inspector, by the way? He handle you rough?"

"Him, sir? Oh, no, he was fair enough."

"You'd met him before?"

"Oh, yes. We did a job for him, or rather, George did. Coming down the road here one evening about three months ago, and someone came out of Denbigh Lane. A bit foggy it was, and this chap caught him fair and square. Smashed his headlight and stove his wing in, so he let the car coast down to here. A Zephyr, it was. Almost new. Quite a good job we made of it and very satisfied he was."

"Well, I must be going," I said. "One thing, though. The Chief Constable isn't going to like it if he knows you've been talking to me. You're not supposed to do any talking till you get police permission."

"That's all right, sir. I shan't mention it if you don't."

"You bet your life I shan't. And don't you either. You've got worry enough on your hands without that."

"Don't you fret about me, sir. I know when to keep my mouth shut and when not."

"I'm sure you do. It's tonight, isn't it, you're making a statement?"

"That's right, sir. They rang me up a minute or two ago. Suggested I be there at half-past six, but, as I told them, I had to close down and go home and have a bit o' tea and tidy myself up, so I'm due there at half-past seven." He gave me an enquiring look. "You connected with the police, sir?"

"Yes, but not the Sandbeach police." I held out my hand. "Well, thanks again. And don't forget about tonight. Just stick to what they ask you and you'll get along fine. We're your servants, you know, not your masters."

"True enough, sir," he said. "Though you wouldn't think it sometimes."

It hadn't been too bad a quarter of an hour. I drove on to the Laneford turn and reversed, and when I got back to the hotel Hallows was in the dining-room, well into his lunch.

15
LOOSE ENDS

JUST after four o'clock Hallows came in with a couple of newspapers—special editions of the *Evening Gazette*. We'd had word that they'd be coming out and he'd been waiting in a one-man queue.

There was even a bigger front-page spread than after the killing of Blayde. I didn't learn a great deal from it. Triller and Overson hadn't been exactly lavish with information: no doubt they'd assumed that everything was under my nose, and no need to dot i's and cross t's.

From what I read I could fill the details in. Davitt had drawn the blinds earlier in the evening. When he came in with Blayde's killer he'd fetched two bottles of beer from the little kitchen and two glasses. He'd probably switched on the electric fire and taken off his jacket and hung it on the back of the chair, but before he could even pour out the beer he'd been shot. The killer had left both bottles on the table but had put back a glass. That was the assumption since the glass had been put on the wrong shelf. He'd then switched off the fire and left. That he'd come to Sandbeach by car was almost a certainty, and that the two men had used it to drive to the neighbourhood of Lower Carter Street. Davitt's own car had definitely not been out that night.

But the really interesting thing was in Overson's personal statement. I'd evidently wasted my time in calling surreptitiously on Jarrett.

The extraordinary thing is that I'd seen Davitt more than once before. I'd had a little repair job done there and dropped in once or twice for petrol. I suppose there's hardly a garage in the town I haven't been in in my time, but when I'd seen him he'd always been wearing a boiler suit with the sleeves covering his arms. That's why that tattooing caught my eye. And then l began to think . . .

There was another interesting thing. That Regency job was reviewed and Davitt's connection with it revealed. Triller spoke about that.

"Oh, yes, we knew about Davitt. The point was not to alarm him wherever he was. Sooner or later he'd do another job and that'd give the police a chance. Which is what happened. Not that we ever imagined a sequel like there was . . .

Plenty of pictures, too: Triller, Overson and one of Davitt that had probably come from the *Police Gazette*. One of the front of Jarrett's garage and two of Davitt's place: one a general view and one of the actual room where he'd been killed, taken just back from the top of the steps with the open door making a kind of frame. I ran the glass over that one. When I'd been leaving that room a few hours before I'd noticed that Davitt had painted the woodwork of the inside windows. Now it looked as if he'd been painting the inside of the door. It had been one of those machined jobs—deal and roughly panelled—and there was a slight difference in the colour of the panels, as if he'd intended later to make the final coat pick the panels out.

Hallows carefully folded his paper and slipped it into an inside pocket.

"Not much more than what you told me. More than enough, though, to kybosh the case."

"You're satisfied?"

"Not by a long chalk," he said. "Doesn't matter about us, though. They've got a cast-iron case. Mr. Hill can start getting out his fountain pen."

"What about Hiddon? What about the unbolted door? And Davitt not wearing gloves? And what about Bob Quarley?"

"I know," he said, and waved a hand. "But it's what's in that paper that counts." He waved a hand again. "I'm not a quitter. You know that. Neither are you, sir, but you know when you're beat."

"Maybe I do," I told him. "But not now. In fact, I'm going to surprise you."

He looked surprised already.

"Instead of that paper kyboshing the case, I think it does just the opposite. I think it's told us a whole lot that we badly wanted to know. There's just one little thing missing and I might be able to find that in town. And one other thing—a local job. If ever we're going to pull it off it's got to be tonight."

"What sort of a job?"

"Breaking and entering," I told him. "Let's get upstairs and try to work it out."

It hadn't been too light a day and dusk was in the sky soon after seven. At half-past Overson would be taking Jarrett's statement and at five-and-twenty past we checked it by ringing Jarrett's private address. Mrs. Jarrett said he'd just gone out in the car.

We gave it ten minutes more. We used Hallows's car. When we got to Churchill Avenue we went on past the last of the bungalows, turned the car where the road petered out and left it on a rough piece of ground with the lights off. It was now so dark that back on the road we couldn't even see it. We walked back to Overson's bungalow and we didn't see a soul, and there wasn't a sound except the blaring of a radio from the second of the two bungalows. The one we wanted was the third, fifty yards on.

The first street lamp was a bit farther on. The gate was open and we cut quickly through. The garage was empty and the door open. We went round it to the back, only a foot at a time, but the concrete path soon showed faintly as our eyes got used to the dark. We passed a window with its curtains drawn, and a yard or two on was the back door. Hallows ran his gloved fingers gently over the lock. I hardly heard his whisper. "All right if it isn't bolted."

I can manipulate a Yale lock myself, if you give me time. He had that door open in seconds. I didn't even know it was open till he drew back. I went through the door and closed it quietly behind me. I flashed the pencil torch and saw I was in the kitchen. The torch made a tiny pool on the floor as I moved forward. The door facing me was ajar and I drew it back with my gloved hand.

I stepped into the sitting-room. It was dark as a pit at midnight, and I wondered why the blinds had been drawn. I stood there for a couple of minutes, trying to visualise the layout of the place. I moved round a table and played the torch on the wall to my right, and there was the door; not the front door, but a door that opened into the lean-to garage. The bedrooms must be on my left.

I moved back round the table. The torch showed me a door half-way along the wall. I felt easier now. My feet made no sound on the carpet and Hallows would be on the watch across the road. I circled the big radio-gramophone, reached for the handle of the door and turned it. I slipped quietly through.

There were two windows, both heavily curtained. The room—Overson's bedroom—had a faint scent of cigarette smoke and hair cream. The bed was a double one. A discarded shirt lay on the counterpane and a necktie across the foot. A blue serge jacket was draped over the back of a chair under which was a pair of brown shoes. In the far corner was what I wanted—a tall, fumed-oak wardrobe.

To my left was another door. I went cautiously through and was in a bathroom-lavatory, and, at the end, just beyond a wash-basin, another door. There were no blinds in that bathroom so I kept the torch to the ground. I went through the door and found myself in a small, almost unfurnished bedroom. It, too, had a door to its left. I didn't look through it. There was only one place to which it could lead—the kitchen.

I had a line of retreat and I went as carefully back. I checked the blinds on the windows of Overson's bedroom, then made for the wardrobe. It was the usual type: drawers and small partitions on the right-hand side and a wide space for hangers on the left. He seemed to have plenty of clothes and it took me a couple of minutes before I found what I wanted. I replaced the hanger and closed the door. And then I heard the noise.

It was as if a car had lost control and was about to crash into the house, and then, when it was almost frighteningly near, there was a silence, and I knew what it was. Overson must have come back. I heard the garage doors closed and the sound of a key in the lock.

"Da-a-ve?"

I recognised the voice, even from that. A moment and the sitting-room light was switched on and I was so petrified that for a moment I lost my nerve. As I slipped through into the bathroom I heard her humming. Further I couldn't go. The kitchen door was ajar and at any moment she might go through.

I strained to listen. I could still hear the faint humming and then there was music—loud at first and quickly turned lower. It was louder again as the bedroom door opened, and she was humming the same tune. I could hear her fussing around as I moved towards that other bedroom door, and then I heard the sound of a bell. The humming stopped.

"Damn! . . . Who the hell's that?"

There was a silence as I slipped into the kitchen. I nearly moved back again: the light from the sitting-room was coming through the half-open door. The bell went again—the front-door bell. A few moments and it opened and I heard Hallows's voice. Another couple of seconds and I was tiptoeing along the grass beside that concrete path. As I rounded the garage I heard the front door close.

I waited a good minute, then made my way to the road. I looked each way before I moved out. A couple of minutes and I was back at the car. Hallows was already there.

"Everything all right?"

"Think so," I said. "Nearly dropped dead, though. She'd only to open the bathroom door and there I'd have been."

He moved the car on.

"Took me by surprise, too. Shut her lights off down the road and then switched them on, and was through that gate and into the garage like a streak. Then I had to think up an excuse. Asked her if it was Kosy Kot—that one there."

We slowed past the bungalow, but it was merely a blackness against the sky. At the end of the Avenue we went straight over and round the park and the cemetery. It was well after eight o'clock and we didn't want to meet Overson's car on its way up.

I was up early in the morning and I didn't want to make the journey by road. I took only a small attaché case with me, and Hallows drove me to the station. The seven-thirty was as good a train as any in the day. I could have had breakfast on it, but I didn't. There might be time to kill at the other end.

I took a taxi to the Yard and asked for Superintendent Jewle. He mightn't be in till half-past nine so I left an urgent message for him, and went round to a little place near the Embankment and had breakfast. I took my time over it and I was just at my last cup of coffee when Jewle came through the door. You'd have thought I was a rich uncle.

Now that George Wharton had at last retired, Jewle was the best friend I had at the Yard. I'd known him for twenty years and we'd worked together on quite a few cases. The very last case had brought him promotion, but we might have been back in his sergeant days for all the airs he gave himself. He had a cup of coffee and we yarned a bit and then I got in my question.

"You've heard about that Davitt business down at Sandbeach?"

"Have we not," he said. "It's being checked now."

"You anything to do with it yourself?"

"No," he said, and "Why? You got some information?"

"Mind if we go back to the Yard?" I said. "It's quite a long story and I'd like your advice."

There were only a few yards to walk and I didn't tell him anything more than why I'd gone to Sandbeach. When we were in his room I opened out: in fact, I gave him a day-to-day progress report that must have taken me over half an hour. He heard what I could prove was true and the evidence that backed it up. He heard what I only suspected, and what was needed to prove it true. He was looking pretty serious by the time I'd got to the end.

"A nasty business. It might stir up a lot of dirt."

"Whose side are you on?" I said, and was ashamed as soon as I'd said it.

"You don't have to ask that," he told me quietly. "The thing that worries me is what I can do. Where's the place to start?"

"Just a suggestion," I said. "You people are trying to get in touch with men who did jobs with Davitt, which means you've been asked to do it. That makes you interested parties in the whole thing."

"Yes?"

"Well, go to the higher-ups in confidence and tell them what you've just heard from me, and it's fifty-to-one they'll do something about it. And it ought to mean your being sent down to Sandbeach. You're now in a strong position and there's a first-class excuse. If you're going to lend Sandbeach a hand in the Davitt case, surely you ought to confer with Triller and Overson on the spot?"

He smiled.

"You were always one for making things sound easy. Still, it might be worked that way. Anything else now you're here?"

"Yes," I said, and gave him the attaché case. "Don't forget this. And a couple more things. What in your experience do the usual provincial forces do with the *Police Gazette*? Keep it filed?"

"Depends," he said. "The bigger ones file and index. I doubt if Sandbeach would. They probably keep a year's issues and then dump or scrap. After all, they can always get back numbers from the C.R.O."

It was just what I wanted to know.

"The other thing's about prints Early yesterday morning a set of Davitt's was sent here for checking, but what I can't understand is this. I had it on the authority of both Triller and Overson that on the morning of Sunday the 20th, after the Regency job, either the torch or the photographs of the prints were sent here."

"Just a moment," Jewle said. "When you say you had it on the authority of both Triller and Overson, don't forget that Triller might have been speaking as ultimately responsible. Overson would run their C.I.D., and unless it was anything very serious, Triller would only be speaking from what Overson told him, if you get what I mean. Carry on."

"Well, there's the problem," I said. "If Sandbeach had Davitt's prints confirmed on the 20th, why send them up again yesterday morning?"

Jewle frowned. "Queer, as you say. Wouldn't mind knowing the answer. You got time to wait while I do some checking? It might take some time."

I said I'd time enough. The train I wanted to take didn't leave till twelve-thirty. It turned out to be over half an hour before he was back. He gave me the empty attaché case.

"Sorry to be so long, but the job had to be done thoroughly. You're going to be surprised. Take the *P.G.*. Overson applied to the C.R.O. on 31st December last for two months' back issues, and this is the point. They included the issue with the Davitt particulars after his escape from the Scrubs."

It was so apt I could hardly believe it.

"Thought it'd surprise you. But listen to this. No photographs and no torch were sent to the F.P.B. on the 20th of this month. I repeat, no photographs or torch. A complete set of prints *was* sent yesterday morning. You can take all that as gospel. Those chaps don't make mistakes in their records."

I whistled softly. "Terrific. You realise what it means?"

"I think so," he said. "Looks like the final clinching. Some-one'll certainly have to do something now. But about you. Sure you can't stay on for a bit?"

I had to get back. Other loose ends wanted tying up. I gave him the number of the Clarendon and said there'd be someone at the end of the line. He said he'd be getting busy at once.

I took a taxi to the Agency and had a word with Norris, then went on to the flat. I collected one or two things I was running short of, and by then it was almost time to catch the train. I remembered something else and put the previous year's police directory in the case. Then I rang Hallows about the train. He'd paid his really last visit to Laneford as arranged, but there wasn't time to tell me about it, and when I got to the station it was with only a couple of minutes to spare. Lunch was on as soon as we pulled out, and then I went back to my seat and studied that directory. I hoped it wasn't too old. Even a year can make a difference.

The train was almost dead on time: probably a record for British Railways. Hallows had only just arrived. It was the afternoon of Blayde's funeral and he'd been held up by the procession. I asked if he'd spotted the widow.

"Can't say," he said. "I missed the first two or three cars. Triller was there, though. Didn't spot Overson."

I asked the desk to put calls straight through to my room and we went upstairs to talk things over. I wanted to know how he'd got on at Laneford.

"Got it straight from Woods, who got it straight from Wellard," he told me. "The house and contents and money for upkeep and maintenance come under a trust. The lady can live there unless she marries again and then the whole thing goes to the National Trust. She gets two thousand five hundred a year, which drops to a thousand if she marries. Wellard gets an annuity of five hundred. Those are the main items. The rest are largely charitable bequests."

It looked as if Mona's wings had been somewhat clipped, and we wondered what she'd be thinking about it. But time was pressing. Unless I was prepared to show my hand too soon, I couldn't very well stay on for more than forty-eight hours. We talked and talked. What Jewle would do we didn't know, but our best contribution seemed to be to make Shirley talk. To show the knots into which we tied ourselves, take one of Hallows's suggestions. It was so ingenious that I nearly fell for it.

"Look," he said. "We buy an *Evening Gazette* and in that one copy we insert an item in the Stop Press. Something like–

MRS. CHARLES DOVELL–SENSATION

How she told our reporter that she was marrying again very shortly and a hint thrown in about Overson. Shouldn't take all that working out. Then we push it through Shirley's letter-box—it'd be in coloured ink, of course, so she couldn't help spot it—and a few minutes later you pay a call. Overson's been got out of the way so she can't telephone."

I said an item would have to be put in by hand on a flatbed machine and who'd do it for us? He said what about a Gestetner, but we hadn't a Gestetner. Even if we had, it would depend on the position of the Stop Press space. Trowton might help, but I doubted it. After all, you couldn't exactly call it ethical.

Tea had just come up when the telephone went. It was Jewle. "You're coming down?"

"I'm nearly there," he said. "Ringing from Chemworth. What I wanted to do was warn you not to take any precipitate steps till I've seen you, and that mayn't be till some time tomorrow. Won't do for me to spread any alarm. Just a mutually informatory visit. When I've got what I want I'll see you, and then we can decide."

He chuckled when I asked him where he'd be staying.

"Where d'you think?" he said. "Plumb in the lion's mouth: the Regency."

And that was that. Othello's occupation was momentarily gone, but we weren't too sorry to stop going round in circles. What I knew was that, unless I got out of the hotel I'd never be able to keep my mind off things, so I had a look at the amusement guide and treated myself to an evening at the Majestic. French was having an easy, too. No point now in any further watching of Shirley Blayde. What Hallows was going to do I didn't know, but his idea of a holiday is to stick with some interesting job of work. My guess was that he'd be hovering unobtrusively in the neighbourhood of police headquarters; keeping an eye on Jewle and trying to anticipate his lines of action. As it happened, I wasn't to be far wrong.

He wasn't in for dinner. I was late myself and I didn't see him till it was almost time for bed. Hallows, by the way, knows Jewle well. Like myself, he's worked with him quite a few times.

"The Super's had a pretty long night," he told me casually. "Wasn't in the station more than a few minutes when the whole caboodle went down to that place of Davitt's. Had about an hour there and then back to Lower Carter Street. Best part of another hour down there and back to the station. Must have had sandwiches and coffee there. He's only just gone back to the hotel."

16
WAYS AND MEANS

IT WAS not till the mid-afternoon the following day that Jewle rang. Hallows, ferreting about as usual, had reported that Jewle had been all the morning at the hotel and his only caller had been Triller, who'd stayed for about half an hour. I was a bit worried. I hoped that Jewle hadn't jumped the gun.

It was about four when he came to the Clarendon, and we went straight away up to my room. Hallows was there. Jewle said it was a regular family reunion.

"I think everything's set," he told us. "I got the evidence we wanted at that place of Davitt's and I've just had word that it checks. All that's left is the show-down. You any ideas?"

I said that primarily I had to look at the whole thing from the point of view of United Assurance. I had to be in a position to prove to Hill that the claim should be rejected, and that was why

I'd had in mind bringing pressure to bear on Shirley Blayde. If we got an admission it wouldn't only conclude the case from that point of view, it would also be a kind of foundation for the other case. Furthermore, if Garlen were implicated, it might be just what was needed for the start of an enquiry into the death of Quarley.

"Yes," he said, quite amiably. "And what do you propose about putting on the pressure?"

I said the first thing was to isolate Overson. No communication either way between him and Shirley, and the way I was proposing to do it was to ring him as a certain detective-inspector who had information to impart about Davitt's associates and who was actually on his way. That would keep Overson tied down to his room for whatever time we cared to arrange.

"Ingenious," he said. "Seems a pity to change it, but the fact is I'd already thought of something like it. I've actually made arrangements for Overson to go to the Yard tonight by the seven o'clock to look over some records."

That was the first deflation. I felt like some small boy who'd announced some grandiose scheme to an elder brother and been suitably sat on. Not that I'm younger than Jewle: I'm a good bit older.

"But about the pressure," he went on. "What've you got in the way of thumb-screws?"

I had a better plan of campaign than Marlborough had at Blenheim.

"First of all, impress her with the power of the company, then shake her with various things she'd never suspect we know. After that, switch to Mona Dovell, whom she hates like poison. Prove to her that Overson is hand-in-glove with Mona and may even marry her. Look at these."

I showed him the prints of little Doris Franks and told him how and where Hallows had got them. I said it had only been suspected by a very few that Mona had taken that long holiday to give birth to the child. Shirley was one who'd suspected, and if she were shown those prints at the right, panicky moment and told to see the obvious resemblance to Overson, she would see it, whether it were there or not. I'd also be in a position, owing to the isolation of Overson, to try a bluff. I'd challenge her to ring Overson and, when she couldn't contact him, tell her there was a good reason. At that very moment he was at Laneford Hall. I knew because I had a man planted there. If her reactions were what I expected, I'd promise immunity if she admitted her share in the Regency job.

"Yes," he said. "I like that first part. It's a very good gambit."

Then he laughed "You ought to set crosswords, you know, not solve 'em."

"And what do you mean by that crack?" I asked him virtuously.

"Well," he said. "Let's look at it seriously. Don't you think it's cracking a nut with a steam-hammer?"

"Ten days we've been here trying to crack a nut," Hallows told him. "Far as I'm concerned, I don't care how it's cracked: even if we have to use an H-bomb."

"I think we can make it a bit more simple," Jewle told him. "If you're going to interview the lady, why shouldn't I be there myself?"

"You mean it?" I said.

"Well, why not? There's always ways and means of getting people to talk. By seven o'clock I'll probably have thought of one."

"I bet you will," I said. "I bet you've got it planned out already."

"Just an idea or two," he said mildly. "Seven o'clock, shall we say?"

It suited me. Seven o'clock at the Clarendon. French could be observing the flat and could ring us from the call-box as to whether she were in.

"She was back on duty today," Hallows said. "The early shift, eight-thirty to five."

"Shouldn't take much more than half an hour," Jewle said. "I've got a nice big room at the hotel and I thought of getting Triller to come round at, say, eight. Hallows might have to stay at the flat, but you'd be there."

I mentioned Trowton. He was an interested party, especially in the matter of Quarley. And if there was anything which Triller might wish to hush up, he'd be stymied from the start. Trowton wouldn't stand for soft-pedalling.

"Right," Jewle said, and got up to go. "I'll see to Triller and you to Trowton. Room twenty-four. And seven o'clock here."

He wouldn't stay for a cup of tea. He'd have a pretty long speech to make that night and he wanted to have everything pat. We went down with him. Hallows went off to see French and I got out the car.

Trowton was in; it was he who opened the door. I said I hadn't come to stay.

"It's really an invitation from Superintendent Jewle of Scotland Yard," I told him. "He's been down here the last day or two and he's holding a kind of private press conference in his room at the Regency at eight o'clock. Room twenty-four. He'd particularly like you to be there."

"Jewle, did you say?"

I spelt the name for him and repeated the number of the room. He said he'd be there.

It was I who rang the bell and it wasn't more than a few moments before the door was opened. It was going to be a lazy night at the flat: slacks and a jumper and bright red slippers with yellow pompons. They suited her better than a formal get-up.

"Do you mind if I trouble you again, Miss Bright?" I said, and stepped well into the light.

The quick look shifted from me to Jewle. He looks younger than his forty-two years and she guessed he was the nephew I'd told her about. Or that's what I thought.

"That's all right," she said. "Won't you come in?"

We went in. Hallows had stayed by the car. If she had recognised him as the bungalow caller of the Tuesday night there might have been reactions.

"If it's to look at the flat, it's awfully untidy. You know how it is when you get home." She tittered slightly. "To tell the truth, I was just going to wash my hair."

She'd been looking enquiringly at Jewle. I introduced him.

"A superintendent?" she said, and, "Oh! I didn't mean to be rude. Mr. Travers is the insurance inspector and you're the superintendent. Won't you sit down?"

She took what was apparently her favourite seat—the divan corner. We had the chairs. She smiled and gave a little click of the tongue.

"I'm so sorry. I ought to have offered you a drink. Will you have it now or after you've seen the flat?"

"To tell the truth," I said, "we haven't come to look at the flat."

She stared.

"And my friend here isn't from the insurance company. He's a superintendent of police. From New Scotland Yard."

It was a shock. She was trying to speak, but the words wouldn't just come.

"It's the same business I came down here for," I told her. "That jewellery robbery at the Regency."

She pulled herself together. "Yes, but what's it to do with me?"

"I'll tell you," I said. "United Assurance is a very wealthy company, and when it's suspicious about a claim it spares nothing to get to the facts. I've had two men working here with me, and we've now got most of the facts. Some of them concern you."

"Me?" The laugh was only a titter. "How can it possibly concern me?"

"Just be patient for a minute and I'll explain. The facts do concern you: in fact, we've learned things about you that you'd never have suspected, not in a lifetime."

"Oh?" she said. "And what facts?"

"Well, take the night after Mr. Dovell died. You remember? You took your car to Dave Overson's bungalow and brought him back here. He wasn't seen because he was in the back of the car and stooping down, and you drove straight into the garage and then he got out and went in at the back door. He spent quite a time with you in that bedroom there."

Her cheeks flushed.

"It's a lie. You're making it all up. You wait till I tell him about it."

"Very well," I said. "But you've heard of tape-recorders that can register conversations and can be played back. I expect you have, but let's talk about the night before last. At a quarter to eight you drove to his bungalow, shut off your lights when you approached and turned them on again as you drove straight into the garage. You shut the doors from inside and let yourself into the sitting-room with your own key. You called, 'Da-a-ve!' just in case he was there, then you checked the curtains and switched on the light. You chose a record and put it on. It was a hotted-up version of a very old tune—*Japanese Sandman*—and you were humming it when you went into the bedroom and did a bit of tidying up. Then there was a ring at the front-door bell. You didn't answer till it had rung a second time." I smiled. "But why go on? Or would you like to hear a play-back of what you and Overson talked about and even what you did?"

Her cheeks had gone scarlet. There was nothing she could say. Jewle chimed in. There's something very impressive about Jewle. Maybe she'd never been in the least afraid of me—till a minute or so ago—but he was someone you couldn't just disregard.

"We know what your share was in that robbery," he told her, "and I'm here to make you an offer. We know it, as I said, but we want it in your own words. If you're not prepared to do that, then I shall have to take you into custody."

"You mean . . . arrest me?"

"Yes," he said. "But there's something else. I'm not threatening you, but I want you to realise that you're liable to a term of imprisonment. One year? Two? I can't say. On the other hand, if you make a voluntary confession I might be able to keep your name out of everything. In fact, I think I can do that."

Suddenly there was a last hope.

"But how do I know this isn't a trick? How do I know who you really are?"

He gave her his warrant card. She looked at it and it almost dropped from her hands. He reached forward and took it. We waited a minute or two and still she couldn't speak.

"Let me help you," Jewle said quietly. "You put sleeping pills in Hiddon's Thermos. You unbolted the service door. Is that right so far?"

Her lip puckered and she began to sob. She turned away, head buried in the divan corner.

"That's right," Jewle told her. "Get the whole thing out of your system. We've got plenty of time. And don't try to shield Overson. I doubt if you'll see him again for a very long time."

Some of it hadn't registered: some of it had. That bit, for instance, about Overson. She was rubbing her eyes with her knuckles. Her handbag was on a side table and I gave it to her. She found a handkerchief.

"Inside another hour Overson will be arrested," Jewle told her. "Tell us frankly what your share in it was and we'll see that you don't have to give evidence. And don't rely on him to shield you. We know that he's prepared to do anything to save his own skin."

There was no more fight in her. A little careful questioning and the whole thing came out. She'd put the dope in the Thermos at Overson's direction. And drawn the bolts. And she'd already given him an imprint in plasticine of the safe key.

Jewle wanted it in writing, but that took a lot of persuasion. I signed as a witness.

"Just a question or two further," I said. "Strictly in confidence. It was Overson who found the money for this flat?"

Some of it, she said.

"He was going to marry you if you could get a divorce?"

He was.

"And that little scene between you and him that first day I came round here: that was pre-arranged?"

He'd rung her just before we'd arrived and told her what to say.

"You made a good job of it, both of you," I told her. "It took me in for quite a time. But just one last question. Where'd he get his money from? From Garlen?"

"You're not going to bring it against him if I tell you?"

"We shan't need to," I told her. "Besides, this is in confidence."

"Well, yes," she said. "I know Mr. Garlen was giving him money."

"And were you paid for what you did?"

She looked indignant. Quite a flash of spirit.

"I'd never have taken it. I only did it for him. I didn't even know why. He said it was a trick being played on Mona Dovell."

I opened the front door. Hallows came in. He was wearing sun-glasses and though she gave him a quick look, I didn't think she'd recognised him.

"Well, that's all," Jewle said. "We shall keep our word, Mrs. Blayde. Mr. Hallows, here, will stay with you till nine o'clock. That's only in case you should be thinking of telephoning to anybody. After that you're free to do what you like."

She got slowly to her feet: she was trying to speak.

"Yes, Mrs. Blayde?"

"Dave. . . . It was true what you said?"

She was sobbing again when we left her.

We stood for a minute by the car. We should have been elated, but somehow we weren't. There'd been a tawdriness about it all: even perhaps a kind of pity.

"What women will do for men," Jewle said, and grunted. "Still, perhaps we were lucky. All the same, I'd rather deal with fifty men than with a woman."

"Wonder what she'll do when she knows the whole of it?"

"Don't know," he said. "Probably want to run as far away from here as she can get." He looked at his watch. "Nicely on time. Don't know about you, but I feel like a wash and brush up."

We drove back to the Regency. As we came out of the cloak-room we saw Trowton making for the lift. I did the introductions. We stood chatting for a minute or two. It was still not quite eight o'clock but we went up. It was a large room, as Jewle had said, and a couple of extra chairs had been brought in. We'd just lighted our cigarettes when Triller arrived. His eyes opened a bit at the sight of me, and even more when he saw Trowton.

"Make yourself comfortable," Jewle told him. "We all know one another, which is always a good thing."

"What's it about?" Triller said. "I wasn't expecting anything like this."

"A longish story," Jewle told him. "But sit down. Have a cigarette."

"Thank you, no." He sat down and he turned to me. "We're not back at that old Regency business again?"

"Just a kind of general review," Jewle said. "This might be as good a start as any."

He took that signed confession from his wallet. Triller felt for his glasses, found them and put them on. He read a few words.

"What's this? How'd you get it?"

"Read it all," Jewle told him. "We'll go into details later." He read it. Jewle took it practically from his fingers and passed it to Trowton.

"Just a minute," Triller said. "This is confidential business. There's no proof. It's just a statement."

Trowton had read it. He was handing it back.

As I've said, there's something impressive about Jewle. Like many big men, he has an air of what I can only call gentleness. He rarely raises his voice and maybe it's that quietness that gives an authority.

"Look," he said gently. "We're four reasonable men. Men of experience. All our lives we've been listening to this and that and then making our own judgments. So why not go on doing it? Let's listen to some evidence and act as a kind of jury. No one commits himself till he's heard what there is to hear. That sound fair and reasonable to you, Triller?"

"Yes," he said, but somehow even the one word wasn't said too graciously.

"And you, Trowton?"

"Sounds fair enough to me. But just one question. This evidence we're going to hear. It's in confidence?"

"Absolutely so. The only thing is, that when you've heard it you'll give a sort of verdict. Included in that verdict will be the decision as to whether or not it's to stay so. It'll be up to you. That satisfy you?"

"Couldn't be fairer," Trowton said.

"Well, let's hear it." That was Triller, curt and impatient.

"You shall," Jewle told him. "I have some notes here to which I may have to refer. And I don't want you gentlemen to get impatient. I'd like you to let me tell everything in my own way. It may sound a bit roundabout, but that can't be helped. I should also say that practically all this evidence was supplied by Travers. During my stay here I've checked it pretty thoroughly and that's why I've asked you to come here tonight. So let's begin. A fairish way back. Six or seven years ago."

"You're sure that's necessary?"

Jewle looked up from his notes. His tone had something different.

"I'll tell it my own way. This is an open meeting. No one's forced to stay and listen."

Triller didn't say a word. He shuffled uneasily in his chair and his thick lips clamped together. Trowton was leaning forward. I sat back in my chair, eyes closed.

"Six or seven years ago," Jewle said, "and the way I see it, things were like this."

17
END OF THE ROAD

HE MIGHT have been using my own words. He took those four people: Shirley, then something of a prude and on the lookout for the main chance; Mona, from a disrupted kind of home and man-crazy from the start; Overson, dominating and a philanderer, and Blayde, a kind of acolyte and always a weak brother.

Time went on and the four were even closer. There was a cooling off when Mona got that job at Laneford Hall, and when she married Dovell the breach between her and Shirley was more than complete. Mona had married a kind of fairy prince: all Shirley had got was a man she had soon realised was only a shadow of someone like Overson. Intimacy began between her and Overson. There were risks in it and it was decided she was to leave Blayde.

"I'm pretty sure Overson wasn't decided at first about marrying her," Jewle said. "He'd been having an affair at the same time with Mona Dovell, and we can't tell what was in his mind—"

"You have proof about Mrs. Dovell?" Triller wanted to know. "Or is it just scandal?"

"Proof enough," Jewle told him. "Even Blayde visited the lady at times. She wasn't particular. I'm not moralising or blaming: I'm merely stating provable facts. You'll admit she hadn't much sex life with her husband, but the way I see it, she revolted Overson, and that brought him closer to Shirley. During the last three months or so he was definitely wanting to marry her. The trouble was that Blayde wouldn't do anything about a divorce. I hope that background makes it more clear about the confession that Shirley signed tonight. If it doesn't, I think you'll see things more clearly later, so let's shift to Davitt.

"We know that Overson, as he himself admitted, had used Jarrett's garage. Davitt actually did the repair job on his car, and that's when Overson spotted him. The snub nose, perhaps, or Davitt might have been working for once with his forearms exposed. But Overson wanted to make sure. He'd just vaguely remembered that escape from the Scrubs and he knew roughly when it was, but he couldn't find the actual *Police Gazette* to refer to. He knew it was roughly about two years ago so he applied to the C.R.O. for copies to cover the period. Then he made it his business to see Davitt privately, probably at that place of his."

"You've proof? Or is this just theory?"

"All in good time," Jewle told him mildly. "In a minute or two I think you'll see that things just had to be that way. Davitt probably offered him money, and Overson took it. Even five pounds a week would come in handy. At any rate, Davitt went on working at the garage and Overson didn't arrest him. And then a few days ago something happened.

"Overson was in Sam Garlen's pay. The evidence isn't strong at the moment but subsequent events make it stronger. An enquiry into his accounts and a search of his bungalow might produce actual evidence, but my own view is that he'll be only too glad to throw Garlen to the wolves. But to get back to the happening. Mona Dovell had got heavily into Garlen's debt. There was a respite when everyone thought her husband was going to die, but he recovered and Garlen closed down. We don't know the amount of the debt. A well-known local character—your friend Quarley, Mr. Trowton—had got wind of something and thought he had a contact in Garlen's office. The contact sold him to Garlen and the next night Quarley fell over a cliff. We'll come back to that later.

"What I say is that Garlen, Mona Dovell and Overson rigged the jewellery scheme between them. The confession you've read shows how it was worked. Overson did the job, and there's one thing I must impress on you. It's vital to everything: I mean the fact that Overson was always the one man against whom nothing could be proved. If he ever had the bad luck to be found where he shouldn't be, he was there on his job. What's more, he was the sole arbiter. He made reports to you, Triller, but I've gathered you're the kind who leaves a man he can trust to do his own job. I think you were right.

"But to go back. I don't know who had the jewellery, but almost certainly Garlen. Mona Dovell would get the insurance money and Overson got what money was in the safe. He also had something else. He'd wanted to plant something of Davitt's there, so he'd probably paid him another visit and taken something with Davitt's prints on—a torch. And this is the proof. *On no account did Davitt have to know.* If the news of that torch had got out and Davitt had been pulled in, the gaff would have been blown. Even if the news had merely been published, Davitt would have seen it and Overson couldn't judge his reactions.

"Now, you assumed, Triller, that the torch or photos of the prints had gone to the Yard, otherwise the discovery wouldn't have been made that the burglar was Davitt. That was the impression Overson wanted to create. But no torch or photos were ever sent. If they had been, and if the Yard had known about Davitt, there'd have been the hue and cry. Davitt's name would have been in the Press, and so on. You see? The gaff would have been blown. You're with me so far?"

"If what you say is fact."

"There's further proof," Jewle told him. "And now we come to the really important part. Everything from Overson's point of view had gone off swimmingly. Travers here was a bit of a fly in the ointment, but luckily he gave Overson the impression that he was satisfied. And that made Overson cocksure. It brought another scheme into his mind. A way to kill two birds with one sure stone and round off the whole thing. I'm referring to the killing of Blayde."

"My God, no!" Trowton said.

Triller sat staring. He didn't say a word.

"Yes," Jewle said. "The killing of Blayde. Planned for the night of the fight. Travers given Overson's seat, which left Overson free to be everywhere and nowhere. But let's approach it from Overson's own angle.

"I don't know where he got the gun; that doesn't matter in any case, but what he did was make an appointment with Davitt for the Saturday evening at, say, eight o'clock. That tallies roughly with the established time of death. He shot Davitt straightaway, took off his jacket and hung it over a chair, brought in two bottles of beer to establish the presence of two people, and so on, and put out the light and turned off the electric fire. His mistake was in turning off the light, but we'll come to that later. What he then did was to go to that warehouse and jemmy a door and do a bit of hacksawing. Then he went on to the fight.

"He showed himself to Travers and settled down to pick the right moment to leave. The big fight came on and everyone—inside attendants and all—would be keyed up. Even the attendants would be having a look through the main stadium doors. Then when the fight suddenly ended, he slipped out. In a minute he was at the call-box reporting something strange at the warehouse. Then he went on and waited for Blayde—"

"Wait a minute," Triller said. "A squad car should have been there. What about that?"

"He had luck," admitted Jewle, "but did it really matter? Overson was Chief Inspector Overson. He could have told the squad men to do this and that and, as soon as he was alone there in the dark with Blayde, he could have shot him and started shouting for help and chasing the killer or killers." He smiled grimly. "I think he'd have preferred it that way. There'd have been more honour and glory in it. Police inspector chases armed killers. A pretty good headline, that.

"What he did do, of course, was to move off in the dark and make his way to where he'd parked his car, and then place the gun where it was found. Then he went on to the station, ostensibly to see if Travers and Blayde were back. He heard the news about Blayde and went to the scene of the killing. I gather he put in a tireless night. I also hear he was pretty heartbroken about Blayde's death.

"All he had to do then was sit back and wait till Davitt's body had been discovered. He was on the scene before you were, Triller, so we'll not know what faking of evidence he did. He did get a search going for the weapon and, of course, he made the sensational discovery that the dead man was Davitt. Up went the prints to the Yard and then the gun and the bullet. Davitt it was, and the gun the same one that killed Blayde. Next was the hand-out to the Press: telling just so much and keeping so much back. And you never had the least suspicion, Triller?"

"Should I have had? Would you have had? Besides, I'm not satisfied yet. There's far too much conjecture."

Jewle must have had something I didn't know about in his mind, or he wouldn't have tackled Triller like that.

"You asked if I'd have had suspicions. One answer is that somebody did have suspicions, and that's Travers. Take just one question: how could Davitt have known that the night of the nineteenth was just the one night when that jewellery would be in the Regency safe? Davitt had been keeping himself to himself for a couple of years, and doing it well. How could he know anyone connected with the Regency? Take the original doubt in Travers's mind. Why should Davitt, an old pro., not have been wearing gloves? Why would he need a torch at all? Then there was the question of the night porter, Hiddon. Why wasn't he questioned more closely? It was Travers who did that and tumbled to the drugging and the crack on the skull being given chiefly for show, and because Davitt had been known to use a cosh."

Triller moistened his lips.

"You can't have it both ways. First you say I was right to let Overson run his department, and now you're virtually ascribing negligence."

"Oh, no. That's not my job. That's for an Inspector of Constabulary."

Triller stared. "You mean . . . ?"

Jewle shrugged his shoulders.

"You're a Chief Constable. This thing isn't going to be hushed up. Before it's over it'll be another Brighton Case."

"No! . . . No!"

"Leave it," Jewle said. "I promised you some definite evidence, and this is it. Remember I said Overson had been foolish to turn out the light before he left Davitt's place? I ought to have said he was unlucky, and this is why. He had to work quickly. Davitt had been painting the interior wood-work that afternoon and it was still wet. The outside of the door hadn't been painted, but when Overson went out by that door, he was close to wet paint. That paint was dry when you took Travers round there, but the place still reeked of it and that's what gave Travers the idea.

"You remember what clothes Overson had been wearing that day. You must have seen him in them. He had them on when he lunched with Travers, and he was still wearing them at the fight. How he did it I'm not prepared to divulge, but Travers managed to get hold of the tweed coat. There was a paint mark on the right sleeve: not a big one—just sufficient. He brought it to me. Yesterday I took a sample of the same paint and our tests show an absolute identity. So there's your final proof."

"Incredible," Trowton said. "I don't mean it doesn't satisfy me. It does. It's unanswerable."

"I thought so," Jewle said. "Otherwise I'd never have asked you both here."

Triller just sat there, heavy body slumped down in the armchair.

"How about you?" Jewle asked him. "You're satisfied, too?"

"Yes," he said. "It crucifies me to say so, but . . ."

The words trailed off.

"Then you've your choice," Jewle told him. "That sending of Overson to the Yard was a blind. He's there by now, and our people are marking time till they hear from you."

"You want him held?"

Jewle shook his head. "You still don't realise things. It isn't what *I* want. It's what you think it's your duty to do."

Triller still sat there.

"Look," Jewle said. "This is your way out. You asked us to lend a hand about Davitt. Very well. Ring the Yard and ask them to take over as from now. Trowton will stretch a point for once. He can let it be assumed that we took over from you when you first asked for help two days ago. That'll put you into the background."

Triller got heavily to his feet.

"There's the telephone," Jewle told him. "Better get it done now."

Triller moved across the room like an old, old man. Trowton made as if to get up but Jewle's hand held him back.

Ten minutes later Triller had gone and Jewle had done some telephoning himself. The three of us went down the stairs without waiting for the lift. Jewle asked us to have a drink, Trowton said it would have to be a quick one, though he certainly wanted a drink. That half-hour in room twenty-four was going to be something he'd remember.

"Nothing's to be printed," Jewle warned him. "I'm in charge here from now on, and I'll give you the all clear as soon as I'm allowed. Might be early tomorrow morning."

There weren't a lot of people in the bar and our drinks were at a table well back. Trowton had something on his mind.

"About Quarley. You think anything can be done?"

"Oh, yes," Jewle said. "It may take a lot of time but we'll get there."

"Like the mills of God," I said. "A slow grind but there won't be much uncrushed."

"Garlen's tricky. You don't think he'll have covered his tracks?"

"We've too many witnesses," Jewle told him. "Overson's sure to crack. Then there's the Dovell woman. I'm betting that within twenty-four hours Garlen'll be under lock and key. He may even give us Romsie to protect his own skin."

Trowton left. Jewle and I had another drink: not festively, we didn't feel like celebrating. If anything we were suddenly tired. Two old friends who just wanted to sit quietly over a drink.

"Matthews will be coming down?" Inspector Matthews was Jewle's side-kick, another old friend.

"Some time tomorrow," he said. "You going back early?"

"Don't know," I said. "If I feel like I feel now I won't have breakfast much before nine. Might get away about ten, after I've rung Hill."

"Good," he said. "That's about the time I'll be going to Laneford. What about you coming with me? Won't be far out of your way."

I hadn't thought of that. Now I knew that I'd like to be there when Jewle saw her, and I don't think there's about me anything specially vindictive.

"Right," he said. "I'll be looking for you about ten o'clock in Henry Street. You can go first and show me the way."

It wasn't a good morning: drizzling, muggy and no wind. Jewle was just behind me as we drew up outside the Hall porch. He'd rung to make sure the lady would be in.

Wellard opened the door. He looked surprised, but not displeased at the sight of me. I congratulated him on his annuity.

"Yes, sir; money's always useful, not that I hadn't something put by."

I introduced Jewle. I asked when he'd be leaving and he said at the end of the week. The madam, he said, was in the master's old room.

"This way, gentlemen."

We were ushered in. There was a fire, as there'd been that day I'd first seen her, and she was sitting in the chair that had been Dovell's. The same stool was on her right and she laid the magazine on it as we went in. She looked taller and more slim: the tightish black skirt, perhaps, and the black jumper with just a touch of white at the neck. Me she ignored: she looked enquiringly at Jewle.

"I didn't quite catch your name on the telephone."

"Jewle. Superintendent Jewle."

"I'm glad," she said. "It's about time the insurance company sent down someone who could deal with this matter. My solicitors say that it's just shilly-shallying. Almost a fortnight now, and nothing done."

"The inspector has some news, I think."

She allowed herself to look at me, and I might have been something that had crawled from under a stone.

"It's about time, too. You've brought the cheque?"

I didn't waste words. I wanted somehow to get out of that room. I thought of another downstair room, and she and Blayde, and a dead man upstairs.

"No cheque, Mrs. Dovell. The company refuse to meet the claim. It's up to you and your solicitors if you wish to sue."

Her hands clenched. I almost thought she'd have struck me if Jewle hadn't spoken.

"Mrs. Dovell, would you mind looking at this? A copy, by the way."

Her hand was shaking as she took it. She read it, and her face was flushing long before she reached the end.

"Shirley Blayde. . . . That little liar! You never could believe a word she said."

"Maybe," Jewle said. "We happen to know it's true."

"But why come to me? I knew nothing. It was Sam Garlen who asked me to leave the jewellery at the hotel. I didn't know it was going to be stolen. And what about Shirley Blayde? She owns up to what she's done."

"Maybe," Jewle said. "But let me correct a wrong impression. I'm not a company superintendent; I'm from Scotland Yard. And it's my duty to warn you. . . ."

I couldn't help it if my lip curled. All the bounce had gone and, back in that chair, the veneer had been stripped and left her what she'd always been. Common as dirt was what they'd have called her in my young days. Overson had had a coarser word.

"If you like to make a statement you're at liberty to do so," Jewle told her.

"I've told you," she said, and I thought for a moment we were in for more tears. "I don't know a thing. All I did was what he told me."

"Right," Jewle said. "I'm afraid I shall have to take you into Sandbeach. I don't know how long we'll be keeping you, but you'd better pack a night bag."

There was the old refuge of tears. Jewle put an end to it. He went to the door and called Wellard. She didn't wait; she was hurrying up the stairs, handkerchief to her eyes.

"Think I'll be getting along," I told Jewle while Wellard waited in the background. "Don't go easy with her. She's probably up there thinking up a whole collection of new lies."

"Don't worry," he told me. "She'll sing before the day's out."

"And Triller? He'll have to resign?"

"I think he'll be glad to. A tired old man waiting for his pension." He held out his hand. "Like me to keep you informed?"

I left him talking to Wellard. A mile or so down the road I drew up the car at the verge. I wanted to light my pipe, but even when it was going nicely I still sat on. What was it Lord Goddard had said about the causes of crime? Greed, love of money, jealousy, lust and cruelty, and in that Overson Case I'd had them all. Most cases left a nasty taste in the mouth, and this had been worse than most: there was not a soul in it that I'd remember with even a trace of respect.

Or was there? I felt for my wallet, took out those two prints and looked at them. A nice little girl, Hallows had said, and she looked it. Natural, no affectation, just charming: the sort of young daughter I'd have liked to have myself. She'd be a beauty one day, according to Hallows, not that that was everything. Look where it had got her mother.

When I'd left Sandbeach that morning all sorts of thoughts had rankled. I'd even anticipated the gesture of taking those prints from my wallet and handing them to Mona Dovell. I'd seen the sneer and heard the riposte.

"Your daughter?"

"No, Mrs. Dovell. *Yours!*"

Now I was feeling something very like shame, and the gesture was not a bringing together of mother and daughter but a kind of isolation as I flicked my lighter and let the flame lick at the edges of those prints. When the flame touched my fingers I opened them and watched till the last faint red had gone. Then I moved the car on.

THE END